A RIVER CONNECTS US

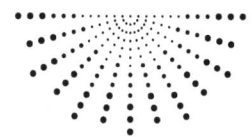

ALLIE WINTERS

Copyright © 2025 by Allie Winters

All rights reserved. No part of this publication may be reproduced, stored or transmitted in any form or by any means, electronic, mechanical, photocopying, recording, scanning, or otherwise without written permission from the author. It is illegal to copy this book, post it to a website, or distribute it by any other means without permission.

This novel is entirely a work of fiction. The names, characters and incidents portrayed in it are the work of the author's imagination. Any resemblance to actual persons, living or dead, events or localities is entirely coincidental.

www.alliewinters.com

First edition.

CHAPTER ONE

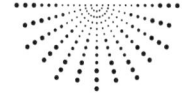

GRAYSON

*S*hit.

It's Mom.

My hands flex on the steering wheel as the center console screen flashes her name, a familiar sense of dread coiling in my gut the longer I let it ring. I should pick up. She knows I'm driving down to Crescent Pass, that I'm a captive audience right now. I'll only hear about it later if I don't answer.

I reach out, finger hovering over the green phone icon on the screen, but I don't press it, and the call goes to voicemail. A wash of relief and guilt passes over me, but I set it aside. You're not supposed to drive distracted, right? And Mom is the ultimate distraction.

I already know what the call will be about. My brother texted me a heads up, as if I didn't know it would be an issue when I RSVP'd.

God forbid I show up to a wedding *sans date*.

If it's not a problem for my brother and sister-in-law—the actual bride and groom—I don't see why it should be one for my mother, but c'est la vie.

A ping from my phone a minute later alerts me I have a new voicemail, and I wince, unsure why I'm surprised she left one. I should feel worse about sending my own mother to voicemail. Actually, I shouldn't be afraid to answer her calls to begin with. I'm twenty-nine years old and haven't lived with her for over a decade. It's ridiculous.

Maybe afraid isn't the right word... No, afraid is right.

I bite the bullet and play it, wanting time to craft a response to the tirade I'm about to hear.

Honey, I know you're probably driving down from Seattle right now, but this can't wait. How come I'm just finding out you're not bringing a date to the wedding? Owen said you RSVP'd as only yourself.

And there it is. Why she's taking it as a personal affront, I have no idea.

You told me you didn't need any help getting a date. How many times did I offer to find a nice girl in town for you to take? I've had so many women ask if you were single because they want to go. Harper's set an exclusive guest list and it's all anyone's talking about.

That's because nothing exciting ever happens in Crescent Pass. Of course the wedding of the town recluse and his bubbly bride would get people interested. Especially since Harper only moved there about six months ago.

Little does everyone else know they've legally been married all this time, and this wedding is just a party to celebrate it.

It's going to look so foolish if you're the only one of your siblings without a date, Mom continues over the voicemail.

I nearly snort aloud. Is she crazy? There are three of us, one of which is the freaking groom, and the other has her live-in boyfriend as her date.

Well, call me back. I have a list of girls who would be perfect for you to take.

The line goes silent, and I scrub a weary hand down my face. My first instinct is to turn the car around and pretend I have some deathly, communicable disease that prevents me from attending the wedding.

No, I can't do that to Owen. He never asks for anything, and he asked me to be his best man. I have to show up for him. But I can't listen to Mom harp at me for the next week about how *if I only settled down with the right girl...*

Now that both my brother and sister have found significant others, that leaves only me for Mom to focus her full matchmaking attention on. Unfortunately, living four hours away hasn't dissuaded her in the slightest.

I itch to call Owen and see if he has any advice for me, but he's probably stressed enough about the wedding. So I do the next best thing and call my sister.

Kristen doesn't answer the phone like a normal person, though.

"Oooh, you're in trouble," she says in a sing-song voice, sounding more like her seven-year-old daughter than herself.

"Damn it," I mutter. "You heard?"

She makes a *pssh* sound. "Of course. Mom is physically incapable of keeping her thoughts to herself. You'll apparently bring great shame upon our family by having the audacity to be dateless." Her voice turns to mock outrage. "How could you do this to us?"

"Can you be serious?" I ask her. "What the fuck am I going to do?"

"Why are you surprised she's mad? I heard you tell her you have a date. Did you actually?"

"No," I admit sullenly.

"So, what? You thought she'd magically forget?"

I shrug, not that she can see me. "I was just going to say the girl broke up with me, or she's sick or something."

"Great plan." Her voice drips with sarcasm, but that's nothing new coming from her.

"Can you be a good sister and help me for a change?"

"Help you? I'm still mad at you."

Mad at me? What the hell? "For what?"

"For giving the kids that stupid Super Smash Bros. game. It's all they do. I'm so sick of listening to it."

I roll my eyes. "Jesus, Kristen. It's not like you even have to play it with them. I bet Eli's the one who does."

"That's not the point. They get so riled up. Worse than Mario Kart."

If that's the worst of her problems, she's got it pretty good. "Fine. Sorry for being a terrible uncle and getting your kids a game they love. Send me an approved present list next time, okay? Now will you help me?"

She chuckles lightly. "What do you want me to do? This is a mess of your own making."

I mean, she's not wrong. But that's also not helping right now.

I run a hand through my hair, then rub at my temples. "I don't know. But I need to get ahead of this before Mom starts parading me through town setting me up with girls."

"So find someone to take. I'm sure she has a list."

She literally does. Who does that?

"I'm not leading on some girl from town," I tell her. "Calling me after the wedding to figure out when we can meet up again."

"So let her know from the beginning it's only as a date for the wedding. Nothing after. Hell, tell her it's only to appease Mom. That way she knows straight from the get-go."

Hmm. That's not a bad idea. It'll get Mom off my back for the next week. Why did I even agree to come down a week early? Just because Harper made all these plans for the wedding party doesn't mean I had to follow them.

Well, it's too late now. I'm already on my way. Now I only have to figure out who I can trust that won't blab to Mom.

"Listen," Kristen says, interrupting my thoughts, "I don't have all day to fix your problems. Harper's going to be over soon to put together wedding favors. We need to get them done so Abby has time to package them this week."

I sit up straighter in my seat. That's it. Abby.

My sister's long-time best friend is more than familiar with Mom's brand of crazy. I wouldn't even need to explain why I need a date to get her off my back. And it would be the perfect reason why I didn't RSVP with a plus one. Abby was already invited herself.

"You're a genius."

"What?"

"Abby could be my date."

She laughs, long enough that doubt creeps in.

"What? Is she already bringing a date?" I thought she was single.

She recovers a few moments later. "Sorry." There's still amusement in her voice. "Just the idea of you and Abby."

I frown. "Why's that funny?"

"I don't know. You've always set her on edge."

I have? "You don't think she'll go for being my fake date?"

"You can try."

From the way she says it, it's clear she doesn't believe Abby will agree, but I have to take a chance. Abby's the perfect choice.

"Give me her number. Let me ask her."

"Nope."

My jaw clenches. "What do you mean, *nope?*"

"I'm not roping my best friend into this. Ask her if you want, but I'm not getting involved."

God, she's infuriating. Why are little sisters so annoying? "She still works at the library?"

"Not getting involved," she reminds me in that same sing-song voice from earlier.

"Fine. I'll stop there when I get into town."

"It's funny, I never have these kinds of conversations with Owen. Only you."

My ire melts away. "That's because I'm your favorite brother."

"Right..." She can't hide the smile in her voice.

"You coming over for dinner at Mom's tonight?" I ask her.

"Yeah, we'll be there. Harper wants to go over the plan for the week with everyone."

That's right. The itinerary. She'd emailed it to me, but I'd only taken a passing glance at it. I'm just along for the ride this week. Wherever they tell me to go, I'll go.

"Well, I'll see you then. And hopefully with the good news that Abby's my date."

She grumbles something under her breath, then says audibly,

"Even if she does agree, make sure you don't leave her to deal with your mess once you go back to Seattle."

My brows knit together. "What do you mean?"

"I don't want Mom hounding her about the two of you."

Shit. She's right. That would be wildly unfair to Abby.

"I'll make it extremely clear to Mom that she's not to bother Abby at all, okay?"

"*If* Abby agrees."

"Yeah, yeah," I mutter. "And I thought you weren't getting involved."

She grumbles something else, then we say our goodbyes.

My thumb taps on the steering wheel in a staccato rhythm, thinking everything over. What the hell was Kristen talking about that I set Abby on edge? I've known her for as long as I can remember. With her and Kristen practically joined at the hip, she was a fixture at our house growing up. Sure, I never hung out with her one-on-one, but why would I? She was Kristen's friend, not mine. Did she take offense to that?

Since leaving Crescent Pass, our interactions whenever I'm back in town are usually minimal, but we've always gotten along fine. Yeah, she's on the quiet side, but it's not like she could get a word in edgewise with the rest of us blabbermouths. The only one ever quieter than her was Owen.

So, how can I convince her to be my fake date for the wedding? Should I offer to pay her? No, that seems so... mercenary. Maybe she won't even need convincing. Maybe if I ask it pathetically enough, she'll take pity on me and agree right away.

Wow, what a brilliant plan.

I glance at my GPS, but it's still showing another two hours until I get to town. There's no way I can wait that long with this looming over my head. Kristen won't help me, but maybe Owen will.

I call him up, surprised when he answers on the first ring.

"Thought you'd be busy with wedding prep," I say, shifting in my seat. Maybe I should stop at a rest area to stretch my legs soon.

"Just finished making the bower," he says in that easy way of his.

"The what?"

"The wedding arch," he clarifies. "Harper wanted it for pictures."

So instead of buying one, he made it? I don't understand him sometimes.

"Um, cool. Listen, do you happen to have Abby's number by chance?"

There's silence across the line for a few seconds. "Abby Walsh?"

What other Abby do we know? "Yeah."

"No, but Harper does. Give me a sec."

I don't want more people involved, but I guess they'd find out anyway if we end up being fake wedding dates to appease Mom.

"Hey, Grayson." Harper sounds way too chipper. "What do you need Abby's number for?"

"Because."

She laughs lightly. "I'm the one with the number."

If Kristen isn't careful, Harper will push her out of the top spot for most annoying sister, even if she's only an in-law.

I sigh and tell her my plan, bracing myself for another laugh the way Kristen did. She doesn't, though, asking instead if I'm sure about this.

"Yeah, why not?"

"Your mom is going to be at most of the events we have planned for the next week. You'll have to keep up the ruse all week, not only next Saturday."

Oh, I didn't think about that. Still, it shouldn't be a big deal. We'll act a little flirty with each other in front of Mom, then tell her it didn't work out next Sunday when I leave.

"It'll be fine. But do you think Abby will agree? Kristen said I kind of set her on edge, whatever that means."

Harper makes a half-laugh, half-hiccup kind of noise before she clears her throat. "She should be willing to help you out. I can't imagine her saying no to this."

Really? That lifts a weight off my shoulders.

"But you have to promise me something," she continues.

"Yeah, sure."

"Don't lead her on," she tells me in a serious tone.

What? "It's fake," I repeat. "I'm not really asking her out."

"Okay. But be clear about that."

I'm pretty sure Abby will get it right away. She's smart. She's a freaking librarian.

She sure has some protective friends, though. I guess it's good she inspires that kind of loyalty. Would anyone in my life look out for me like that?

Okay, not the time to think about that.

Harper gives me the number, only for me to realize I have nothing to write it down with.

"Text it to me," I request, then thank her profusely.

After hanging up, I do some finagling with my phone to call Abby, trying to keep most of my attention on the interstate. It rings, nervousness growing in the pit of my stomach the longer she doesn't pick up. What if it's the wrong number? What if she doesn't agree? I've gotten my hopes up way too much about a plan that doesn't even exist yet.

Hi, it's Abby. You know what to do.

Her voicemail beeps for me to leave a message, and I get flustered for a moment, unsure what to say.

"Hey, it's Grayson. Um, Taylor. You know, Kristen's brother. Of course you know that." Shit. I'm rambling. Why am I so nervous? It's only Abby. "Listen, I wanted to talk to you about something important. You're probably working, but I'd like to stop by the library and ask you... Well, maybe this should be an in-person kind of conversation. Shit, I'm messing this up." Wait, did I say that out loud? "I'll talk to you later, okay?"

I fumble to press the end call icon and clench my jaw, shaking my head at myself. I'm acting like some middle schooler, nervous to ask his crush out to the winter formal.

I put back on the podcast I was listening to before Mom's call interrupted it and silently stew until I get a text twenty minutes later.

Abby: *The library closes at six tonight, so I'll be there until then. Or you can stop by my house after.*

Perfect. I'm supposed to get to Mom's at five-thirtyish, but I'll tell her traffic was bad. I need to have an answer before I see her.

I keep my hopes up during the rest of the drive and pull into the gravel parking lot of the Crescent Pass Library at five-fifteen. There are only a few cars parked here, including what I'm pretty sure is Abby's gray Elantra.

Shutting the car off, I take a moment to inhale and exhale before I head inside, releasing my worry. If Abby doesn't agree, I'll just have to come up with something else.

I have no idea what that something else is, but that's a problem for future Grayson.

Opening the double doors to the library, I spot Abby at the reference desk in the center of the open room, looking like the quintessential librarian with her cardigan and dark blonde hair pulled back in a bun. All she needs is a pair of glasses held by a chain around her neck to complete the look.

As I approach, she turns to greet me, her mouth opening and closing as recognition hits. "Grayson," she murmurs in that soft voice of hers, her brown eyes widening.

Huh. I never noticed they're lighter in color than the usual brown, more like a honey or amber hue. Guess there's a lot I'll be learning about her over the next week.

If she agrees, Kristen's voice echoes in my mind.

Here goes nothing.

CHAPTER TWO

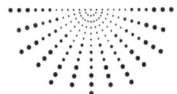

ABBY

Grayson's presence catches me off guard every time I see him, as if I forgot just how tall he is, how broad-shouldered, how he seems to take up all the air in the room.

Then again, I only see him a few times a year, usually around the holidays when he makes the long drive from Seattle to Crescent Pass. In the times between, I tell myself I must be misremembering how blue his eyes are, how his face lights up when he laughs, how my brain seems to turn to mush when he speaks directly to me.

Which is hardly... ever.

But then he shows up again and it all comes rushing back. The crush I've had on him since we were teenagers never really faded, even with time and distance.

Not that he has the first clue about that.

"Abbs," he says in greeting, using the nickname he gave me as a kid, and smiles. His grin has always been a little crooked, lifting more on the right side. He leans across the desk to give me a hug. "How are you?"

Oh, okay. This is happening.

His arm encircles the backs of my shoulders for a moment, and I lean in, my hand hovering above his back, unsure what to do. He's gone before I can decide, and I let it drop awkwardly.

"I'm fine," I say, giving him a small smile.

"Great. Do you have a minute to talk? You're not busy or anything, are you?"

I glance around the nearly empty library. Susan is shelving books over in the corner, and our regular, Stan, is reading the newspaper in one of the comfortable chairs.

"I have time. How about over there?"

I point toward the children's section, where we're least likely to be heard by the others.

Wiping my sweaty palms on my pants as I follow him, I think again about Harper's frantic call earlier, telling me that Grayson wants me to be his fake date for the wedding. It had taken a good five minutes to unravel the full story out of her, unsure what she was saying in her excitement. Even once I understood her, I half-thought she was crazy.

If Grayson's here, though... Maybe not.

He pauses in front of the *spring into a good book* display I made, featuring picture books about flowers, gardens, and springtime. Reaching out, he fingers one of the paper flowers I taped to the edge of the shelf.

"Is this origami?" he asks curiously.

I nod. "It's a cherry blossom. There are roses and lilies, too. And tulips on the bottom."

He steps back and studies the whole display. "You guys bought these?"

"I made them."

He glances at me, his dark brows pulled together in confusion. "You made them? Like, all of them?" He waves a hand to encompass all of it.

My fingers fiddle with the hem of my cardigan. "Um, yes. I like doing paper folding projects."

"This looks advanced. I didn't know you could do stuff like this."

My head tilts to the side as I meet his gaze. "Why would you?"

When I do get the chance to talk to him—which is rarely—we stick to safe, neutral topics. *How are things in Seattle? How are your folks doing? Can you believe how big Jamie and Jenny are getting?* I've never had a reason to tell him that origami and gift wrapping are totally my jam.

"Right." He gestures toward the paper flowers. "Well, it's very impressive."

I give a slight nod in thanks. "But I'm guessing you didn't drive over here to admire my children's book display."

His mouth lifts in that crooked grin again. "No."

He stuffs his hands in his pockets, then immediately takes them out and crosses his arms over his chest, the sleeves of his fitted tee pulling tight around his biceps. "I, um... Well, I wanted to ask..."

I wait for him to continue, but he doesn't. Instead, he's chewing on his bottom lip, seemingly lost in thought.

Wait, is he nervous? Grayson? He's normally so unflappable. Then again, this is a supremely weird request he's about to ask of me.

"Harper told me," I say, putting him out of his misery. "You want me to be your fake date to her wedding so your mom will get off your back."

He blinks in surprise before he sighs. "I should have known she couldn't keep that to herself. Where my brother's a vault, she's an open book."

He's definitely not wrong with that analogy.

"So..." His gaze flicks to me and away as his fingers curl into the muscle of his upper arm. "Are you game? You'd really be doing me a favor."

I shrug, trying to appear casual, even as a thrill runs up my spine. Despite it being fake, I'm still going to be Grayson's date. Teenage Abby would die. "Yeah, sure. That's what friends do."

"You think of us as friends?"

My mouth opens, unsure how to respond as the thrill dissipates, leaving an empty heaviness in its wake. Does he think so little of me?

"I mean, we are," he backtracks, appearing alarmed. Was my disappointment that obvious? "I just always thought of you more as Kristen's friend. I didn't realize it extended to me and Owen, too."

I hide my wince. Bringing his brother into the mix? If he says he thinks of me as a sister, I'm going to spontaneously combust.

Giving him a half-smile, I turn and straighten a few books on the display, not that they weren't already perfect to begin with.

"Thank you," he says, filling the now-awkward silence. "This means a lot to me."

He squeezes my arm in thanks, the area tingling even after his hand returns to his side.

I nod unsteadily, hating how he affects me. I'm twenty-eight-freaking-years-old. I shouldn't still have this stupid crush on him.

"Harper said she has some events planned for this week?" he continues, his voice lifting at the end, making it a question. "I don't know, I didn't really look at the itinerary she sent. But she mentioned my mom will be at some of them, so we might have to pretend, too, before the actual wedding."

"Yeah, that's fine."

"It could be a good thing, you know? Another way to sell it to my mom."

How important is it that she believes I'm his date to this thing?

"Are you coming over to dinner tonight?" he asks. "At my mom's?"

"Oh, no. I think that's only for family. We're all going out tomorrow night, though. Over in Kirkwood."

There's a beat of silence, and I resist the urge to fill it as he seems to inwardly think.

"Can I stop by your house in the morning?" he finally asks. "So we can get on the same page about everything?"

"You mean come up with our alibi?"

He laughs, almost like he's surprised, and gives me a searching look. "Yeah, exactly."

I nod. "Sure. Just text me."

Since he has my number now and all, apparently.

He says his goodbyes and as he leaves, I let out a whole body sigh, tension releasing from me.

So, that just happened.

Before he's even out the front door, the library assistant, Susan, is pushing her book cart toward me, nosiness radiating from her. God help me in this small town of busybodies.

"Was that Grayson?" she asks, as if she hasn't been in the stacks texting to let her gossip network know the once-prodigal son has returned. "What's he doing meeting up with you?"

Ouch. Is it that unbelievable that Grayson would—

Okay, yeah. I can't even finish the outraged thought. She has a point.

"We have some things to coordinate for Owen and Harper's wedding," I tell her, surprised at how breezily it comes out. Not that it's a lie... It's just not the full truth.

"I can't believe you're taking off a full week for that," she grumbles. "It's not until next Saturday."

I don't bring up the fact that I haven't taken a vacation in years. I've already reminded her numerous times.

"Well, Harper has a lot of stuff planned for us since her friends are visiting from Chicago."

"Yeah, but a whole week?"

I give her a shrug and walk away. She's only salty because she wasn't invited to the wedding.

It's not long until it's six o'clock, and I go through the closing procedures on autopilot, my mind obsessively going over everything. Can I really convince Mrs. Taylor I'm her son's wedding date? And why wouldn't I have mentioned it before now if it was true?

I mentally add it to the list of plot holes we'll need to resolve tomorrow. I should have asked him why he needs to convince her in the first place, but I have a feeling I already know the answer. His mom can get a bit... forceful when it comes to pushing her kids toward her idea of what's right.

When I get home, my orange tabby, Leo, chatters loudly at me, telling me it's past dinner time.

"I know, bud," I murmur, setting my bag down on the kitchen table. "Give me a sec."

He circles my ankles, nearly tripping me as I open the pantry door and peruse the selection.

"Is it an ocean whitefish and tuna kind of night? Or salmon and beef?"

I hold out the two cans of cat food to him, and he rubs the side of his face against the first option.

"Excellent choice, sir."

I plate it for him, his interest in me long forgotten as he chows down, licking up all the gravy before chewing the shreds of meat. I watch him, not in any rush to start dinner for myself. There's still this unsettled feeling in the pit of my stomach, like I'm on a precipice, ready to tumble into the unknown.

This thing with Grayson... Spending time with him, getting to know him better... It could lead to something. An actual something. That's what happens in rom-coms, right?

Get real, an inner voice snarkily whispers. *The man hasn't looked twice at you in the two-plus decades he's known you.*

I think back to this past Thanksgiving, seated next to him but barely saying a word throughout the whole dinner. At Christmas, hardly able to string two words together when he'd greeted me.

A lump forms in my throat, and I swallow hard to get rid of it, not liking the reminders of all my failings when it comes to him. Of all the ways he's never noticed me, of how anxious I get around him.

No, no. Today was different. I'm turning over a new leaf. I'm going to be fun, bubbly Abby, the perfect fake date for his brother's wedding. So perfect that he'll wonder why he never paid attention to me before, how I've been under his nose this whole time. How we'd be perfect together.

A soft laugh escapes me, tinged with an edge of hysteria. I'm delusional, aren't I? I need to cut back on the romance novels and Hallmark channel.

Even if nothing happens between us, though, this feels like a wake-up call. I'm tired of life passing me by, waiting for something to happen. If I want things to happen, I need to make them happen.

And who better to try that with than the man I've always wanted?

CHAPTER THREE

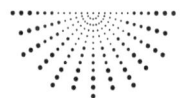

ABBY

I eye the living room for approximately the ten millionth time this morning, making sure everything is just so. The throw blanket folded along the back of the couch and trio of unlit candles on the side table lend added touches of warmth without being overbearing. The open curtains make the room bright and inviting. The charcuterie board on the coffee table will tempt Grayson to stay longer.

I bite at my thumbnail, eyeing the spread. It's too much, isn't it? What if he doesn't like prosciutto? Is it too pretentious? Should I have put out breakfast items instead? It's nearly eleven-thirty, though.

Rubbing at my temple, indecision wars within me. I should scrap the whole thing. It's giving *trying way too hard* vibes. But as the doorbell rings, the decision is made for me.

I smooth my palms over my jeans. "Be cool," I mutter to myself. "Just… don't be embarrassing."

My smile must look normal as I answer the door because Grayson doesn't run for the hills, giving me a returning smile.

He takes off his aviators, his unshaven jaw looking more modelesque than scruffy. "Mom hasn't kidnapped you yet?"

My brows draw together. "Kidnapped?"

"When I broke the news to her last night that you were my date for the wedding," he explains. "I thought she might've snuck over here to kidnap you and hold you hostage the next week so you won't change your mind."

My stomach makes a slow turn, unsure how to feel about that. "So *Operation Trick Your Mom* is a success so far?"

His eyes crinkle at the corners. "Think we can get that trademarked?"

"Might ruin the whole keeping it a secret thing."

He nods, still smiling. "True. See, you're always two steps ahead. This is why you're the perfect fake date."

Heat touches my cheeks, and I step aside, ushering him in the house. Okay, things are good so far. We've got some banter going and I'm not freezing up like an idiot... I can do this.

"Are you having people over later?" he asks, gesturing to the charcuterie board.

My blush intensifies. "Oh, no. It's for you," I tell him lamely. "Just some stuff I had in the fridge, in case you're hungry."

I knew I shouldn't have put that together. It was way too much effort. He probably thinks I'm crazy for—

"Awesome, I love this."

He helps himself and I breathe a sigh of relief. Overthinking things as usual, Abby.

"You liked the one I brought a few Thanksgivings ago," I say, taking a seat on the couch.

He pauses, his mouth full of meat and cheese. "You remember that?"

"I..." Sweat blooms under my arms. "My brain's funny like that." I tap the side of my head. "I'll remember what we ate for Thanksgiving years ago, but couldn't tell you what I had for breakfast yesterday."

I tack on a nervous laugh, resisting the urge to fan my armpits.

He returns my smile, apparently accepting my explanation, and sits in the overstuffed armchair. "I think I'm the opposite. No problem with the short-term stuff, but my long-term's shot. At least, it seems that way every time I come back home. Everyone's always talking about things from when we were kids I swear I don't remember."

I study him for a moment. "You were so intent on leaving here. Maybe you were so focused on the future, you forgot to experience what was happening around you."

He sets down the cracker he's holding loaded with salami and cheese, and stares at me.

Oh, crap. I did it again, didn't I? Making it obvious how much I pay attention to him.

"Sorry," I mutter. "Ignore my psychoanalyzing."

"No," he says slowly. "You might be on to something." He seems lost in thought for a moment, then shakes it off, focusing back on me. "Anyway, Mom completely bought our story. Said she's always sensed something special between us."

The words would carry more weight if they weren't accompanied by an eye roll.

"And she didn't question why things have changed now?" I ask. "Considering how long we've known each other?"

He shrugs. "No, not really. I laid it on thick that it's a casual thing, though. And that I don't want her to put pressure on you."

I nod. Good. When Cheryl gets an idea in her head, she's like a dog with a bone.

"So when she inevitably gets pushy," he continues, "it'll be her fault for ruining our relationship."

"Hmm." I lean back against the cushions, getting more comfortable. "If I didn't know you better, I'd say you're pretty devious."

"Come on, that's brilliant," he argues. "She'll have no one to blame but herself."

"You're kind of setting her up to fail."

"Hey, whose side are you on?" he asks with good humor. "If she wasn't so hell bent on me having a date to begin with, this wouldn't be an issue."

"Fair enough." I trace my finger over the couch cushion, making a figure eight pattern along the soft fabric. "Why is she so insistent on that?"

He rolls his eyes again. "She keeps saying I need to settle down. That I'm turning thirty soon and need to get started building a family. As if I'm some Regency-era spinster on the shelf."

My brows pop up. He's familiar with that kind of stuff?

He must notice my surprise because he waves a hand in explanation. "Mom and Kristen made me watch *Pride and Prejudice* about a million times. Anyway, she thinks it'll make her look bad if I show up dateless when she's talked me up to everyone she knows." He heaves a sigh, annoyance flashing over his face. "This is so dumb I have to even get you involved to begin with."

"It's okay," I murmur.

"And seriously, if she gets pushy about anything to you, you tell her you want to keep things between us private and she should talk to me about it. I don't want her hounding you."

My stomach flutters at his intensity. "Well, that's very chivalrous of you."

He snorts. "I'm the one who roped you into this. The least I can do is keep her off your back."

There's a beat of silence, then he rubs his palms on his jeans. "Guess we should go over some ground rules," he says.

"Right."

"I figure we just need to be a little flirty with each other in front of Mom. Make her think we're interested, but not too crazy. I don't want her planning our wedding or anything."

That flutter in my stomach pulses stronger and I ignore it. Get a grip, Abby.

"And how often will we be around her?" I ask, reaching for my phone on the coffee table. "Let me pull up the itinerary."

Grayson shakes his head. "I still can't believe Harper made that."

"Well, she has a lot planned for the week."

"Why is she jam-packing everyone's schedules, anyway? What if I wanted to relax?"

My lips tip up at his disgruntled expression. "She wants to make sure everyone has a fun time while they're here. Her friends from Chicago haven't visited yet and you're hardly ever here. It's kind of a once-in-a-lifetime opportunity."

"I guess," he mutters. "So what is it we're doing again?"

I open the attachment Harper emailed last week. "Tonight's the dinner in Kirkwood."

"Yeah, Mom'll be there for that."

"Tomorrow is the hike, then Monday during the day we'll go horseback riding. Monday night is game night at Owen and Harper's place, then Tuesday she's spending with Elena and Kelly. But Tuesday night we're all going to Harry's Bar. Wednesday is the trip to the winery. On Thursday the girls are getting manicures and pedicures and you and Owen are going fishing. Friday we're setting up for the wedding during the day and having the rehearsal dinner at night. Then Saturday is the wedding."

"Holy fuck, that's a lot." He scrubs a hand down his face. "Is Harper some kind of masochist?"

I press my lips together to keep from laughing. "She likes being busy."

He wisely doesn't comment. "Well, what other ground rules should we have?"

I tuck my hands under my thighs so I don't fidget. "I guess it all depends on how far we're willing to go with the ruse. If there will be touching or…" I swallow heavily. "Kissing or something."

His eyes widen. "No, we won't go that far."

I nod in agreement, even as disappointment splashes in the pit of my stomach.

"I might put my hand on your arm or your lower back or something," he says. "Is that okay? I don't want to make you uncomfortable."

"I trust you, Grayson."

The words slip out unconsciously, and I don't think it's only my imagination that I put more emphasis than I needed into them, based on the way his eyes widen.

"I mean, yes, of course it's okay," I add. "And it's all right if I do the same? Or hold your hand?"

He nods, shifting in his chair, his gaze moving away from me.

Did I go too far? Is holding hands too much?

A thick kind of tension fills the air between us, but there's nothing sexual about it. More... awkward.

Lovely.

"Well, as long as we're on the same page, everything will be fine," I say brightly, in an attempt to get things back on track. "And we can always readjust our plan throughout the week depending on what happens."

He looks again at me, his discomfort gone now. "Right. And again, I appreciate—"

I hold up a hand to stop him. "You don't have to keep thanking me."

"Is there anything I can do for you in return? I feel like I'm taking advantage of you."

A wave of heat rolls through me as that daydreaming part of my mind wishes he'd take advantage of me in a different way.

No. Bad Abby.

"I could pay you," he continues. "What's a fair rate for being my fake wedding date?"

I hide my wince, not liking turning this into a transactional arrangement.

"It's fine," I tell him. "Seriously, I don't need anything. I'm happy to help a... a friend."

He'd commented earlier that he didn't think of us as friends—which hadn't been a blow to the ego at all—even if he had a fair point. He's right that I've always been his sister's friend, not his.

But I want him to notice me now. First as a friend, then maybe something... more.

"Okay, well let me know if anything comes to mind I can do to even the score." He places his hands on his knees, then stands. "I'll get out of your hair. Give you the rest of the day to yourself before dinner."

I nod and follow him to the front door. "Do you need a ride to Kirkwood?"

"Kristen's taking me. Jamie and Jenny begged me to ride with them in her Mom-mobile."

"It's hard to say no to them." I smile, thinking of Kristen's precocious twins.

"Yeah, especially since I missed their birthday last month."

"You're still a good uncle."

He gives me a half-smile, rubbing at the back of his neck. "See you tonight."

"See you."

After shutting the door behind him, I lean against it, my forehead touching the cool surface. That could have gone worse, I guess. Could have gone better, too, but it's a start.

CHAPTER FOUR

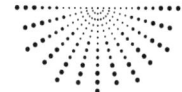

GRAYSON

"Just like the time Duke barked at Grandma!"

Everyone at the table laughs loudly at Jenny's comment, and I glance around cluelessly, no idea why Owen's dog barking is funny.

Kristen must notice my confusion because she says to me, "You had to be there," while wiping tears of laughter from her eyes.

It's not the first time someone has referenced something I've missed out on. Usually it's no big deal to shrug it off, but it's not as easy today for some reason. The whole car ride here was full of inside jokes between Jenny, Jamie, Kristen, and Eli. I thought Kristen's boyfriend would at least be the odd man out along with me, but he seems at ease among the family, fully in on all the references.

Guess that's the price I pay for moving away.

The relief I feel at the sight of Abby entering the restaurant surprises me momentarily. I've never particularly cared if she was at any of our family events over the years, but after our talk this morning, there's a sense of... kinship between us. If anyone else were to understand what it's like to be an outsider among this group, it'd be her.

"There's Abby," I murmur, getting up from my seat.

I'm conscious of Mom's gaze on me as I head towards the entrance, and step in close to hug Abby.

"Mom's watching," I whisper.

She's smiling as I lean back. "Ready to put on a show?"

Thank God she agreed to this asinine plan. "As ready as I'll ever be."

Mom is out of her seat before we even get to the table, nearly sprinting to Abby to get her own hug.

"I'm so glad you could join the family tonight," Mom says. "You know you're practically family already." She pauses for a moment, seeming to collect herself. "And now you're dating Grayson—"

"You're dating Uncle Grayson?" Jenny shouts, her hearing exceptionally good in this crowded restaurant.

Shit. This is getting away from us.

"We're going to the wedding together," Abby says brightly to the twins, both staring wide-eyed at her.

I try my best not to grit my teeth. "Let's not put too much pressure on it," I remind Mom.

"Right, right," she says, miming zipping her lips even as her eyes twinkle with delight.

From her spot at the table, Kristen rolls her eyes. She better not blab to Mom about the truth of our arrangement.

Or apparently to the kids now. They'd be the first ones to spill secrets to their grandma.

"Should we call you Aunt Abby?" Jenny asks, brazenly forging ahead with the topic.

Abby's cheeks pinken, her gaze darting to me and away again.

I rub at the back of my neck, hating how awkward this has turned. "No, it's not..." I trail off, about to say it's not anything serious before I remember I want Mom to believe it's serious enough to not set me up with anyone else while I'm in town this week.

Damn. When did this get so complicated?

"You can still call me Abby," Abby says to Jenny, her composure recovered.

Jenny shrugs. "Okay, cool."

We're saved from any more on the topic as Owen, Harper, and two women who must be her friends from Chicago arrive. One is short and blonde, the other a taller brunette with legs for days.

In the chaos of their arrival, I gently grab Abby's arm and guide her to the other end of the long table, away from any more questions from nosy moms and nieces.

We're introduced to Kelly and Elena, the other two bridesmaids in the wedding, and our server stops by to introduce herself and take our drink orders. As the conversation turns toward the two women's travel from Chicago to here, I whisper to Abby, "Sorry about all of that."

"That's okay. Jenny's just… precocious."

Yeah, that's one word for it.

"I guess I didn't think this all the way through. It was one thing to pretend in front of Mom. Now we'll have to do it in front of the twins, too." A thought occurs to me. "Oh, shit."

"What?" Abby appears startled at my tone.

"What about these two?" I jab my thumb toward the two women to our left. "Can we trust them to keep the secret?" I'm too deep in this lie to risk getting caught now. I'd never hear the end of it from Mom.

Abby chews at her bottom lip. "I don't know. Harper did say she was a little worried about Elena when we go to the bar and winery later this week. I guess she likes to overshare when she gets drunk."

I couldn't care less if Elena gossips about Harper's past. But I don't want her accidentally letting loose that I'm tricking Mom into thinking Abby's my date for the wedding so she'll stop meddling in my love life.

"Has Harper already told them?"

"Let me find out." She pulls out her phone to text Harper, and a second later Harper picks up her phone, then shakes her head at the two of us.

"So we'll keep up the ruse in front of them, too," I say, ignoring the apprehension pooling in my gut. "Like I said earlier, just a little flirty with each other. No biggie."

"Yeah, of course. And not every couple is super obvious. I mean, look at Kristen and Eli. They're dating and you wouldn't even know it from looking at them."

At that moment, Eli whispers something in Kristen's ear and she blushes, turning to face him as he looks at her adoringly.

Disgusting.

"Okay, maybe not the best example," Abby amends. "They're usually not flashy about their relationship."

I glance over at Owen, the same goofy expression of adoration on his face as he watches Harper chat animatedly with the brunette, Elena. Does being in love automatically turn you into a sap?

"What are you two lovebirds whispering about?"

I jump in my seat as Mom's voice registers from behind us. When did she sneak over here?

"N-nothing," Abby stammers. "Just, um, the hike tomorrow."

Mom slips into the empty chair next to us. Why couldn't we have an even number in our party so there are no extra seats?

"I'm sure you two are looking forward to having some time to reconnect." Mom smiles fondly at us. "How long has it been since you've last seen each other?"

Abby's hands twist the napkin in her lap. "I stopped by Kristin's place at Christmas, but we didn't get a chance to talk. We sat next to each other at Thanksgiving, though."

That's right, I forgot about that. Good thing she has a functional memory.

I stretch my arm across the back of Abby's chair, my fingertips grazing her shoulder. Mom's gaze zeroes in on the action, just like I wanted.

Unfortunately, Abby startles in her seat, ruining any kind of intimate effect I was hoping for. Time to save this another way.

"Yeah, I forgot how funny Abby is. She was cracking me up with some story about her dad." That's a safe lie, right? Mom's not going to ask about the actual story, will she?

Mom reaches a hand forward and squeezes Abby's upper arm briefly. "Oh, honey. I've been meaning to ask you about him. Is he doing any better?"

Oh, shit. Is there something wrong with Abby's dad? Something I presumably should know about?

Abby gives a half-hearted smile. "He has his good days and bad days. Actually, more bad days lately."

My arm drops awkwardly from her shoulder. "Is everything okay?"

She waves off my concern. "Yeah. My dad has dementia."

Oh. I had no idea. I don't remember much about her parents other than they always seemed so much older than my own.

"Well, you let me know if you need any help with him," Mom says.

She takes her leave then, and an uneasy silence falls between me and Abby.

"Sorry to bring the mood down," she whispers.

"No, no. I shouldn't have made up that stupid comment."

"It's fine."

She smiles, but it doesn't reach her eyes.

We're interrupted by the server bringing us our drinks and taking our food order, and I mentally smack myself for letting my mouth get away from me. As someone interested in her, I should have known that about her dad.

"I don't think Cheryl cares you didn't know about it," Abby whispers, seeming to read my mind. "It's not like it's a first date kind of subject anyway."

I roll my shoulders to loosen the sudden tension in them. "Was this whole ruse a mistake?"

"No," she says vehemently, surprising both of us.

I glance over at her, her cheeks pinkening again. She must be an easy blusher.

"We've already made it this far," she continues, composed now. "There's bound to be a few hiccups along the way. And would you rather go to the wedding with me—who doesn't expect anything of you—or someone your mom picks? Because you know she won't let it rest if you say you're going solo."

My brow creases. When did our roles reverse where she's the one convincing me to do this? And why?

"I... I don't want to get caught in a lie," she whispers, reading my mind for a second time. Does she have telepathic powers?

I shake my head. What's gotten into me? "Yeah, of course. We'll keep it up."

I grab her hand for good measure, as much to comfort her as to put on a show. Her palm is soft, skin pale against my tan. A sudden urge to stroke a finger down the length of her palm strikes me before I push it away. That was weird.

She smiles, a genuine one, and my stomach makes a strange twinge in response. Also weird.

I'm just... glad I could give her something to smile about.

That's all.

CHAPTER FIVE

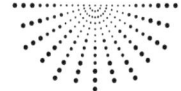

ABBY

I wipe my hands surreptitiously against the worn cotton of my yoga pants, ridding them of the dampness that always seems to happen when I'm around Grayson, then take a swig from my water bottle in an attempt to counteract the dehydration. When will my body adjust to being around him?

Then again, I'm not used to such concentrated doses. Usually, I get a fleeting encounter two or three times a year. Seeing him for the third time in as many days is an overload to my system.

"You good?" he asks, sidling closer to me as we continue our hike down the winding forest trail.

I nod, hyper aware of him next to me. It would be a romantic scene with the dappled sunlight coming through the trees overhead and the far-off gentle burble of water from a nearby stream, if not for the overexcited seven-year-olds ahead of us.

"The left side of the path is mine," Jamie whines to his sister. "Stay on your own side."

"I am," Jenny insists. "You're the one who's going too far over."

"Jesus, it's constant with these two," Grayson mutters under his breath. "How does Kristen do it? For that matter, how does Eli?"

Before I have a chance to respond, he quickens his pace until he's in between the two of them. Stooping, he wraps his left arm around Jamie, then does the same to Jenny with his right. He spins around, the kids' annoyance with each other transforming into shrieks of delight.

"Faster, Uncle Grayson," Jenny yells, her braided hair flying out around her.

"Too dizzy," Grayson says, slowing and placing each kid back on the ground.

"No, please. Again." Jenny hangs on his arm, giving him puppy dog eyes.

From this angle behind the trio, I can't fully see Grayson's face, but I still glimpse the affection there as he returns his niece's gaze.

"You'll have to give me a few minutes. I might accidentally—"

He makes an overdramatic lurching motion, as if he's going to vomit on them, and I chuckle as the twins squeal with a mixture of disgust and amusement.

"Why don't you pick some flowers?" I ask, gesturing to the field to our left with an array of wildflowers in bloom. "I can help you make one of those flower crowns I was telling you about."

"Ooh," Jenny exclaims. "Yeah, come on."

She drags her brother off into the field, and I shout after them, "Find ones with long stems."

"Good idea," Grayson comments, keeping an eye on the kids as they keep pace with the group while also ripping flowers out of the ground with a little too much gusto. "Keep them occupied so they'll stop bickering."

A zing pops through my chest at his praise. "You did good, too. Breaking up their argument like that." I twirl my finger around the same way he spun the kids. "You're great with them."

He gives a half-chuckle, half-snort. "I'm just the fun uncle. I don't think they'd actually take me seriously about anything."

That's true. Every time I've seen him with them over the years, he's been the novelty goofy entertainment.

"Yeah, but they need some silliness in their lives. You know Kristen isn't exactly... silly."

A grin spreads over his mouth. "No, she isn't."

There's another zing knowing I made him smile like that, but it slowly fades as the conversation stalls. Up ahead, everyone else in our hiking party is grouped in pairs along the narrow trail—Owen and Harper leading the pack, Elena and Kelly behind them glancing around wide-eyed at the beautiful scenery, then Kristen and Eli, holding hands as they follow the others. There's a gap where Jenny and Jamie had been, then me and Grayson bringing up the rear. Cheryl didn't come on the hike, citing her bad knees.

We continue on in silence, discomfort growing in my chest the longer it lasts. This is the perfect opportunity to talk to him. How am I ever going to get him to like—

Nope. Don't go getting your hopes up, Abby. But still...

"Do you want kids?" I blurt out, saying the first thing that comes to mind that's somewhat related to our previous conversation.

He squints at me suspiciously. "Did Mom tell you to ask that?"

A chuckle escapes me. "You think I'm a double agent now?"

He strokes the stubble on his jaw. "Can't say for sure. You're surprisingly sneakier than I thought you'd be."

"You just don't know me that well," I respond without thinking.

Wait, I shouldn't have said that. I should be playing up our connection, not the distance.

"I'm coming to see that," he says slowly, his gaze lingering on me.

A full-body flush overtakes me, and I duck my head, hating my body's overeager response to any kind of interest from him.

Not that it was even interest. He was only looking at me as he responded. Like a normal human does.

"I guess we've never gotten to know each other as adults. We should hang out more when I'm in town."

I smile, unsure how sincere it looks. His offer feels like a throwaway invite, one of those things you say you'll do that you'll never actually make good on.

"So, are you going to answer my question?" I ask, getting back to the topic at hand. "No double crossing, I swear."

He laughs, then blows out a breath. "I don't know. The right woman would have to come first. And that still hasn't happened yet, so I'm not worrying about something that may never happen anyway."

Up ahead, Kristen calls out to Jenny to be careful as she does a cartwheel out in the field and loses half the flowers stuffed in her hand.

"Have you seriously dated anyone?"

Grayson's never brought a woman with him to Crescent Pass as far as I know, but that's not to say he hasn't dated. How could he not? He's handsome, funny, smart, financially stable… Okay, no need to rehash all his good qualities. But how could someone not have snatched him up by now?

He shrugs. "A few weeks here and there. Nothing ever really pans out, though."

Why, I desperately want to ask. What's the problem?

"How about you?" he asks. "Kristen's never mentioned anything, but I assume you're not seriously seeing anyone if you agreed to this asinine plan."

I nearly snort. "Me? No. All the guys in town…"

They're not you.

I obviously can't say that, though.

"There was a guy in college," I add. "But it didn't work out."

"He the one who got away?"

"Oh, no. No. I was the one who ended it." Peter had proposed after only four months of dating, which had derailed everything. Turns out he was way more into me than I was into him. "But, you know, it's fine. I like my life. I have a great job, a great house, a great cat." Okay, that sounded pathetic. "I would rather be single than be with someone I don't care about."

He nods. "I need you to write that down so I can memorize it and say it to my mom. Maybe that'll get her off my back."

We both chuckle and he looks over at Jenny and Jamie in the field of wildflowers, then ahead, one of the mountains that surrounds our town rising in the distance.

"I forgot how pretty it is here in spring. I've only visited during Thanksgiving and Christmas the last few years."

"It's not nice in Seattle?"

"No, it is. Just different. I guess I don't go outdoors much."

There's a plaintive note in his voice, something I haven't heard before.

"You and Owen used to practically live in the forest as kids."

A small smile touches his lips. "Yeah, we did." He gestures toward the front of our line of hikers. "He seems really happy. Happier than I've ever seen him."

Up ahead, Harper says something to Owen, using her hands to animatedly make a point, and Owen grins, the smile transforming his face from his usual stoic expression into one filled with life. Even from this distance, it's obvious how much he loves her.

"They're great together," I tell Grayson. "And head over heels for each other."

He nods distractedly. "He called me last year, after she left to go back to Chicago." He pauses, seeming to collect his thoughts. "I thought he was going to start sobbing. I didn't know he could even feel that strongly."

My brow furrows, confused. "Owen can feel."

Owen and I aren't the closest, and yes, he's reserved, but he's expressive enough when he needs to be. Especially when Harper's around.

"No, I know. I just... Maybe I mean that I don't think I... I could feel that strongly."

He's staring ahead at his siblings, but it's more like he's looking through them.

"I guess the right person will do that to you," I murmur.

Have I felt like that about Grayson? Like there's a hole in my heart when he's not here?

No, but we've never shared the kind of experiences Owen and

Harper have. I've never opened up to him, put myself out there. I've never truly thought he'd be interested in me in return. And how could he be if I keep myself hidden?

"Do you feel like you're missing out?" I ask.

He's quiet for a bit before responding. "I didn't before this trip," he finally says. "But yesterday at dinner, everyone was talking about things that had happened without me. I swear Jamie and Jenny are a foot taller than the last time I saw them. And now looking at Owen with Harper, and Kristen with Eli..." He trails off for a moment. "Sometimes I think of Crescent Pass as a time capsule. Everything should stay the same as I left it. But it doesn't. Everyone's moving on without me."

I reach for his hand, emboldened by the way he held my hand at the restaurant last night, even if it was for his mom's benefit. "I know the feeling," I tell him, unsure what else to say. Everything he said is true. His family *is* moving on, and it wouldn't help matters to remind him it was his choice to move away.

He squeezes my hand in return, then lets go as Jenny rushes toward us, her brother on her heels, both of their arms filled with long-stemmed wildflowers.

"We got the stuff," Jenny says breathlessly.

Grayson calls ahead to the others to pause, and we find a nearby fallen log to sit on. Elena, Kelly, and Harper all ask if they can make flower crowns once they realize what we're doing, and thankfully, the twins have gathered more than enough flowers for all of us.

Surprisingly, Grayson stays for my demonstration as I show them how to braid three stems together, then add in a new flower every inch or so until the chain is long enough to wrap around your head. My fingers make quick work of it, used to the actions from all the paper folding I do, and tuck the ends into the start so it's a circle. I place the finished product on Jenny's head, who immediately runs to her mom to ask her to take a picture so she can see what it looks like.

As Jenny exclaims in delight at her appearance, Harper and her friends select their flowers and begin braiding them together.

"Did you want to make one, too?" I ask Grayson, motioning toward the leftover flowers.

I'm only joking, so I'm a little taken aback when he grabs three flowers from the pile and holds them in his lap.

"I watched you do it, but your fingers were moving too fast to make sense of it."

"Oh, you just braid it."

He grins sheepishly at me. "I've never braided anything in my life."

A laugh escapes me. I guess there aren't many opportunities for a grown man to practice braiding. "Think of it as crossing strings over each other in a pattern. Start with the right one and cross it over the middle one."

He does as I say.

"Then the one on the left goes over the middle one."

"The original middle one or the new middle one?"

"The new one."

He does it, but without holding onto the ends, it all unravels. "Hey," he exclaims.

"You have to keep tension on it," I explain, "especially since these stems are thick and naturally want to stay straight. Here."

Our fingers brush as I show him what to do, and I quietly enjoy the tingles that race up my arms. Is it pathetic that I get this much pleasure from this little contact? Probably. Am I going to stop? Hell, no.

The girls are done faster than him, but spend so much time taking selfies afterward that it evens out. I help him tuck in the ends, then realize the crown is too small.

"Wait, you need to add more flowers to fit your head."

"No, I made it for you."

He takes it from me and places it atop my head. There's something solemn about the way he does it, and when I look up at him, his expression is more serious than I was expecting.

"It looks good on you."

Heat floods my face, but I don't duck my head like I instinctively want to, afraid the crown will fall.

"Thank you," I whisper, warmth also filling my chest. "That's really thoughtful."

His gaze roams my face, but I'm not sure what he sees. Or what I want him to see.

"Aw, that's so sweet." Kelly's high-pitched voice interrupts whatever kind of moment was happening. "He made her a flower crown."

Grayson clears his throat and stands, stepping away from the log and remainder of flowers strewn everywhere. "We ready to keep hiking?" he asks, looking over at the rest of the group hanging out on the side of the trail. Deliberately not looking at me.

I stand, too, brushing petals and bits of stems off my lap as a heaviness fills my stomach. I can't explain why, but something seemed to shift.

And I don't know if it was for the better.

CHAPTER SIX

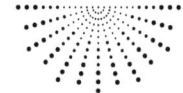

GRAYSON

"Grayson Taylor, you son of a bitch. You said you'd never step foot on this ranch again."

Aw, shit.

The grizzled old man comes forward, and it's hard to make out his expression from underneath his cowboy hat, but his words aren't promising.

"Hey, Rodney." I rub at the back of my neck, aware of everyone's gaze on me. Most are curious, but Mom looks like she's about ready to blow a gasket. The only thing is, I'm not sure if she'll attack me or Rodney.

He pushes the brim of his hat up so his weathered features are visible, and a grin splits his face, his tobacco-stained teeth on display. "I'm just yanking your chain, boy. Good to see you again."

He claps me on the back, and my insides go loose with relief. Didn't want to fight a man who has to be nearing his seventies by now.

Next to me, Abby quirks a brow up, clearly asking me to explain what that was about.

"I worked here one summer in high school," I tell her. "Rodney was my boss."

"And you said you'd never come back?"

My weight shifts from foot to foot before I force myself to stop. "Not exactly. He wanted me to keep working here during the school year, but I had football practice and couldn't. Things got a little heated when I put in my two weeks."

When he told me I was lucky he gave me a job in the first place, I told him he was lucky I was willing to shovel horse shit all day for minimum wage and that it'd be a cold day in hell before I did it again. He'd laughed long and loud about it, so I don't think he was too mad, but true to my word, I haven't been back since.

Horseback riding is on Harper's *itinerary* today, though, and Lucky Ranch is the closest place to Crescent Pass to offer something like this.

"Well, Grayson here is already a pro," Rodney announces to the group, a twinkle in his eye, "but the rest of you will need to listen to the safety briefing."

Our group today consists of everyone from yesterday, plus Mom, and minus the kids, who are in school. They listen as Rodney goes over how to mount and dismount the horse, and how to use the reins to steer and stop, but my mind wanders, having heard the same spiel a hundred times during that summer over a decade ago.

The earthy smell of manure is pungent in the air, but mixed with the fresh air and sweet scent of hay from the bales next to us, it's not so bad. It's nostalgic in a way, and I take a deep breath, remembering how I'd become nose blind to it before. Mom would yell at me as soon as I'd come home to put my clothes in the washer and take a shower. Kristen would theatrically plug her nose if I got near her, but Dad and Owen never cared.

And Abby. She was there too a lot, holed up in Kristen's room, sometimes peeking out from the door frame to see what the fuss was about. She was a regular fixture in the house, but I never paid much attention to her.

I glance over at her now, studiously listening to Rodney's instructions, and feel again that tug in my stomach, the same one from yesterday when she'd looked up at me with the flower crown on her head, happiness radiating from her. It had been so unexpected, I'd unthinkingly blurted out that it looked good on her. And all thoughts of asking her to take a selfie to send to my mom had fled as she'd blushed prettily in response, somehow heightening that joy.

Did she do it because Harper's friends were watching? That's the only thing I can figure.

But that doesn't explain my reaction. How beautiful I thought she looked. I've never thought of Abby like that. She's just been... Abby.

She glances up at me, like she sensed my gaze, and I look away toward the stables where our horses are waiting for us in their stalls. Would it matter if she caught me looking at her? No. But do I want her to catch me?

Before the past couple of days, I wouldn't have given it a second thought. But now, I don't know. Something's... changed.

I'm just not sure what.

I breathe a sigh of relief as another thought occurs to me. I'm only on edge because of this stupid lie I told Mom. That's why I'm thinking of Abby differently. Not because there's anything actually different.

The answer is so simple, I almost smack my forehead with the obviousness of it all. And now that I know, it won't happen again.

Rodney is leading the group over to the stalls and I hurriedly catch up, breathing in the musky scent of leather and horse. Golden patches of light filter in through the wooden beams overhead, the silence interrupted by the occasional soft nicker from a horse or rustle of hay.

A boy who looks to be in his late teens joins Rodney to assist him as he matches each person to a horse and gets them mounted.

"Grayson, get the two at the far end over there for you and your girl," Rodney calls out, gesturing toward the back of the stables.

I startle for a moment at the mention of Abby as my girl, but to be fair, I've been standing close to her the whole time, aware that Mom's keeping an eye on us. Even so, is that what people see when they look at us? I guess that means we're doing a good job with the act, at least.

Abby doesn't comment on his assumption as she follows me.

"Looks like we've got a chestnut and a gray," I tell her as we approach the last two stalls. "Take your pick."

"This gray one seems sweet." She looks at the placard on the front of the stall. "Houdini. That's a cute name for a horse."

Looks like I'll be taking Kentucky then.

The horses are ready to go, but I double check the tack, making sure everything is secure before I lead Houdini out of the stall for Abby.

"When was the last time you rode?" I ask her.

She shakes her head. "Never. It's my first time."

I grin. "Come on, even the Chicago girls have ridden before."

Her lips twist ruefully. "Yeah, I'm not super adventurous. But I'm working on it."

"Really? How?"

Her mouth opens and shuts before she finally says, "Just trying to get out of my comfort zone lately. This week being one example."

Fair enough. "All right, well come face the horse here and give me your left leg."

Her brow furrows in confusion. "My leg?"

"Yeah. Bounce up with your right foot while I lift you, then swing your right leg over."

She's lighter than I expected as I help her up, and I wait until she has the reins firmly in hand before I get on Kentucky.

I motion for her to follow me a little ways away from the rest of the group still mounting, and she blinks at me, then the horse, as if she doesn't know what to do. Houdini eventually does it for her, instinctively following my horse.

"You comfortable?" I ask her. "Saddle okay?"

She gives me a shaky smile, clearly nervous. "This is higher up than I thought it'd be."

"You'll be fine," I assure her. "Houdini knows what to do."

"Grayson, you take the back of the line," Rodney calls out as he leads the rest of the group onto the trail, his palomino one I don't recognize from before. He used to have a spitfire bay stallion.

But a lot can change in nearly fourteen years.

Mom takes the lead behind Rodney, followed by Kristen, Eli, Owen, Harper, Elena, and Kelly. Abby's horse falls into line behind Kelly's and mine brings up the rear. We move ahead at a comfortable pace as the trail winds through the forest, the towering trees overhead providing shade against the midday sun.

A cool breeze lifts Abby's dark blonde hair from the back of her neck, her body swaying in time with Houdini's gait, and I watch her for a moment, surprised again remembering yesterday and how easy it was to talk to her, how she'd somehow gotten me to open up about things I hadn't even fully articulated to myself, let alone another person. Is it because she's so unassuming? Because something about her feels trustworthy? Or because she's become my accomplice in this deception we have going on?

I shake my head, trying to put thoughts of her out of my mind, focusing instead on the rhythmic clip-clop of hooves on the forest floor, the creak of the saddle underneath me, the distant chatter of the group ahead of us, Rodney too far to even see now at the front of the line.

I've forgotten how meditative nature can be out here, a sense of peace stealing over me the same way it did yesterday on the hike. The resinous scent of evergreens and damp earth swirls in the breeze, and I let my mind float, unable to remember the last time I relaxed like this. Like I told Abby, I hardly even go outside anymore back home. There's always work to do.

The reminder of work and all the emails piling up over this weeklong vacation has my shoulders tightening until I consciously loosen them. Work will be there when I get back next week. And my boss told me not to check in, that they have everything covered while I'm gone.

My horse stops moving, jerking me out of my thoughts, and I

realize Abby's horse has stopped ahead, distracted by a patch of grass it begins grazing on.

Abby ineffectually tugs at the reins. "Houdini, um… this way." She points ahead, to the gap forming between her and Kelly's horse.

I grin to myself and ride up next to her. "Here." Taking the reins from her, I show her how to redirect the horse until it moves again, albeit at a snail's pace.

"Houdini, we're going to lose the group," she says. There's a bend in the trail up ahead, and as Kelly's horse rounds it, we lose sight of the rest of our party completely. "Come on."

She digs her heels into the horse's flank in an attempt to get it to move faster, and Houdini shies away, jerking Abby in her saddle.

Something in my chest drops to my stomach as Abby tries to reseat herself and in the process somehow spooks Houdini further, causing him to bolt away from the trail and through the forest undergrowth.

"Abby!" I choke out, spurring my horse to follow hers, a surge of fear snaking around my ribs.

She's precariously close to falling off, her body listing to the left, her hands white-knuckled on the reins. And the worst part is she's not even screaming, but making these strangled gasps that are somehow worse.

The scrub is too thick here to get beside her, so I follow as close as I can, telling her I'm here, urging her to right herself, but she keeps getting bumped and banged around too much to do anything other than hold on to the little purchase she has, sliding even further down Houdini's side. Her right foot flails for the stirrup, but she's nowhere near it now.

We scrape past outstretched tree limbs and thick brush, everything rushing past at a blur, and my heart lurches into my throat as Houdini jumps over a fallen log, unseating her even more.

I take Kentucky over the same log and there's finally enough room to maneuver next to Abby. I grab her under the arms and yank her toward me, her left foot thankfully dislodging from the stirrup and reins going slack in her grip as she drapes sideways over my lap.

Houdini continues on crashing through the undergrowth, no change in his stride now that Abby's off his back. Best to let him tire himself out and he'll eventually find his way back to the ranch.

I slow Kentucky to a halt and guide Abby to the ground, where she crumples in a heap. My pulse is beating painfully in my ears as I dismount, running my hands over her, checking to see if she's hurt anywhere.

"Are you okay?" I ask her, over and over, unsure if the words are even making it past my lips with the way my brain's moving a million miles a minute. She could have broken her arm or leg, cut herself, got a concussion—

"I'm okay," she replies shakily, and I crush her to my chest, my heart still pounding, adrenaline racing through me.

She clings to me in return, both of us in an awkward position kneeling on the forest floor, but I don't care about that right now as relief pours over me. So many things could have gone wrong. One slip-up and she could have been seriously injured, or worse. Maybe if I hadn't chased Houdini he would've calmed on his own, but how could I chance it with Abby at risk?

"I couldn't catch my breath," she says, still struggling to breathe. "And it only kept getting worse."

"I know." I smooth a hand over her hair, dislodging a leaf out of the strands, unable to say anything else. I want to tell her she's never getting on a horse again. I saw how nervous she was to begin with. I should have ensured she had a calmer horse, one who wouldn't spook. Thinking about it now, Houdini was probably named for his temperament, disappearing off the trail like that with no warning.

"I'm sorry," she says, finally pulling away. "God, I'm so stupid. I can't even ride a horse right." She wipes under her eyes, smearing the dirt on her face around.

"Hey, no." I move her hands from her face, hating the tears forming in her eyes. "None of that was your fault. Houdini's a fucking jackass."

A grin reluctantly crosses her lips, even as a tear slips down her cheek. "He's a horse."

"Well, Rodney needs to take him out of rotation for trail rides. Or make sure he at least only has an experienced rider."

She nods, wiping again at her eyes. "He looked so sweet. I guess looks can be deceiving."

Yeah, they can. Like how I've never given Abby a second look before, and now… she's all I can see.

Wait. Where the hell did that thought come from? That's not what's happening. I was only so worried about her because she's… because she's my sister's best friend. I've known her forever, of course I care about her. I mean, care if something happens to her.

That's all this is. It doesn't mean…

My breath catches for a moment before I exhale. It doesn't mean anything else.

"Looks like I lost my horse," she says, standing.

"Yeah." I stand, too, my heart rate finally back in normal range, and try to gauge how far we are from the trail. "He'll find his way back. It's us I'm more concerned about."

Abby looks around uneasily. "I hope the rest of them aren't worried. If they even noticed we're missing."

Right. The others. Shit, did we mess up Harper's itinerary?

I pull my phone out of my pocket. "I'll text the family group chat and let them know we'll meet them back at the stable."

She glances over at Kentucky, the horse calmly waiting for direction from me. If only I'd put Abby on this horse to begin with. "Can we both ride your horse back?"

Normally, I'd say no since it's uncomfortable for both the riders and horse to double up like that, but the last thing I need is for Abby to trip over something out here in this dense scrub and break her leg for real.

"Yeah, just until we get back to the trail. Might be a little squished, though."

I hoist her up in the saddle and follow. The only way to do this is for her backside to be fully flush against my front, one of my arms around her waist to make sure she's secure.

I swallow heavily as she presses against me, hesitating for a moment before giving Kentucky the signal to go. This shouldn't be a big deal. It's an emergency kind of situation.

But wasn't I thinking earlier how something has changed?

No, I decided that's because of this fake interest we're putting on for Mom's benefit.

Then why am I reacting to Abby like this?

CHAPTER SEVEN

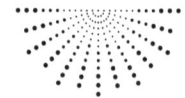

ABBY

I'm the biggest screw-up in the history of screw-ups.

I not only practically fell off a runaway horse, but then lost the freaking horse, too.

"There's the trail." Grayson points ahead of us, his words rumbling in his chest behind me, where I'm scrunched against him like a sardine.

When I suggested we ride back together, I thought it might be romantic, but he was right when he said it'd be uncomfortable.

He swings off the saddle when we're on even ground and holds the reins in one hand as he leads us to the stables. He's unusually quiet, his shoulders tense, and while my newfound plan to find ways to connect with him is still in place, I stay silent, too. My eyes are itchy from crying and all I want to do is go nurse my bruised ego in peace.

He's probably over there rethinking this entire farce. Could he have picked a worse person to feign interest in? Once everyone hears what happened… My face flushes at the thought.

We're silent the whole way back, but as we enter the stables,

Grayson helps me off the horse, his hands spanning my waist for the briefest of moments before he's gone.

"Are you afraid of horses?"

I nearly startle at his question after silence for so long. "Um, no. Just unfamiliar, I guess. I had no idea what to expect."

"You want to learn how to groom one? That might make you more comfortable."

I blink up at him stupidly. He wasn't figuring out a way to get rid of me before the wedding this whole time?

Nodding mutely, I follow him as he leads the horse into its stall, saying something about clipping her into cross ties to get the tack off. I don't know what it means, but I nod again in agreement, watching him move confidently around the stall. I had no idea he knew so much about horses.

Grayson points under the horse's belly. "We'll start by loosening the girth—that strap holding the saddle in place. Don't take it all the way off yet. Just loosen it so Kentucky can breathe easier."

"Wait, you want me to do it?" Didn't he see how my last experience with a horse went?

He runs a hand down the horse's side. "Kentucky here is a hell of a lot calmer than Houdini. I wish I would've known something about their temperaments first or I would've put you on her."

I shrug. "Lesson learned."

He eyes me. "You're taking what happened pretty calmly."

"More like trying to block my mortification," I mumble, loosening the strap he pointed out.

Thankfully, Kentucky doesn't react.

"Bridle comes off next. Hold her head gently and we'll slip it off."

I move in front of the horse, her big brown eyes gazing back at me docilely. Tentatively, I reach a hand out and stroke her snout as Grayson unhooks the reins, then removes the bit from her mouth. He slides the bridle off over her ears, and she thankfully doesn't startle, letting me pet her head the whole time.

"Yeah, Kentucky's more my speed." Today might have been a success if I'd had her to begin with.

He moves to her side and finishes undoing the girth, then lifts the saddle and removes the pad underneath. "You have nothing to be embarrassed about. It could've happened to anyone."

And yet, I was the only one it happened to. I give him a tight smile instead of saying it aloud, though. "I'm sorry if I worried you."

He shakes his head, some of the tension from earlier still in him. "No, I overreacted. It must have been the adrenaline."

A lot of what happened is a blur, but I do remember him hugging me tightly afterward, the sense of safety from being in his arms doing more than he knew to finally calm me down.

"You were like an action hero saving me like that."

He looks up at me in surprise from where he was checking Kentucky's side. "To be honest, I was scared out of my mind."

He was? He'd seemed like he had everything under control.

"You care that much?" I blurt out without thinking about it.

"Of course. You're... you're an old family friend. Kristen would have my head if something happened to you."

I give him some semblance of a smile before turning away. A family friend. His little sister's best friend. I can't forget that's what I am to him.

Even if that's not the way I feel at all.

The reminder of Kristen sends an additional stab of guilt through me. She'd asked me the other day how I felt being roped into Grayson's fake wedding date scheme, and I'd downplayed the whole thing. I've never told her about my crush on Grayson.

"Can I brush her?" I ask, noticing the brushes along one wall of the stall. Maybe giving my mind something else to focus on will stop me from begging Grayson to see me in a new way. Someone other than the invisible girl I've always been to him.

"Yeah, of course. Let's start with the curry comb." He picks one up and hands it to me. "Use small, circular motions to loosen up the dirt under the horse's coat."

I slide my hand through the handle and tentatively reach out to Kentucky's side, afraid I'll mess this up somehow. "Like this?" I sweep it over her side in a circle.

"Smaller." His hand covers mine, warm and rough as he shows me what to do. I savor the contact, hating how I cling to these small scraps of connection even as I wish he wouldn't let go.

He starts in on her other side, then hands me a hard brush to flick off the dirt I've loosened.

"Be careful around the legs and belly," he tells me. "They're more sensitive there."

I nod, more confident now, and finally finish with a soft brush in long, gentle strokes. There's something relaxing about doing this, almost like we're giving Kentucky a mini massage.

"Might be nice to be a horse just to get this kind of attention," I say, half-joking.

He looks up, giving me a half smile, but it doesn't reach his eyes.

I set the brush back on the shelf. "Is everything okay?"

Now that I really look at him, there's a tightness to his movements, his shoulders rigid.

He nods, but I don't believe him.

"Grayson."

His gaze cuts to me, then away. "I... I keep thinking about the whole thing," he finally says. "How close you were to falling."

"I'm fine."

"Yeah..." He blows out a shaky breath. "But what if you weren't? Something bad could've happened."

Oh my God, he's actually worried about this. Even if I am only a *family friend*.

I walk around Kentucky, laying a hand on Grayson's forearm. "Don't kill yourself with the what-ifs. I'm fine. Really."

I take a chance and hug him, half-surprised when he hugs me back, pressing me in tight to him. My eyes drift shut, basking in the simple pleasure of being in his arms, this time not in the aftermath of a high-stakes situation. His hands burn hot through the cotton of my shirt, and I know I'll be reliving this moment later.

"Don't worry me like that again," he murmurs, his breath tickling my ear, and a shudder runs through me.

"I won't," I promise, my voice faint and wispy. Way to seem unaffected, Abby.

As he pulls away, our gazes lock, and I swear there's an infinitesimal pause, a wealth of possibilities in the air. It's broken, though, when he turns again to Kentucky to finish brushing her coat.

I sigh, knowing I was imagining it, but wishing it was true all the same.

"That's so scary," Harper says, concern all over her face. "Why didn't you say anything when we got back from the ride?"

I shrug, sipping from the can of sparkling water she gave me. Everyone else has wine or beer, but I've never been a drinker. I don't get how people enjoy the taste of alcohol.

"I didn't want to make a big deal of it. It was embarrassing."

Kristen gives me a sympathetic smile, but Harper's look is full of pity. She's the only one who knows how I really feel about Grayson.

"They shouldn't have that horse out for trail rides if it's doing stuff like that," Kristen says.

"That's exactly what your brother said."

"Well, he gets things right every once in a while." She ducks her head out from Harper's kitchen to check on Grayson, Owen, and Eli in the living room. "Is it going okay with him?"

I roll my eyes. "Yes, Mom."

Her lips purse, but I can tell she's hiding a smile. "Just making sure. I still can't believe he's trying to pull one over on Mom like this."

"It seems to be working," Harper says. "From what I've seen, at least."

"And it's only been, what? Four months since you were single?" I remind Kristen. "Are you saying you don't remember what her matchmaking efforts were like when they were focused on you? Can you blame him for wanting to head her off at the pass?"

"Yeah, I guess," she grumbles.

Harper grins. "Maybe you're jealous he found a way to beat Cheryl at her own game."

Kristen laughs at that. "Maybe I am. But seriously." She looks at me. "I hate that you're caught in the crossfire. I don't want you having to clean up his mess once he goes back to Seattle."

I pat her arm. "I'm a big girl. I'll be fine."

There's a knock at the front door and Harper rushes to get it, knowing it's Elena and Kelly.

Kristen steps in closer, her gaze on the two women entering. "What do you think of them?"

Ooh, are we gossiping? "I haven't talked much to either of them, but they seem nice. Why? You have something to report?"

"No, I just noticed Elena keeps checking out Grayson."

She has? I've been so wrapped up in trying to put on a good performance in front of the others that I haven't paid attention to anything else.

"It's too bad he made the deal with you before she showed up," she continues. "Honestly, that would have been a better scenario for him. They both leave after the wedding and Mom doesn't have anyone to badger about why it didn't work out."

I give her a weak smile, muttering some kind of agreement, but my attention is laser focused on Elena now, her glossy dark hair hanging loose down her back, a pretty red sundress complementing her bronzed skin. She's smiling at something Harper says and all I can think about is how beautiful she is, how much better of a match she is for Grayson. I know Kelly is engaged, but Harper never mentioned Elena having a husband or boyfriend, and her left ring finger is bare.

Jealousy and shame swirl in my gut. Elena's done nothing wrong. Kristen's probably imagining it.

Kristen sets the two women up with drinks, and as they wait, I watch Elena surreptitiously. See, there's nothing—

Her gaze cuts to Grayson as soon as Harper turns her back, and I push down the insane sudden urge to scratch her eyes out.

Oh God, this is going to be a long night.

CHAPTER EIGHT

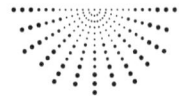

GRAYSON

"All right, this is the last point," Harper says, looking at everyone dramatically to create tension. "If Abby gets this, you guys win."

I lean forward, strangely invested in this game of charades we have going on.

"But if you don't, we win."

She motions to her, Owen, Elena, and Kelly—the opposing team. The losers, more accurately. Because our team is going to win.

"No pressure," Kristen says, patting Abby's knee. "It's been a fun night, no matter what happens."

I give my sister a skeptical look. "When did you get so uncompetitive?"

Eli snorts a laugh next to her, but wisely says nothing.

Kristen rolls her eyes. "Since I became an adult." She nudges her index finger into my shoulder. "Unlike you."

I grin, loving riling her up. It's my job as her big brother.

Abby stands, wiping her palms on her jeans.

"You've got this, Abbs," I tell her.

She nods but doesn't look like she believes me as she approaches the basket in the center of the table with the clues. We wrote clues for the other team, and they wrote ours, so me, Kristen, and Eli have no clue what's on the slip of paper Abby draws.

She studies it for a moment, then sighs. I can't tell if that's good or bad.

She gestures to indicate it's a movie and one word, but after that flounders a bit as she makes what looks like a rectangle in her hands that breaks in half.

"Um, snapping," Kristen says. "*Jaws!*"

For someone who claims she's not competitive, she's certainly invested in getting the right answer.

Abby shakes her head, then wiggles her arm around and theatrically lowers it to the ground. What the hell?

She tries again, but no one knows what she's doing, so she moves on, making a circle shape around her neck next.

"A necklace," I shout, unsure why I'm yelling. Getting into the spirit, I guess.

Abby nods, pointing to me.

"*Pretty Woman,*" Eli says. "*Breakfast at Tiffany's.*"

Kristen gives him a *what the fuck* look. "Those aren't one word."

"Right, sorry."

"Ten seconds," Harper says smugly, holding up her phone with the stopwatch app displayed on the screen. Thirty seconds is criminally too short a time to guess some of these.

Abby glances around frantically, then pulls me up to join her, moving me so I'm standing behind her. Her hands find mine and bring them to her waist, then she spreads her arms out wide.

It happens so suddenly, I'm startled, frozen in place as I stare down at her, the crown of her head right at the level of my nose. I inhale unthinkingly, her scent both familiar and heady.

Damn. She smells really good.

At her waist, my fingers flex, unable to help myself. I'd held her against me on the horse earlier, but that was different. Or, rather, I'd told myself it was. That was an emergency. This...

I'm interrupted from my internal dilemma as Kristen screams, "*Titanic!*"

Abby jumps up and down in response, my hands tightening around her instinctively, fingers pressing into her hip bones. She stops, glancing over her shoulder up at me questioningly, and I force myself to let go, returning to my seat.

I take a swig from my beer bottle, accepting Eli's clap on my back as Kristen gets up and hugs Abby.

"Good to see you're still not a poor winner," Owen says to Kristen in a rare public display of teasing. It's usually me who does that.

Kristen lets go of Abby. "I'm celebrating, not rubbing it in your face. Besides, Grayson's not showboating nearly as much as I expected."

All eyes turn to me and I take another swallow of beer. "Maybe I've matured."

Kristen laughs at the thought. "Yeah, okay." She turns around and hugs Harper, then Owen goodbye. "Thanks for the fun night. But me and Eli have to go relieve Mom of babysitting duty."

Which means Mom will be home soon. And since I'm staying at her house this week, it's another night of watching *CSI* reruns with her. If I have to watch one more person get murdered on that show, I might kill myself, too.

"You ready to go?" Kristen asks me, since I rode with her and Eli here.

"Kelly and I can give you a ride later," Elena says, curling a finger around a long strand of her dark hair. "If you want to hang out here a little longer."

Hmm, it would be nice not to have to go home yet. But I don't know if I want to listen to Harper and her friends yap to each other, either. Every time I've been around the three of them the past few days, they're all up in each other's business gossiping.

"I'll take him," Abby says, curling her hand around my upper arm.

She stares at Elena, who stares back for a moment before smiling and nodding her head.

What was that about?

"Yeah, sure," I tell Abby. "If it's no trouble."

We say our goodbyes, too, and as we get in her car, I ask, "Could we actually not go to my mom's yet? She keeps making me watch police dramas every night with her."

"We could hang out at my house," she suggests, U-turning around Owen's wide front yard back toward the dirt road that leads to town.

I gladly agree, ignoring a small voice of warning in my head that remembers the strangeness of holding her waist, of being terrified for her when her horse had nearly unseated her.

This is just hanging out. I've known Abby forever. It's not like anything is going to… happen.

When I enter her house this time, there's an orange cat lingering by the doorway who definitely wasn't there the other day. He takes one look at me and bolts, scrambling around a corner to what looks like the kitchen.

"Leo," Abby says in exasperation. "You'll like Grayson, I promise."

"Leo? Because he looks like a little lion?"

Abby smiles. "Exactly."

She turns the same corner and a moment later there's a shaking sound. I peek in and spot her on the floor with a bag of treats, trying to coax the cat out from under the kitchen table.

"I don't want to invade his space," I say, feeling bad now.

"No, he'll be fine. He just needs a minute. If he can handle Jenny, he can handle you."

Good to know my reputation isn't as bad as my niece's.

Leo slinks out from under the table and sniffs the treat in her hands before devouring it. He lets her pet him a few times, then turns to me, meowing balefully.

I hold up my empty hands. "I don't have anything for you."

"Here." Abby gives me the bag of treats. "To butter him up."

I crouch down and shake out a few treats in my palm and hold it out.

The cat looks at my face, then my hand, and back at my face, studying me.

"Can he see into my soul?" I whisper.

Abby presses her lips tightly together, holding in a laugh. "Sometimes I swear he can understand me. I've asked him to blink twice if he's a person trapped in a cat's body, but he hasn't done it yet."

Leo decides to give me a chance and approaches carefully, then gobbles up the treats as fast as he can.

"Treats won you over, huh?" I ask him, stroking my hand down his side. "Wow, he's soft."

"Yeah, he's my fluffy boy."

See, things are normal between us. Those off the wall thoughts I had earlier were a freak occurrence.

"You don't have any pets, do you?" she asks. "Your family never did growing up."

Mom had resisted all attempts of ours to bring home an animal, claiming the three of us were wild enough animals already.

"Nah, Owen's the only one who ever branched out into pet ownership." I continue petting Leo, surprised when he rubs the side of his face along my outstretched fingers. "I guess I've never thought about it much."

"He likes you. Maybe you're destined to get a cat."

"Yeah, maybe. Better than a dog, at least. I'm not home enough to take them on walks."

She gets up and fills the tea kettle on her stove with water. "You work a lot?"

"Yeah. Fifty-to-sixty-hour weeks are the norm at my job."

"You know, I'm not sure what you actually do. Kristen said something in finance?"

I chuckle. No one in my family has ever taken an interest in my job. "I'm a financial analyst."

She smiles as she opens the cabinet to the right of the stove. "Sounds complicated. Tea?"

She holds up a mug and I nod, then settle in one of the kitchen table chairs.

"Not to sound rude," she continues, "but I thought you'd always end up doing something more exciting."

"I can see how you'd think that. I was kind of a daredevil, huh?"

"Yeah, you were."

I shrug. "Guess I got it all out of my system when I was younger. I'm boring now."

"I don't believe that for one minute."

I breathe out a laugh. "Why?"

"Because you were always the most exciting guy in town."

She reaches back into the same cabinet and gets two tea bags, but all I can do is stare at her back. She thinks I'm exciting?

There's that strange pull in my stomach again, something that's never happened around Abby in all the years I've known her. Before this week, that is.

But I haven't really known her, have I? Or rather, bothered to get to know her.

I ask her how things are going at the library and she chatters on happily as she cuts thick slices of banana bread and slathers them with butter, then sets the plate in front of me.

Man, I love banana bread. What are the chances she'd happen to have some?

I nod and *mm-hmm* at the right places as she speaks, but I'm more interested in watching her move around the kitchen, preparing a plate identical to mine for herself, readying the tea, placing a steaming mug in front of me along with saucers of milk and sugar. There's something graceful about her movements as she flits from table to counter, keeping her hands busy, idly petting Leo every so often. And though I have no idea why we're eating banana bread and drinking tea at nine o'clock at night, I'm not complaining.

"Oh my God," she says, finally pausing. She's standing behind me, so I have no idea what she's referring to.

"What is it?"

"You have this awful scratch. Here, on the back of your neck."

A cool fingertip brushes the nape of my neck, sending a tingle down my spine. I turn around in my chair, not wanting to be caught off guard again.

"What?" I ask thickly, not sure what my body's response meant.

"I bet the tip of a branch got you when we were speeding through the forest. One got me, too." She pushes up her left sleeve to reveal a Band-Aid. "I can put some antibiotic cream on it."

"Um, sure."

I agree without thinking about it, and I take a huge bite of banana bread, comforted by the mellow, sweet flavor.

She's back a minute later with the cream and a bandage, and stands behind me, pulling the neckline of my shirt down slightly.

I swallow heavily, that tingling sensation back as she applies the cream.

It's just Abby, I tell myself as she puts on the bandage next, her fingers delicate where they sweep against my oversensitive skin.

Abby, who I've known forever.

Has she ever touched me before this week? I can't remember a time she would have.

Jesus Christ, what is wrong with me? Why am I getting worked up over a little touch? I swear I've felt less sensation during hook-ups than this.

"All better." She smiles as she takes her seat across from me at the table.

But all I can think of is her hugging me at the stables when I'd admitted I was worried about her, how she placed my hands on her waist for that *Titanic* clue during charades, of her unexpected touch on my neck.

And how I want her to do it again.

CHAPTER NINE

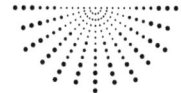

ABBY

I blow on my tea, cooling it before taking a sip, and try not to fidget, aware of Grayson's gaze on me. His attention must be good, right?

Better than indifference, at least.

It'd been a stroke of luck when he asked to hang out at my place rather than call it an early night, and I'd done the first thing I could think of when we got here, which was to ply him with his favorite snack.

I'd baked the loaf of banana bread last night, trying to come up with a way I could organically give it to him without it being obvious I'd made it specifically for him, knowing he loves it. And here an opportunity has fallen into my lap.

Everything went well during game night, too. I'd not so sneakily suggested the teams, making sure Elena was *not* on Grayson's team, and I was. Do I feel a bit guilty about that? Sure. Would I do it again? In a heartbeat.

"We made a pretty good team for game night," I say.

He nods in response. "We did."

He's still looking at me, almost like he's trying to figure something out, but I don't know what the question is. I'm not sure if he does either.

"You know, when Harper said game night, I thought she meant card games. Her, me, and Kristen usually play poker together."

His brows raise. "You three play poker?"

I act mock affronted. "You think I can't play?"

That crooked grin I was hoping to tease from him makes its appearance. "Only one way to find out. You have a pack of cards around here?"

I set down my tea. "Wait, you want to play now?"

He shrugs. "You got something better to do?"

He's right. And why in the world am I not jumping on the chance to keep him here longer?

I get up and find the deck of cards and poker chips I keep on my bookshelf in the living room, then return, handing him the deck.

"Wow, you've got chips, too?" he asks, eyeing me speculatively. "I underestimated you."

I should tell him I'm not that good, that it was Harper that brought the chips over, but I hold my tongue. There's something exciting about him seeing me in a new light.

"I have a lot of hidden talents you haven't seen."

Oh my God, did I actually say that out loud? It sounded an awful lot like flirting. And I'm not a flirter. Especially with Grayson.

I open my mouth to take it back, then shut it just as quickly. How can things ever change between us if I don't push for it? Force him to see me differently?

He smirks in response, something like interest in his gaze as he settles in his chair. "We'll see about that. I've got a few tricks up my sleeve, too. Texas Hold 'em?"

I nod, praying he doesn't notice my blush as he shuffles and deals while I distribute poker chips, the number meaningless since there's no real money behind it.

I take the two private cards he deals me and glance at them. A ten and a four.

"You have a good hand?" he asks. "Don't think I missed that smile."

I was smiling at his response to my quip, not my cards, but I keep that to myself. I shrug one shoulder. "Who knows? Maybe I was bluffing."

His grin grows. "Right."

I put in two chips for the blind and Grayson calls it, matching my chips.

"Let's see what the cards have to say."

He reveals the first three community cards—the ace of hearts, seven of diamonds, and ten of spades.

My heartbeat picks up as I look between my private cards and the flop. Looking good.

"You're not a good bluffer."

I quickly school my expression. "Maybe it's all part of my strategy."

Grayson checks but doesn't bet, and I put in four chips.

He laughs in response. "Bold move. But I'll play along."

He calls my bet and tosses his chips into the pile forming in the center of the table, then deals the next card—the king of clubs.

Hmm, that doesn't help me.

"Not your card, huh?"

Damn it. I guess it's a good thing he wasn't paying attention all those years or he would have known—

He raises the bet by six chips and I narrow my eyes, unsure if he's messing with me or has great cards. In for a penny, in for a pound, though. I call.

He deals the final card. It's the two of hearts. Neither of us can make a flush or straight with this board, so it's up to what's in our hands. I attempt to maintain my poker face, even though my pair of tens isn't as strong as I'd like.

Grayson raises again, this time by ten chips. Good Lord. Then again, he's always been one to go all or nothing.

Unlike me.

"You think you've got me beat, huh?" I chew at my bottom lip, stalling. I could fold now and cut my losses. Grayson wouldn't raise so much unless he has a decent hand.

He smirks again. "I know I do."

But this week is about putting myself out there. Taking chances.

"I think you're bluffing." I call his bet and match his chips.

We reveal our cards, but my pair of tens can't beat the king of hearts and king of diamonds in his hand. No wonder he bet so high.

"Looks like I wasn't bluffing," he says, scooping up the pile in the center of the table.

No, guess not.

I sit up straighter in my seat. "How about we make things more interesting?"

He gives me a lazy smile as he stacks his chips in neat columns. "Sure. What do you have in mind?"

I swallow, knowing it's now or never. *Take a chance.*

"How about strip poker?"

The poker chips he's setting on the last of his columns clatter to the floor, his gaze swinging to me.

"Didn't think you had it in you to suggest something like that," he finally says.

I inhale a deep breath but stand my ground. Fake it till you make it. "I can be full of surprises."

His grin goes crooked in that way I love. "And hidden talents, right? Well, let's see how far you're willing to go then."

The knot forming in my stomach loosens at his agreement. I don't know what I would have done if he refused, but it looks like my bluff paid off.

"Don't expect me to take it easy on you," he teases, shuffling the deck again.

"Likewise."

He laughs. "Oh, so you let me win the first round?"

I hold up my hands. "I can neither confirm nor deny."

He strokes his jaw, then bends to look under the table. "If you take one shoe off, we should be even."

I do a quick mental calculation. Shirt, jeans, bra, panties, two socks, and two shoes. Presumably he's not wearing a bra, which leaves me with one extra item of clothing.

I toe off one of my shoes and kick it behind my chair. Leo takes offense to that and stalks out of the kitchen. It's near the time he winds down for the night, anyway.

"Anything else?" I ask.

"Hmm. No betting. And no folding."

So only luck then. Even if I'm dealt a bad hand… I'll have to strip. But so will he.

"Deal."

He grins again as he passes out our cards. "You ready to lose more than just your chips?"

I gather my two cards. "Oh, don't worry. You'll be the one losing."

I have no idea where I'm pulling this banter from, but I like it. I like being Flirty Abby. Bold Abby.

So different from Shy Abby, the way I normally am around him.

And even more, I like the way he seems to be flirty right back. I've seen that side of him with other women, but never with me. Sure, we agreed a few days ago that we'd flirt to sell the ruse to his mom, but that meant in front of others.

Not alone.

Grayson deals the first three community cards and I hide my excitement when I realize I have a two-pair already of queens and nines.

I glance up at him, but his poker face is excellent. I have no idea if his cards are good or bad. Really, though, is there a downside to winning or losing? If I win, I get to see him, and if he wins, he gets to see me.

Does he want to see you?

I stop short at the small voice inside my head. I hadn't thought that far ahead. What if I undress and he doesn't care? Or worse, is repulsed or embarrassed or something? This idea could majorly backfire.

"You have a tell," he says.

I put an end to my mental criticism and paste on an intrigued expression. "What's that?"

"You blush."

The ever-present heat in my cheeks intensifies. I almost tell him it's rude to point that out, but bite my tongue instead. "Okay, but what you don't know is if it means I have a good or bad hand."

He opens his mouth to respond, then shuts it. "Damn." He chuckles. "You're right." He toys with the deck. "Ready for the next card?"

I nod.

It's the three of hearts, which doesn't help me at all, but doesn't hurt either.

"So what does the blush mean?"

I swallow, avoiding his eye. I have no idea how he's just now realizing I blush around him constantly. Maybe he wasn't paying attention before.

It seems he is now, though.

"It means you should turn over the final card."

"Okay, keep your secrets. But I'll find out before the night is over."

My face is practically scorching now. His comment makes it sound like we'll be spending the whole night together. Which we're obviously not.

What do I think will even happen at the end of this game? One of us will be nude and then… What? He'll take one look at me and be seduced? Flip the kitchen table over and come at me like a rutting bull?

Or maybe cross over to me and gently pull me out of my seat, his hand softly cupping my jaw, gazing deep into my eyes. Telling me he's never noticed me before, but now… now he finally sees what he's been missing all these years. His gaze filled with lust, traveling down my face until it lands on my mouth, his lips parting in response. Then leaning in until we're a whisper apart, anticipation crackling in the air.

"Last card," Grayson says, and I snap out of my daydream, the hot flush over my entire body now.

Shit. I need to stop reading so many romance novels.

He turns over the king of spades and I glance at my cards again. I've still got my two-pair—a pretty strong contender.

"You look nervous," he says, and I'm pretty sure there's a teasing note in his voice. "Afraid I'll keep up my winning streak?"

I don't respond, instead laying out my hand. "Two-pair. Queens and nines."

He winces as he reveals a ten and a six. He has nothing.

My shoulders sag in relief. Yeah, I talked a big game, but the thought of actually stripping...

Grayson grabs the back of his shirt and pulls it over his head, his muscles shifting and contracting. His chest is broad with a light dusting of hair, shoulders wide and rounded, biceps thick. His pecs lead down into defined abs that disappear at the edge of the kitchen table.

Have I seen Grayson shirtless before? Maybe swimming or something? Even if I had, that would have been years ago as a teenager. Nothing compared to now, as a man. A handsome, muscular, sexy—

"Want me to turn around for you? Do a little spin?"

My gaze flicks to his, mortification spreading through me as I realize I was visibly ogling him.

Mirth dances in his eyes, a smirk over his mouth as he waits for my response.

I swallow past the thickness in my throat and honestly say, "I mean, if you want, I won't stop you."

He laughs at that, but doesn't do it. Instead, he picks up the cards and shuffles the deck.

"So no starting with socks and shoes?" I ask, trying to defuse the situation.

"Nah. I figure if we're doing this, I gotta commit, right?"

A weak chuckle escapes me. I definitely won't be starting with my shirt. That'll be one of the last things to go.

The rounds move quickly as we continue playing, since there's no betting or folding. With it being entirely luck-based, we're pretty evenly matched half an hour later. We're both barefoot by now, and I'm left in my shirt, bra, and panties. My jeans were abandoned two rounds ago when he beat me with a pair of aces. And while normally I'm a little chilly in my house, I'm practically sweating now, nervous about both losing or winning this next round. If he wins, I take off my shirt. If I win, he's left in just his boxers.

"Final card," Grayson teases, drawing it out in slow motion. He seems to be having a great time, at least, cracking jokes and making quips throughout the game, but especially this last round. I'm not sure if he's doing it because he feels like it, or specifically because he can sense the growing tension in me.

He finally flips the card over onto the table, and my belly goes loose and light. It's a four, giving me three of a kind.

I lay my cards out and he groans. "Damn it, Abbs. My ego is a delicate thing."

He grins to let me know he's kidding, then stands, unbuttoning his jeans. There's a dark trail of hair revealed beneath his belly button, disappearing into the edge of his boxer briefs.

Okay, not a boxers man, apparently. The black cotton is snug around his muscular thighs, as well as his…

I look away before he catches me staring again.

"Could be my last round," he comments as he shuffles and deals. "You've got, what?" He takes a quick peek under the table at my bare legs. "Three left?"

I nod and grab the two cards he deals me, internally groaning when they're both low cards—a two and a five of different suits.

The flop and the turn don't help any either, and by the time we get to the river, I know I'm screwed. I have nothing playable, not even a high card.

He wins with a measly pair of threes.

So now I have to decide—will I get rid of my shirt or my panties?

CHAPTER TEN

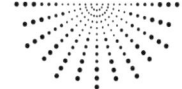

GRAYSON

I do everything but look at Abby as she slowly removes her shirt, not wanting her to feel self-conscious.

Even though I really want to fucking look.

I shuffle the cards. Move my seat closer to the table. Drain the last of my now tepid tea.

I've been trying to make her comfortable throughout the game, lightening the mood despite it being her idea. But as my gaze sweeps up to check if she's ready for the next round, it gets stuck on her cleavage.

I've never seen anything remotely close to cleavage on Abby, who's usually wearing a shirt that covers even her collarbone. Nothing like this creamy expanse of porcelain skin, the bra lifting her breasts to create a valley between them, delicate lace skimming the edges of the cups. She's not big-chested—maybe a B-cup—but I've never cared about cup size.

And why the fuck am I thinking about Abby's cup size? Abby is my *friend*. She's doing me a favor by agreeing to be my fake date to Owen's wedding. I shouldn't be considering her in a sexual way.

But hasn't she been flirting with me tonight? Or is my brain so addled from all the strange thoughts of her today that I'm interpreting normal conversation as flirting? Abby and I have never been interested in one another. And she could have her pick of guys in town. She's smart and funny and caring and beautiful and...

How have I never noticed that before?

"Are you going to deal?" she murmurs, her arms crossed over her chest now. Unfortunately, the action only serves to push her breasts together more. Damn, she looks good like that.

No. I'm dealing cards, not salivating over my sister's best friend.

But she was the one who suggested we play strip poker to begin with. And was definitely checking me out when I took off my shirt...

Fuck. I need to stop.

I deal and stare at my two cards—the nine and queen of spades. Let's see if the rest turn out to be anything.

I flip over the first three community cards without looking at Abby to gauge her reaction. It's been fun trying to figure out her tells tonight, but now that her shirt is off, it doesn't feel that way anymore. It feels... serious.

It's been years since I've played strip poker—college would have been the last time. And even with all those teenage hormones raging in me, I don't remember it feeling this weighty. Maybe I wasn't as attracted to those girls.

Wait. Am I attracted to Abby?

I'd thought to myself she was beautiful the other day, but attraction is different.

My face is downcast toward my cards, but I peek up at her, past her chest to the graceful fall of her hair around her shoulders, the warmth of her honey-brown eyes, the softness of her lips. She's not the kind of girl that grabs your attention right away, but once you look at her, really look at her...

She's breathtaking.

Ah, shit.

I turn over the next card without seeing it, then the next, my mind turning over this revelation.

"I have a straight," Abby says excitedly, laying down the four of hearts and six of diamonds to match the three, five, and seven of spades on the table.

It takes me a moment to focus back on the game. "Wow, that's great. Your best hand tonight." I finally take stock of my hand and the community cards. "I have a flush. All spades."

I lay my cards down, not registering what it means until her jaw drops. I won.

"What are the chances we both have our best hands during the same round?"

A nervous chuckle escapes me. "Yeah," I agree lamely, not sure what else to say.

I know what I *should* say. I should be a gentleman and tell her we can stop the game right now. That neither of us should undress any further. That this might change the dynamic between us.

But I keep quiet instead, waiting to see what she does.

"Guess I have to strip," she says, toying with one of her bra straps.

My gaze zeroes in on where her fingers flirt with the satin material, inching down her shoulder and upper arm. The cup loosens, folding down, and if she does it much more, her nipple will show.

My dick twitches, excited for what comes next.

She pauses, then stands, one hand still on her loose bra strap, the other hooking into the waistband of her panties. "Actually, which do you think I should take off?"

I stare at her, my tongue going thick in my mouth, the blood rushing from my head down to my dick. This is beyond flirting. This is… intimate. Seductive. I didn't know Abby was capable of this.

Or that I would like it so much.

I have the insane urge to tell her to take off both. To tell her to come over here and climb on my lap so she can feel exactly what she's doing to me.

But this is Abby. *Abby.* Kristen's best friend. I can't mess around with her like that.

A phone rings, breaking the charged moment, and Abby lets go of her underwear, blinking at me like she's free from a spell she was under. She turns, digging in her purse on the counter until she finds her phone.

I take the opportunity to breathe in deeply, grateful that something put a stop to it. We were getting too carried away. What would have happened, otherwise? How would I have responded to her?

"Mom, slow down," Abby's saying, worry in her voice. "What's wrong?"

Wait, what's going on?

"He fell?" A long pause. "I'll be right over."

She makes eye contact with me as she hangs up, and there's nothing of the seductress in her anymore. There's distress and fear and an exhaustion I haven't seen in her this week.

The lust that had been rising within me evaporates. "What is it?"

"My dad fell and Mom can't get him up." She sets her phone down and picks her shirt up to put it on, but it's inside out. She tries to flip it right side out, but somehow tangles it up more, the fabric twisting.

I approach her slowly, gently taking it from her shaking hands. "Let me help you with that."

She nods, then turns to pick her jeans up off the floor, but not before I catch her wiping under her eye.

"I'm sorry, I—" She clears her throat. "I have to go. I can drop you at—"

"I'll go with you," I say, untwisting her shirt. "If you need help." She clearly does.

She shakes her head, but I stop her, laying a hand on her shoulder. "Let me help you," I murmur.

She takes her shirt from me and puts it on. "Okay," she finally whispers. She looks up at me, a hint of moisture in her eyes. "Thank you."

Warmth fizzles in my chest, hot and unexpected, but I don't examine too closely what it means.

A small smile breaks through the distress on her face. "But you'll have to put on some clothes."

Right, of course.

I jump into action, dressing quickly, and follow her out the door. She struggles to lock the front door, her hands still shaking, and I take the keys from her to do it myself.

"How about I drive?" I ask, and she nods gratefully.

Once we're in her car, she tells me how to get her to parents' place, which is only about five minutes away. There's a thick silence in the air, neither of us mentioning what happened in the house, how what was supposed to be a fun, teasing game turned into something different. Something more.

At least, it did for me. And from the look in her eye, I'm fairly sure it did for her, too.

When we make the last turn, she says, "Dad gets confused sometimes. He might not recognize you. Actually, he probably won't. It's been at least a decade since you've seen him."

"Yeah, no worries." Even without dementia, I'd be surprised if he remembers me.

"It's the yellow house up here on the left."

I park behind a beige sedan, and Abby is unbuckled before the car's even stopped, then rushing up the driveway to the front door. She rings the doorbell twice and paces, wringing her hands in front of her.

A slight woman answers the door, probably in her mid-sixties, relief filling her face when her gaze lands on Abby.

"Come on," Abby says, forgoing any kind of greeting as she speeds past her mother.

The woman's eyes widen as she spots me, and I give her an apologetic smile as I pass by her, following Abby into the house.

"He's usually in the living—" She pauses as she enters the threshold of another room. "Oh, Dad."

She rushes over to where a man is sprawled face-down on the carpet and attempts to pick him up, but can't. He's a big man, and I honestly don't know if the two women could lift him together.

It's awkward with him being deadweight, but I manage to get him up and into the recliner nearby.

He blinks up at me, like he just became aware someone was helping him, and there's something childlike about it, especially paired with his striped pajamas and bare feet.

His blinks turn into a squint. "Frank?"

I go still, my father's name punching me square in the chest.

He turns next to Abby. "And Nancy? What are you doing here?"

Abby smiles patiently, but doesn't bother correcting him. "Let's get you ready for bed," she says, guiding him out of the chair and toward the hallway.

His steps are careful at first, as if he's afraid of falling again, then more sure.

"You used to babysit little Frankie, remember?"

She makes a noncommittal noise and looks over her shoulder at me before disappearing down the hall. *Sorry*, she mouths.

I nod, not that she needs to apologize. She said he gets confused and wouldn't recognize me.

I rub at the dull ache in the center of my chest. Even though it's been five years since Dad died, the loss never really goes away. Just lessens with time.

"Who did he call you?"

I glance over at Abby's mom at the edge of the hallway, huddled in a pink fleece robe and matching slippers, her gray hair in a loose braid down her back. I can't for the life of me remember her name.

"Frank. My dad."

Her head tilts to the side, then recognition hits. "You're Cheryl's oldest. Kristen's other brother."

"Grayson." I hold out my hand and she shakes it, her thin fingers cold.

"I'm Brenda."

Silence settles between us, the distant sound of water running coming from the bathroom. I glance around the living room, the furniture and decor outdated, but kept neat and tidy.

"Who's Nancy?" I ask, just to make conversation.

"Oh, Abby's aunt. Stephen's late sister. Abby looks very similar to

Nancy when she was younger, especially her hair. He... he sometimes gets them confused now."

There's apology and shame in her voice, and I want to tell her she doesn't need to be sorry, but I don't know her well enough and don't want to call attention to it.

What a cruel fucking disease.

"Did Abby's aunt really babysit my dad?" I ask instead, trying to shift the mood.

She laughs softly. "I suppose she did. She would have been about fifteen years older than him, probably. I might have even babysat him, now that I think about it."

Wow. That's so weird.

"Stephen and I are quite a bit older than your parents," she continues. "I... I was there at his funeral. I'm so sorry for your loss."

"Thank you." I never know exactly how to respond to people's condolences, but I've found that a simple thanks works well enough.

"And I'm sorry I didn't recognize you at first. I suppose I wasn't expecting Abby to show up with anyone so late at night."

She's not nearly as bad as Mom is fishing for details, but there's still an unspoken question of *what the hell were you doing with my daughter?*

I have no idea if Abby's shared with her mother this clandestine arrangement we have going on, so I tell her, "We're both in Owen and Harper's wedding party. We were getting some things ready for the wedding when you called."

Which is a complete lie, but she doesn't need to know that.

She brightens with the simple explanation. "That's right. Her new friend Harper. It's so nice she has more friends. She's only really ever had Kristen."

I keep my grin to myself, knowing Abby's cheeks would be burning red hearing her mom talk about her like this.

"Now, maybe you can explain something to me," she says. "Harper and your brother are already married, but they're having a wedding?"

I let loose my grin, knowing it doesn't make any sense either. I explain how they got married in Vegas nearly six years ago, and by the time I'm done, Abby's returned, weariness radiating off of her.

"Thank you, dear." Brenda crosses the room to hug her daughter, and though Abby's not particularly tall, she still seems to dwarf her mother as she enfolds her in her arms.

"Everything okay with your dad?" I ask her. We didn't check to see if he'd hurt himself during the fall, though he seemed to be walking okay.

"Yeah, he's in bed now."

"I'm sorry I had to call you," Brenda says. "But I couldn't get him up on my own."

"It's fine, Mom. You can call me anytime."

"You're a good daughter," she whispers. "I don't know what we'd do without you."

Abby smiles, but it doesn't reach her eyes.

Brenda pats her arm. "I'll let you two get back to your wedding prep." Abby sends a questioning look my way, but I shake my head slightly. "Thank you for your help, Grayson."

"Yeah, of course."

It's on the tip of my tongue to tell her she can call me again if she needs help, but I stop myself in time. I'm leaving on Sunday. I can't offer help I can't give.

"I'll come by tomorrow to help out," Abby tells her mom before we leave. "Sorry I didn't make it over this weekend."

"Oh, don't you worry about that." Brenda waves her off. "You enjoy your week off."

In the driveway, I try to hand Abby her car keys, but she shakes her head tiredly. "Can you drive?"

"Yeah, I'll, um, just drive to my mom's place."

She nods, staring out the window on our ride back.

I want to ask her how she's doing, but she doesn't seem like she wants to talk, back to the Abby I'm used to from before this week, who's more of a silent observer than participant.

When we get to Mom's, she thanks me again, and though it seems genuine, there's also something perfunctory about it. As if she can't give anything else today, all her energy spent.

"I'll see you tomorrow," I say, keeping things simple as I hand her the keys and get out of the car.

"Grayson, wait."

I pause halfway up the drive, looking back at her.

She gets out of the passenger side of the car. "I'm sorry I'm not myself right now. It has nothing to do with you. That thing with my dad rattled me."

I walk back over to her, taking in her somber expression, the red-rimmed eyes I didn't catch before.

"Go home and get some sleep. We'll talk about it more another time."

The urge strikes me to lean forward and kiss her forehead in comfort, the impulse seeming natural even though we've never done anything remotely like it before.

But I don't. So much has changed today, I can't begin to process it.

And I have a feeling sleep will be a long time coming tonight.

CHAPTER ELEVEN

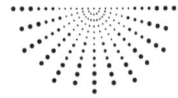

ABBY

"Wasn't that nice of Abby to come make us dinner?" Mom taps Dad's arm, getting his attention.

"Oh, yes. Very nice," he says agreeably, though I'm not sure he knows what he's agreeing to.

"I'll clean up," I say, grabbing my empty plate. "You guys can relax in the living room."

"Nonsense," Mom says. "You cooked, so I'll clean. I'm sure you and Dad can find something you both want to watch on TV."

"I'd rather clean."

Mom falters from where she was gathering Dad's silverware and napkin, glancing over at me with concern. She rubs at the spot on her chest over her heart, as if she has heartburn.

I guess I said that a little forcefully.

"How about I set your father up out there, then we can both clean up?"

I nod, not wanting to argue about it, and continue collecting the dirty plates off the table, bringing them over to the sink. Mom doesn't believe dishwashers fully clean the dishes, so everything in her house is washed by hand.

I scrape the stuck-on food into the trash, trying to focus on the action rather than the looming time. Only an hour now until I'm supposed to meet everyone at Harry's Bar tonight.

And I still have no idea what to say to Grayson.

He'd texted earlier asking what I was up to, and I told him I was busy. Which was technically not a lie. But busy with things that weren't time sensitive. I deep cleaned my house. Finished up the last of the origami for the wedding favor boxes I'm putting together for Harper as my wedding gift to her, including personalized calligraphy for each guest. Then came over to my parents' house and deep cleaned over here, too.

To be fair, they needed it. Mom can't keep up with the cleaning here, not with her health and usually needing to keep an eye on Dad, too. She won't admit she can't do as much as she used to.

I plug the drain in the sink and turn on the hot water, squeezing a glob of dish soap in to bubble up. The last few days spending time with Grayson have been a break from reality. A chance to pretend I'm someone I'm not. I wanted him to see me as fun, flirty Abby. Not Abby who has to take care of her aging parents. Abby who feels guilty for thinking of them as a burden sometimes, even though she loves them and they're the only family she has in the world.

That's not sexy. That's not who he wants.

God, I still can't believe how far I'd gone last night before we were interrupted, how in the moment I was. And, as crazy as it seems, that he might have been, too. I swear there'd been interest in his gaze as he'd looked at me in my lingerie.

What would he have said if my phone hadn't rung?

"Turn the water off, dear."

I startle, glancing down to find the sink nearly overflowing. I turn off the tap and gather the silverware to soak in the hot water and soap.

Mom edges in next to me, handing me a dish rag. "How are you? You don't seem quite yourself."

"I'm fine," I murmur.

"Abby."

Her chiding tone makes my insides twist with guilt for lying. One of the best and worst things about being an only child is that all of your parents' attention is on you.

"Does it have anything to do with Grayson?" she asks, undeterred.

I drop the fork I was washing back into the sudsy water.

"So it does."

I laugh, unable to help myself. If I don't, I might cry.

"Can't tell you how surprised I was that he showed up here last night with you. At nearly ten o'clock at night."

How scandalous. "We needed his help to get Dad up."

Looking back on it now, thank God he'd offered to come. Mom would have strained her back trying to help me lift him.

"He said you were working on something for the wedding?"

"Mm-hmm," I say noncommittally, not wanting to contradict anything he told her. And especially not tell her what we were actually doing.

"How has it been seeing him again?"

"Fine." When is she going to drop this topic already?

She hesitates as she takes a plate from me to rinse. "I… I know how you used to feel about him. In high school."

My fingers slip on the dish I'm holding, but I don't drop it. "What do you mean?"

"That you had a crush on him."

I glance over at her, pink staining her cheeks. I inherited my easy blushing from her.

"W-what?" I stammer. I've *never* talked to my mom about my love life before. Or, rather, lack of one.

She mumbles something, but I don't catch it, and ask her to repeat it.

She sighs in exasperation. "I found your diary, okay?"

"My diary?" I echo, shock radiating through me. Mom isn't the type to snoop.

"I wasn't searching for it," she says, almost pleading, rubbing at her chest absentmindedly. "I just came across it. Under your mattress."

Wow, apparently my very original hiding spot wasn't so secret.

"But not when you were in high school," she amends. "It was once you had left for college. I didn't want the bedsheets to get dusty, so I was changing them, and I found the diary."

I hand her another plate to rinse, not sure what to do with this information. "I forgot to pack it. I think I came and got it during that first Christmas break."

She nods. "I saw it was gone later. And I'm sorry. The house was so empty once you left and I missed you. When I found it, I guess I wanted to feel close to you again. To know your thoughts and feelings, even if they were from years ago."

I try to hold on to anger at the violation of my privacy, but can't. Mom doesn't have a mean bone in her body. She wasn't trying to spy.

"I barely remember what I wrote in there." What kind of teenage fantasies did I spin in that thing?

"Well, as far as Grayson was concerned, how cute you thought he was. How you liked that he helped his family. That he was athletic and smart in school."

Heat flushes my face. This is mortifying. Even if I still think all those things about him.

"But you also seemed upset that he never noticed you. Did you try to get him to notice you?"

I scrub the casserole dish in my hands extra hard, trying to get the baked-on gunk off. "No," I finally say. "I didn't do anything. Just... waited in the background."

That about sums up my life. Waiting for something to happen.

Like I told Grayson yesterday, though, I'm stepping out of my comfort zone this week. Otherwise, nothing will ever change.

"Do you still feel the same way about him?" she asks quietly.

I waver, unsure whether to admit it to her. To put it out into the universe like that, where it means something. I can't take it back if I do.

When I'd told Harper about it last year, it had felt low-stakes. I thought I'd never see her again. Thankfully, she's kept the secret, but telling my mom is different. Like it makes it *real*.

Don't I want it to be real, though?

"Yes," I finally say. "I still like him."

I'm stunned at the relief that flows through me, as if a weight released that I didn't know was holding me down.

"But he lives in Seattle."

Her comment crashes down on me, weighting me again. Like I need the reminder when it's something I'm specifically *not thinking about*.

"I know. It's not like anything's going to come of it, anyway."

Could it have last night? If we hadn't been interrupted?

"I just don't want you to get hurt. The way you seemed upset in the diary."

"I'm fine, Mom. Really."

I hand her the last dish to rinse off, then drain the sink. Grayson and I aren't anything, I remind myself. I can't get hurt because there's nothing there.

And if I want that to change, it's up to me.

"Abby, you came!"

Harper is all smiles as she hugs me, some kind of half-empty cocktail in her hands already.

"Of course," I tell her, squeezing her in return. "It's your wedding week."

She leans back and beams at me. "Well, thank you. I know this isn't normally your scene." She takes a sip of her drink. "But I got Harry to agree to make some different mocktails for you."

A blush works its way to my cheeks. As if I'm some underage girl who can't drink. I don't see how everyone enjoys the taste of alcohol. It's disgusting.

"Everything's on me and Owen at the bar for our group," Harper continues blithely. "So get whatever you want."

"Drinks are on you?" a woman asks. I glance over at Ruth Cooper, our town's token busybody. This woman's got her nose so far up everyone else's ass, it's a wonder she can see her own.

Harper wags a finger at her good-naturedly. "Just for the wedding party. But we'll have an open bar on Saturday, so you can drink your heart out then."

Ruth harrumphs but doesn't comment as she grabs her beer from Harry and disappears back into the crowd.

"You invited Ruth to the wedding?"

Harper sighs. "How could I not? I'd never hear the end of it, otherwise."

That's true.

"Hey, do you know where the bathrooms—" Elena cuts off mid-sentence when she notices me. "Oh, hey, Abby."

"They're over there," Harper says distractedly, pointing to the far wall. "Oh my God, Greg is talking to Kelly. He better not be hitting on her."

She leaves to go intervene in whatever is happening across the bar, and Elena and I stand there awkwardly.

"Congrats on winning game night," she says, smiling at me.

The sudden tension in my shoulders eases slightly. All I can remember is going all possessive with her yesterday about Grayson, wrapping my arm around him and telling her *I'd* take him home, not her. She must think I'm nuts.

"Thanks. I think it's supposed to be one of those things where everyone wins because we had fun."

She laughs lightly. "Yeah, you're right. And, um, I didn't mean to step on any toes about Grayson. Kristen mentioned you two weren't really dating, that it was so their mom thought he had a date."

My shoulders deflate. Wonderful. One fewer person we have to keep up the act for. Which, in my case, is bad.

"No, I'm sorry. I went kind of psycho girlfriend on you there, didn't I?"

Her eyes crinkle at the corners as she smiles. "Oh, that was nothing. I almost got punched at a bar once by a girl who was convinced I was hitting on her man. I only asked if they were using the spare chair at their table."

I wince. "Well, we're not that crazy in Crescent Pass. But I'd appreciate it if you didn't..." I swallow hard. "Well, if you didn't set your sights on Grayson."

She studies me in that same way Harper does, as if she can divine all my secrets. How do the two of them do that? "You like him?"

I nod hesitantly, not sure what compels me to reveal that. Maybe because I did the same with Mom earlier. Maybe it's time to stop living in the shadows.

"But Kristen doesn't know," I blurt out. "Or Grayson."

She mimes zipping her lips. "Your secret's safe with me."

"Thanks." Of course Elena's nice. She's one of Harper's best friends. "Actually, um, do you have any advice for me?"

Her brows pop up. "Oh my God, I love playing matchmaker. Give me all the backstory between you two."

She orders a Moscow Mule and sips at it as I tell her what I can, not that the story is long.

"Okay, so childhood sort-of friends and you want him to see you in a new way," she sums up. "Also, he doesn't live here, so that's an added factor. And he's your best friend's older brother."

I nod, a wave of guilt swamping me. What would Kristen think if she overheard this?

"Are you flirting with him?"

"I did last night."

She squints at me. "Does *he* know it's flirting?"

My stomach drops. Am I that obvious? "I'm not the best at it." As in, I don't know how to do it at all.

She nods decisively. "We need shots. To loosen you up a little."

I open my mouth to tell her I don't drink, but really, what do I have to lose? Maybe this will push me past a barrier that's been holding me back.

She gets Harry's attention. "Three Kamikazes." She looks back at me and drains the rest of her cocktail. "I'm a sucker for vodka and lime."

"You want me to take three shots?" That seems like a terrible idea.

"One for me, two for you. Trust me."

Okay...

Harry lines them up on the counter for us.

"One right after the other," she says, sliding her shot in front of her.

I eye my two. "I'm not a fan of vodka." Or anything.

"Don't think about the taste, just drink."

Before I lose my nerve, I do it, pushing past the burn in my throat. Oh God, that's vile. Like paint thinner.

She grins. "You look pretty lightweight, so give that fifteen or so to kick in."

"Are we doing shots?" Kelly asks, joining us. Greg must have finally left her alone. "Give me a Woo Woo," she says to Harry.

He looks at her like she's got three heads. "What the hell's a Woo Woo?"

"Peach schnapps, vodka, cranberry juice, and lime."

"Ooh, that sounds good," Elena says. "Give me one, too." She turns to me. "You want one?"

I shrug. "Sure, why not?" In for a penny, in for a pound.

Kelly holds up three fingers. "Three Woo Woos, please."

Harry rolls his eyes, mumbling something about out of towners, but sets to making them.

"Abby, are you drinking?" Harper asks as she sidles up next to our group.

"I guess I am." I don't feel any different so far. Elena said it'd take fifteen minutes, though.

"Yes, all right!" she cheers, holding up her empty glass. "Make another of whatever they're having for me," she calls to Harry.

He finishes making the shots. "Y'all might want to pace yourselves."

"It's Harper's wedding week," Kelly tells him, as if that explains everything.

Elena holds up her shot and shouts, "Harper's getting married!"

"Woo!" Harper and Kelly yell in unison, then all of them down their shots.

I grab mine off the counter, wincing down at it, already anticipating the awful taste.

Bottoms up, I guess.

CHAPTER TWELVE

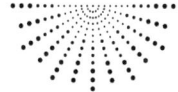

GRAYSON

The parking lot of Harry's Bar is packed, which is weird for a Tuesday night. Then again, I've never been here. I'd moved away by the time I was old enough to drink, and it's not like Owen's the type to hang out at bars and socialize. It's a wonder Harper got him to come here at all.

That girl has him wrapped around her finger so tight, I'm surprised he can walk. He seems to like it, though.

I'd debated forever about coming here tonight. I'd texted Abby earlier, wanting to clear the air, but she'd said she was busy. Was that true or a way for her to subtly let me know she didn't want to rehash what happened last night? Or rather, almost happened. She'd been about to strip for me, like my own private show.

And then barely talked to me after the thing at her parents' house. She'd said she was rattled, but again, was that because she was embarrassed?

Christ, I sound like a girl going on and on about this in my head. If I want to know what's up with her, I just have to ask her.

It's noisy and packed when I enter, the speakers playing some kind of 70s soft rock, maybe America. I look around, but the crowd is too dense to easily spot my group.

"Ah, the prodigal son returns."

I glance over at Ruth Cooper, her gray hair in a bun so tight, her scalp shows through the strands. Of course she'd be here the night I want to talk to Abby. Nothing escapes her notice.

I nod at her politely. "I think that'd imply I'm making a repentant return."

She takes a sip of her beer. "You were always a smart-aleck."

"Takes one to know one, Ruth."

She shakes her head and laughs, seemingly against her will. "Your new sister-in-law is making a right fool of herself over there."

She tips the neck of her beer bottle toward the far end of the bar. Harper's dancing with one of her friends, making a semi-spectacle of herself as she holds up a shot glass, then drains it. Nearby, Owen's on a barstool, scowling at Greg, who's looking at the two women with interest.

Oh God, he's not doing the cliche possessive husband thing, is he?

"Grayson!"

Someone jumps at me and I instinctively catch them. It's Abby, a sloppy grin on her face as she looks up at me.

"You're finally here," she says. "I thought you bailed on us like Kristen."

I peek at Ruth, who's staring at us with unabashed interest. We've never needed a local paper because Ruth spreads news faster than any newspaper ever could. This'll be all over town tomorrow.

"Excuse us," I say, putting Abby back on the ground and leading her over to Harper and her friends.

Abby grabs my hand and intertwines our fingers. "Because we're dating," she says in a loud whisper, then holds her finger to her lips, making a *shh* sound.

Except she uses the finger attached to mine, so my hand knocks into her mouth.

What the hell is up with her? And I swear if Ruth heard that…

"Abby, what—" My question dies when I finally notice her outfit. It's an obscenely short dress, something I can't imagine Abby would actually own. "What are you wearing?" I blurt out, my mouth not catching up with my brain.

"You like it?" She lets go of my hand and twirls, the dress riding up to show off the bottoms of her underwear. "Kelly and I switched clothes. Isn't that funny?"

"Jesus Christ," I mutter, grabbing her shoulders to stop her from twirling.

I look over at Kelly, who's half a foot shorter than Abby, wearing jeans rolled at the cuffs and a shirt that hangs loose on her.

"Are you drunk?" I ask her.

"I had some shots," she says solemnly, as if she's confessing. "At first, I had three. But then you didn't show up, so I had more. I figured, fuck it, right?"

I blink stupidly. I've never heard Abby curse. I didn't know librarians were allowed to.

Then again, they also don't strip in their kitchen and seductively ask if they should take off their bra or panties next.

Okay, not thinking about that right now.

"At first, the taste was awful," she continues. "But I can't even taste them now. See?" She goes over to the bar, picks up a random shot, and swallows it.

Who the hell's shot was that?

I follow her and ask Owen, "What the fuck's going on? Why'd you let Abby get plastered?"

"What?" Most of his attention is on Harper, taking off her heels in the middle of the bar.

"Abby's drunk. And wearing Kelly's clothes?" I have no idea what that's about.

"Yeah, I can't keep track of all of them," Owen says, collecting the shoes from a barefoot Harper. "I figured Kristen could handle Abby and I'd get Harper and her friends. No, don't drink that." He takes a half-full glass out of Harper's hands that's evidently not hers.

Okay, he clearly has too much on his plate. "Abby said something about Kristen bailing?"

"She had to go home," Harper yells, needlessly loud, even with the music and general din of noise in here. "Jamie's sick."

Owen frowns. "She didn't tell me she was leaving."

"She texted our group chat." She wags a finger playfully at him. "No boys allowed." Her finger gets closer and closer to him until she boops him on the nose, then kisses him. "God, you're sexy. I can't believe I'm marrying you."

Owen's normally stoic face softens. "We're already married."

"Mmm. Even better."

I turn away before they start making out. Wait, where'd Abby go?

Scanning the crowd, I finally spot her over by the jukebox, dancing with Greg. Something sharp stabs my chest and I glance down, half-surprised when there's nothing there. That was an internal stab.

I shake off the sensation and stalk over to them, pushing through the other couples on the dance floor. When Abby spots me, she waves excitedly and leaves Greg's side.

He glares at me as he sees who Abby left him for, but I don't care about that right now.

"Abby—"

"You wanna dance?" she asks, putting her hands on my shoulders.

"Um, sure. Listen—"

"Oh, I love this song. *You can go your own way,*" she sings along. Holy crap, her voice is terrible.

I grin, the urgency of finding out how she got like this fading. I've never seen her this way.

She sings the last verse, lost in her own world, and her hands squeeze my shoulders. "You have the best shoulders. Very broad."

"Uh, thanks." It's all I can do not to laugh. There's no way she'd be doing all this sober.

"Do you work out?"

"I do." Although this week my usual gym schedule is completely thrown out the window.

She nods. "I try to work out, but I always forget. Like I'll do it for a couple of weeks, then life gets in the way and suddenly it's a month later and I have to start all over again. Does that ever happen to you?"

It's dizzying keeping up with her rambling and changes in topic. "Can't say that it does."

"That's good. You're very committed. That's admirable. I've always admired you."

She has? "Thanks."

"And I could tell you work out, even before I asked you. When you took your shirt off for me yesterday, it was obvious."

Took your shirt off for me. The way she phrases it makes it sound like I was taking it off specifically for her, not the poker game. Which, I guess I was. It was only us two playing, after all.

She leans in closer, whispering, "You know, when your shirt was off, I saw your happy trail."

I don't know if it's her words or her breath in my ear, but my stomach pleasantly curls with anticipation. "Yeah?"

"I liked seeing it," she confesses. "It made me all tingly."

And my stomach bottoms out all the way. Holy shit. I should tell her to stop talking right now. To not reveal anything else when her lips are this loose.

But I don't. I desperately want to know what else she'll say.

"Tingly in a good way?" I ask.

"Mmm." She gives a dreamy sigh. "Very good. Can I tell you a secret?"

Hell yeah, she can.

There's a tap on my shoulder and I glance over at Greg. "Can I cut in?"

I give him a death glare. *Fuck off,* I mouth at him.

He flips me the middle finger before disappearing back into the crowd.

Fucking prick. I never liked him in school. And now he's trying to edge in on my—

I cut off that train of thought. Abby's not anything to me. Not yet, at least.

No, not *not yet*. Not anytime. Didn't I decide yesterday it was a good thing we got interrupted last night? Things were getting too heated. Starting something up with Abby wouldn't be right. It's one thing to do this fake dating for Mom's benefit. It'd be another thing to do it for real.

Wait, wasn't she telling me about a secret?

She turns her head. "Was that Greg?"

"Yeah. About that sec—"

"You know, he asked me to prom senior year. And I almost said yes, but then I found out he only asked me because, like, ten other girls said no first. And I didn't want to be the eleventh pick."

Oh, I guess we're on the next topic now. "No one wants that," I agree.

"I wish..." She trails off, still swaying to whatever song's playing now. Another Fleetwood Mac maybe.

"What do you wish?"

"I wish you would have come home from college and taken me to prom."

My forehead wrinkles. What? "We barely talked back then."

She sighs. "I know. You never noticed me."

Something like shame swirls in my gut, even though logically I have nothing to feel guilty for. "It's not that I didn't notice you." Actually, that's true. But I don't want her to feel bad about it. "You were my sister's best friend. Off limits."

She stops swaying and looks up at me. Her voice goes husky as she asks, "Am I still off limits?"

My mouth dries. If I wasn't sure about her flirting before, I'm definitely sure now.

But she's drunk. I can't actually answer her. She might not even remember this in the morning.

Out of the corner of my eye, I spot Owen approaching us, Harper stumbling next to him. "I'm taking all the girls home. They're getting out of control."

"You're out of control," Harper mumbles half-heartedly.

"Yeah, good idea. I'll take Abby home."

Abby's grip on my shoulders tightens and she leans in to whisper, "You're going to come home with me?"

A shiver races down my spine, and I pray Owen didn't hear her.

"Come on." I lead her off the dance floor, and it almost feels like Owen and I are doing the walk of shame as we pass Ruth, her judgmental gaze heavy on our pack of drunk girls.

"I can't believe Harry wouldn't serve us anymore," Elena grumbles once we're in the parking lot. "What kind of bar is this?"

"A responsible one," I mutter.

It's like a slapstick show watching Harper, Elena, and Kelly stuff themselves into Owen's truck, but they manage.

"You'll be okay?" I ask him. I don't envy the man.

"Yeah, it's fine. Harper warned me they wanted to let loose tonight."

I apparently missed a lot getting to the bar as late as I did. As I open the passenger door of my car for Abby, I realize I didn't even get a drink there. Probably for the best, anyway. Someone needs a clear head.

Abby keeps up a stream of chatter on the way back to her place, thankfully away from the topic of our limits, and when we get there I open her door, letting her lean on my arm for balance as we head inside.

I flick on the light in the front hallway and Leo peers up at me lazily from his spot on the floor. At least he's not running this time.

"Do you need help with anything?" I ask. It's been a long time since I've taken care of a drunk girl, and even that just mostly involved dropping them back at their dorm in college. "I can make coffee. Might sober you up some."

She shakes her head, hair swinging wildly around her face. "Let's go to bed."

I chuckle nervously, even as an unexpected thread of desire tugs at me. "I'll help *you* get to bed. Then I have to go home."

"Right," she says, tugging me down the hall.

We pass the living room and kitchen and head further into the house where I haven't been yet. The last room down the hallway is her bedroom, and she switches on the light, revealing a cozy room done up in shades of cream and blue. A queen bed with an oversized tufted headboard and fluffy duvet sits in the middle of the room, and there are more bookshelves in here, the books color coordinated on each shelf. How many books does she own?

She slips off her shoes and tosses them in the corner, then tugs at her dress. "How do I…"

"Hey, whoa, whoa. Why don't you undress in the bathroom?" It looks like there's an en suite bathroom attached. "I'll get you some pajamas." I turn toward her dresser, then realize I don't know where anything is. "Which drawer are they in?"

She's still tugging at her dress, to no avail. "Second from the top."

I find her a matching set of top and bottoms, then hand them to her. "Go change."

She leaves and I look around the room. Okay, what will she need? A trashcan by her bedside, in case she gets sick. Oh, and some water and ibuprofen for when she inevitably wakes up with a headache.

I retrieve a glass of water for her from the kitchen, and when I return, she has the bathroom door open.

"Grayson?" she calls.

"Yeah?"

"I can't get this dress off."

I pinch the bridge of my nose. "There's a zipper in the back."

"Can you help me with it? I can't reach it."

I want to ask her how she got it on in the first place, but who knows what those girls were up to before I got to the bar.

She walks over, able to keep her balance now across the room, and presents her back to me, pulling the curtain of her hair over one shoulder to give me better access.

There's something suggestive about it, but I push that out of my mind as I unzip her dress, down, down, revealing a black bra that contrasts with her pale skin. The mood of the room shifts, my gaze traveling over each part I reveal. It's a long fucking zipper, stopping at her lower back, nestled right above her ass.

The dress slides down her shoulders, loose now, and I should look away, give her some privacy. But as she turns around, catching my eye, it's obvious she doesn't want me to look away. She pulls it down further, the fabric sliding over her cleavage, revealing more and more of it. This bra is sexier than the one she wore last night, the cups lower cut, barely skimming the edge of her nipples.

"Abby," I breathe, unable to look away for the life of me.

She pulls the dress down all the way, molding her hands over her breasts, teasing me, pushing them together. "You like that?"

I tear my gaze away, looking at her face, at the desire there.

Holy fuck.

"Are you trying to seduce me?" I ask without thinking.

Her gaze drops to my lips. "Is it working?"

"You're drunk," I reply, needing to say it. She clearly had way too much alcohol tonight. She's not thinking right. She'd never do this sober.

Didn't she take her clothes off for you last night, too?

As part of the game. But this isn't a game anymore. I couldn't take advantage of her like this.

She moves forward, hands settling on my shoulders, mouth pressing to mine.

Her lips are soft and eager as they move over mine, her breasts pushed against my chest. A bolt of lust rushes through me, and I want more than anything in this moment to slant my mouth over hers and kiss her back, to discover how much she wants this, how far she's willing to go.

But I can't.

I step back, telling her gently but firmly, "You've had too much to drink. We shouldn't be doing this."

Her face takes on a mulish expression. "I know what I want."

"You're drunk," I repeat. And besides that, everything is moving way too fast for me to keep up with. I wasn't even attracted to Abby before yesterday. And now she's not only kissing me, but I'm dying to kiss her back?

The stubbornness evaporates as she continues to look at me, her lips quivering the slightest bit. "So you're rejecting me?"

My stomach drops. "Abby, no."

Before I can reach for her, she's across the room, staring at me with accusatory eyes. "Just go."

"Don't you need help—"

"Go," she says in a low voice, then turns and slams the bathroom door shut behind her, leaving me alone in her bedroom.

Fuck.

I stride over and knock on the door. "Abby—"

"Go," she yells, and my hand drops.

I rub the back of my neck, an anguished ache beating in my chest. That was not how I wanted this to go. I'm not rejecting her, I'm being responsible. If I took her up on everything she was promising tonight, she'd be horrified tomorrow. She'd feel violated.

She's not in her right mind. Can't make sensible decisions.

So why do I feel like absolute shit?

CHAPTER THIRTEEN

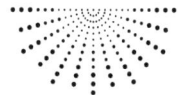

ABBY

"One of the most important things in winemaking is what we call *terroir*—the combination of climate, soil, and landscape that makes our wine unique. Here in Oregon, the volcanic soil is rich in nutrients, and we get just the right amount of rain to help the vines develop deep roots."

The chipper tour guide goes on to explain something about how the cool nights and warm days give the grapes a good balance between acidity and sweetness, but all I can do is wince. The sun is extra bright, piercing through my sunglasses straight to the throbbing pain behind my eyes.

Why the hell would Harper schedule a winery tour the morning after a planned night of drinking? Is she secretly a sadist?

I glance over at her, seemingly unaffected by last night's activities as she leans in to Owen's side, smiling and whispering something in his ear. Why is she smiling? What is there to even smile about?

Okay, pump your brakes, Miss Crabbypants. Just because you're miserable doesn't mean everyone else is.

"Our winery has been family owned since the early 1990s, expanded from five to now fifty acres," the tour guide continues. "April is an exciting time here because the vines are waking up after winter, with the first buds breaking that will eventually develop into grape clusters."

Oh my God lady, no one cares. Actually, Kristen and Eli appear interested at the front of our group, nodding along at the appropriate parts. I guess I might normally find it interesting, too, even if I don't drink wine.

But not today. Today I'm drowning in my complete humiliation, heightened by the headache from hell I'm currently experiencing.

I threw myself at Grayson last night. There's no other way to describe it. Just threw caution to the wind and took my clothes off and kissed him. And what did I get? A big, fat *no*. A *we shouldn't be doing this*.

What did I think would happen? That he'd take one look at me in my bra and be seduced? Get real. I cringe, remembering he'd even asked if I was trying to seduce him. Could I be any more pathetic?

I groan, the headache pounding harder, and massage my temples. This whole idea of breaking outside my comfort zone and getting his attention was a mistake. I've spent my life making safe choices, and for good reason.

You don't get hurt that way.

Over on the other side of our group, Cheryl is talking in a low voice to Grayson. When they both glance at me, I avert my eyes and nestle in further between Elena and Kelly. I've stuck like glue to the two of them since the tour started, praying that Grayson won't try to talk to me about last night if I'm around them. He doesn't know that they know the truth about our arrangement.

I rub my temples again. Damn, this is getting confusing.

Grayson breaks away from his mom, circling around until he's behind me.

"Can I talk to you?"

I stare straight ahead, ignoring him and listening to the tour guide's explanation of the winery's sustainable farming practices.

"Abby."

I squeeze my eyes shut, not wanting to hear the plea in his voice.

Next to me, Elena gently nudges me. "Go talk to him," she urges.

She doesn't know about the mortifying ordeal last night. All she remembers is me telling her I like Grayson.

I smile weakly and turn, heading toward the other side of the vineyard. If Grayson repeats anything that happened, I don't want anyone within earshot.

He follows, then hands me two ibuprofen and his bottle of water. "For your headache."

My resistance melts a little. That was nice of him.

I take it and down the medicine, figuring it's time for another dose anyway.

"Mom's asking about you," he says, sticking his hands in his pockets.

I stare down at the grass as tears sting my eyes. So he's doing this to look good in front of his mom, not because he actually cares.

"Yeah?" I say noncommittally. I have no idea what to say to him today. How to explain away my behavior last night. Not when he doesn't feel the same.

"You've avoided me all morning."

"Have I?"

My response is stupid. I've obviously been avoiding him. Which, yes, is not a good look in front of his mom when we're supposed to be cozying up to each other. It was one thing to do it when I didn't know how he felt, but now that I know...

"Listen, we should talk about last ni—"

I cut him off before he finishes his sentence. "I don't want to."

He shifts, looking over at the group, and I take the opportunity to finally look at him. He's in comfortable clothes—a faded green tee and jeans—and has his aviators on again. His shirt sleeves are tight around his upper arms and I recall seeing him shirtless the other night. How good he looked. How much I wanted him.

How delusional I was.

"I think we should."

Oh, does he? "Well, too bad." I'm too hungover today to be anything but blunt.

There's a stubborn set to his jaw. "You think we're not going to talk about how you—"

"Later," I hiss, glancing around to make sure we're still alone.

"If we don't do it now, you'll put it off forever."

Damn it, he knows me better than I thought.

"We're moving on to the barrel room," the tour guide calls, waving her arm to catch our attention.

I wave a hand back to let her know we heard and slip away from Grayson to join the group.

Cheryl touches a hand to my arm. "You okay, honey?" She looks back toward where I left Grayson, then at me again.

"I have a bad headache," I say, hoping that's explanation enough for not hanging around her son. "I'm not great company today."

She gives me a sympathetic frown. "I'm sorry you're not feeling well. Why don't you have Grayson drive you home?"

I grit my teeth at her solution. "I'll be fine."

The barrel room is blessedly dim and cool, the pounding in my head receding. I'm not sure if it's the change in light and temperature or the ibuprofen kicking in, but I send up a silent prayer of thanks.

"Now this is where the magic really happens," the tour guide announces, her chipper voice echoing off the walls. "After the grapes have been harvested, fermented, and pressed, the wine comes here to age in these beautiful oak barrels. The aging process is critical because it allows the wine to develop more complex flavors and textures over time."

I hold in my snort of disbelief. Every time I've tried wine, it tastes like pure alcohol. How people detect all those different notes and essences, I have no idea.

Grayson sidles up next to me during the guide's spiel about how the oak barrels impact the flavor, crossing his arms over his chest. He bends, whispering in my ear, "We're talking about it today."

I breathe in deeply, not only the scents of oak and earthiness coming from the room, but also of Grayson, something masculine and fresh. The urge strikes me to press my nose to his chest to discover precisely what that scent is, and I just as quickly push it away.

I don't respond, dread pooling in my chest the longer the guide talks about barrel craftsmanship and humidity control and a million other things I don't care about. I don't want to talk to Grayson about this. Don't want him to awkwardly explain how he doesn't feel the same way. To remind me about how I basically sexually harassed him, taking off my clothes and pushing my breasts together in front of him, then kissing him.

Why in the hell did I let Elena convince me to do shots?

When the group files out to head to the tasting room, Grayson holds my elbow, not hard but firmly. I could tug it away, but that would cause a scene. I don't want any more attention on me today.

"We'll catch up in a bit," Grayson says to Owen when he glances back at us questioningly.

The barrel room door shuts, silence permeating the air until Grayson turns to me. "Why are you avoiding me?"

I firm my mouth, internally debating. I guess I can't avoid him forever, even if a part of me wants to head back out to the vineyard and bury myself in a hole so deep, I never have to face the consequences of my actions again.

"Are you embarrassed?" he asks.

I can't help the snort of disbelief that escapes me this time. "That's an understatement," I mutter.

"Why?"

I stare at him, confused by his apparent confusion. Is he seriously asking me why I'm embarrassed? "Because I threw myself at you," I sputter.

He waits quietly for me to finish.

"And..." I swallow hard, my throat suddenly thick with emotion. "And you don't feel the same way."

God, that sounded pathetic.

His brows furrow. "When did I ever say that?"

Doubt creeps its way in before I dismiss it. "You didn't kiss me back. Said we shouldn't be doing it."

"You were drunk."

He says it like it's a complete explanation, even though it's not.

"So?"

"So, I wasn't going to take advantage of you like that."

A laugh burbles up inside me. Take advantage of me? After I did all that stuff to him? "So if I wasn't drunk, you would have kissed me back?"

"If you weren't drunk, I don't think you'd have tried to begin with."

He's right. I wouldn't have. Which is the crux of the matter. This whole deal about stepping outside my comfort zone. And despite my earlier vow to play things safe from now on, that bluntness from my now-faint headache rears its head.

"And if I had?" I ask him, letting the cards fall where they may. What do I have to lose at this point?

Something shifts in the air, a tension present that wasn't there before. "I didn't know if you only did it because you were drunk, or because you actually wanted to."

He's giving me an out. I could say it was the alcohol, not me. But that would be a lie. And I'd be an even bigger coward if I took the easy way out.

"I wanted to," I whisper, not looking at him. I don't want to see the pity in his eyes.

There's a gentle finger on my chin, tipping my face up to meet his gaze. There's no pity there, only searching, like he's trying to figure something out.

"I wanted to kiss you back," he says. "I don't understand it, but I wanted to."

My breath hitches. "You don't understand it?" I repeat dumbly.

One side of his mouth lifts in a smile. "It's like you're suddenly a different Abby than the one I've always known. Or maybe I never really knew you. Didn't see you this whole time."

Time seems to slow as he leans down and presses a kiss to my lips. I'm so stunned, I barely respond to the soft pressure, not until he's pulling away.

"No," I mumble, reaching for him and pressing my mouth to his determinedly. It's clumsy and not my best work, but it gets the point across.

He makes a satisfied noise in the back of his throat that has my knees weakening, and I cling to him, half-surprised when he wraps his arms around my waist, bringing me flush against him. He deepens the kiss and my heart races, letting him take the lead, following the way he guides me, submitting to his exploration of me. Tingles race across my skin where one of his hands roams lower.

And then it's abruptly gone, and it takes me a moment to register Cheryl's surprised voice from behind me.

"Oh, I didn't realize," she says from the now-open doorway. "I thought you were right behind... Well, I'll just let you two..."

She trails off, a sly grin breaking over her face before she leaves.

I look at Grayson, who's looking back at me, guilt all over his face. Why does he look guilty?

Did he... He didn't know his mom would come back in here to find us kissing, right?

Pain lances through my chest. Did he set that up? Knowing she'd come back here? Is he that desperate to make sure she believes we're an item?

"Grayson..."

His brows pinch together. "I'm sorry."

I hold back a sound of distress and make my escape. It was stupid to come here today. Even knowing it was important to Harper, I should have made my excuses.

How many times can I humiliate myself before I learn my lesson?

CHAPTER FOURTEEN

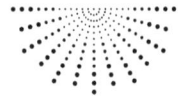

GRAYSON

*A*bby's gone before I can finish apologizing to her. I can't believe Mom barged in on us like that. Of all the times for her meddling to rear its ugly head.

Squinting into the sunlight as I exit the building, I hold a hand up to my eyes, searching for Abby, but it's like she's disappeared. Wait, everyone's supposed to be in the tasting room. Thankfully, the winery has signage directing me there.

"Our Chardonnay has a bright acidity and citrus notes," the tour guide is saying to the group as I sneak in. "But it's our Pinot Noir we're known for. You might taste hints of cherry or raspberry in it, possibly even earthy flavors, too. Let me know what you think."

I slip in unobtrusively next to Harper. "Have you seen Abby?" At first glance, she's not in here.

"She just texted," she says, swirling her wine around in the glass. "Her hangover finally got the best of her so she headed home."

Fuck.

Why the hell had she run like that after Mom came in? Was she that embarrassed?

"Thanks," I mutter, and leave the tasting room, in no mood to pretend to detect notes of whatever is in the wine.

Pulling out my phone, I call Abby, but it goes straight to voicemail. Did she turn off her phone or screen my call?

I jab my finger on the end call icon and shove my phone in my pocket, then pull it back out almost immediately when it vibrates in my hand.

Did Abby—No, it's a text from my buddy, Charlie, asking about the name of an Italian place he wants to take his girlfriend to. I'd taken a date there last year, and though I can't even remember the girl, I can clearly recall the amazing ravioli I'd had.

I text him back the name of the restaurant and I'm about to call Abby again when another text from Charlie pops up.

Charlie: *How's life in Podunk City?*

That's how I've always referred to Crescent Pass to my friends in Seattle, but it rubs me the wrong way now. Yeah, it's a small town with not a ton to do, but there's a lot I've forgotten about it, too. Fresh air. Wide, open spaces. My family and all the time I've missed with them.

And now... Abby.

It's weird, I've barely thought about my real life this week. My friends. My job. My condo. The life I was so desperate to get to at eighteen, wanting to be rid of small towns forever. But being back here for this long feels like I'm in a different life now, even if I'm only playing pretend. Like I'm two different people, one in Seattle and one in Crescent Pass.

But which one do I want to be the real Grayson?

I debate what to text back, my fingers fiddling over my phone. Telling him I'm actually enjoying my time here, that I'm seeing a girl I grew up with in a different way... I don't know, it seems too out of left field. Usually after my trips I'm complaining about Mom prying into my life, about how there's nothing to do in town.

Me: *Going fine. Same old, same old.*

Guilt swamps me almost immediately, as if I'm ashamed of liking Crescent Pass. Ashamed of not telling him about Abby. Truthfully, I don't know what there is to tell. I kissed her and she ran away from me. It's kind of a blow to the ego, now that I think about it.

She wanted me to kiss her, though. I know she did. The way she'd jumped at me as I'd kissed her, then yielded, letting me take control. I like taking charge in the bedroom, and she'd seemed fully on board with that.

Not that we were in a bedroom. We were in a winery's barrel room. Where my mom walked in on us.

I cringe again. Not that she knew what she was walking into, but still. This won't help my case, either. I'd worked hard to convince Mom this was a casual thing with Abby, not a sneaking around and making out during winery tours thing.

I call Abby one more time, but it's straight to voicemail. She clearly doesn't want to talk to me. Well, too bad. Didn't she say the same to me earlier? I don't like leaving things unresolved.

"Grayson."

I spin around, finding Mom there.

She looks around in confusion. "Where's Abby?"

"She went home. Headache." I want to tell her it was because of her, but I can't be fully sure of that. Not until I talk to her.

"Seems like things are going well between you two."

"Mom..."

She holds up her hands in surrender before I can say anymore. "I know, you don't want me to get involved. I think she's good for you, is all."

Normally, I'd leave it at that, but something compels me to ask, "Why?"

She gives me a soft smile. "She balances you out. Where you're stubborn, she's flexible."

I'm not stubborn. If I say that, though, it'll prove her point.

"She'll soften your rough edges."

"I don't have rough edges," I mutter, probably stubbornly, in her opinion. Seriously, what is she talking about?

"You've always been so driven," she says. "Focused on getting out of Crescent Pass, promoting up in your career. You never let yourself breathe. I don't think I've seen you actually relax on a trip until this one. Until you started spending time with Abby."

That's not entirely true. I often pretend like I have *very important business matters* when I'm here, just so I can escape from Mom hounding me about who I'm dating or what's holding me back from getting serious with someone.

"You don't have your nose buried in your phone this trip like you usually do," she continues.

Damn it, how many times am I going to feel guilty today?

"Sorry, Mom. I'll try to be more present from now on."

She smiles and pats my arm. "It's never too late to change. But I'm happy to see you happy. You've been all smiles with Abby."

That's part of the act, though.

Well, not entirely. She's made me laugh more than I expected. And the way she's gotten me to open up about things, see my family and relationship with them in new ways…

A wave of something like longing washes over me. For Abby.

"Come on," Mom says, looping her hand around my upper arm. "Harper set up a catered lunch for us."

I nod and she leads me away, but all I can think is when did I start to miss Abby?

ABBY IGNORED my call again on the drive from the winery back to Crescent Pass, but like Mom said, I can be a stubborn son of a bitch.

I drive to her home, the afternoon sun warm on my back as I stand on her porch and ring the doorbell.

She answers, appearing startled for a moment, but I'm more focused on her faintly red-rimmed eyes.

"Have you been crying?" I ask, forgetting about greetings. "What happened?"

She looks at me helplessly, and everything else fades away but the urge to figure out what's wrong and fix it.

I step inside, taking her in my arms. "Seriously, what is it?"

I'm relieved when she presses her forehead to my chest, but the contact is brief before she pulls away and shuts the door behind me.

She searches my face, then bluntly asks, "Did kissing me earlier have anything to do with your mom?"

"My mom?" I repeat, thrown for a loop. What's she talking about?

"Did you…" She falters, then resolves herself. "Did you kiss me so Cheryl would see?"

My mouth drops open. "No. Why would you think that?"

She lifts one shoulder in a half-hearted shrug. "You looked so guilty after she saw us. And said you were sorry. I thought…" She twists the hem of her shirt. "I thought you wanted to make up for how I wasn't talking to you at the winery in front of her."

It takes me a moment to connect the dots. She didn't leave because she was embarrassed Mom saw us. She left because she thought I orchestrated…

My stomach sinks. Shit. I fucked this up, didn't I?

How can I blame her for jumping to conclusions when I've been vocal this whole time about putting on an act in front of Mom?

Things aren't all an act anymore, though. Everything got more complicated with that kiss.

"I would never use you like that," I tell her, trying to convey to her my sincerity. "I know we have this fake dating thing going on, but I wouldn't kiss you to keep up the lie. Like I told you earlier, I did it because I wanted to. And I only said I was sorry because Mom barged in on us. I thought you were embarrassed."

She stares at me, then buries her face in her hands. "God, I'm an idiot."

"No, you're not. This whole situation is… unprecedented," I finish, not sure how else to put it.

I gently tug her hands away from her face. "Were you crying because you thought that kiss was fake?"

She squeezes her eyes shut. "Maybe."

So it meant something to her.

"Are you ready to talk?"

She gives me a look of annoyance that has me laughing before she nods and leads me to the living room. She sits on one end of the couch, while I take the other. She crosses her legs, then uncrosses them, folding her hands in her lap, fingers clenched. She's nervous.

"This is a first for me," I admit, wanting to put her at ease. "I've never found myself in a situation like this."

Her lips tug up at one corner. "Oh, this is like the fifth time this month I've been someone's fake date to a wedding, then got drunk, made a pass at them, and kissed them the next day."

At least her sense of humor is back. "So just another Wednesday for you?"

"Pretty much." She sighs, rubbing her palms over her thighs. "It's obviously a first for me, too."

She's blushing again, and I can't help following the flush with my gaze down her neck to where it disappears under the collar of her shirt.

"As far as last night, you have nothing to be embarrassed about."

She looks away. "I don't know how I'm going to show my face in town again."

Right, the stuff at the bar. I was only thinking of what happened after. I grin, remembering how she was. "You flashed your underwear to nearly everyone at Harry's."

"Grayson," she half-laughs, half-moans, then gives me a reluctant smile when she catches sight of my grin, just like I wanted.

"I meant with me, at your house afterward." I reach for her hand, glad she lets me hold it. "To be honest, you taking off your dress was pretty hot. And if you hadn't been drunk, I would have kissed you back."

Her blush intensifies, her tongue darting out to wet her lip. "I... I don't know what I'm doing. What *we're* doing, I guess."

"I don't know either. But I really want to find out."

CHAPTER FIFTEEN

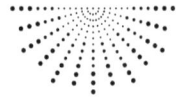

ABBY

*H*e wants to find out what this thing between us is. That's good, right?

"So we're in uncharted territory?" I ask, my palms sweating.

"Map's out the window."

He shifts to face me more fully on the couch. How does he appear so at ease when I'm a bundle of nerves over here?

"Would you be interested in starting something up while I'm in town?" he asks in that same nonchalant tone.

Starting something up, I silently mouth to myself. "What does that mean exactly?"

He looks me up and down, and I swear there's something lascivious there.

I really like it.

"Well, we both seem to be attracted to one another."

He waits for me to respond, but it takes me a moment to get past the fact he outright said he's attracted to me. It was one thing to hope for it, even suspect it. But to hear him say it... I finally did it. Finally got him to notice me.

I nod, trying not to appear too eager.

"I'd be down for... exploring this attraction for the rest of the week, if you are," he says. "As long as we're on the same page about it. That we'll be done when I leave Crescent Pass on Sunday."

A sense of déjà vu sweeps over me. Kristen had a similar agreement with Eli last winter when he'd first moved in with her as her roommate. Is this kind of situation more common than we thought?

"We're on the same page." When it comes down to it, I would rather risk my heart getting hurt if it means having a brief interlude with Grayson. It's no contest. "And I'm very interested in exploring things." I clear my throat, not sure what else to say.

"And when I visit here in the future, everything will be cool between us?"

"Yeah." I shrug as casually as I can, trying to match his vibe. Even though I'm vibrating with energy on the inside. Is this actually happening?

A mischievous grin slips over his face. "All right. You ready to get started?"

My jaw drops. "Now?" I glance around my empty living room. "It's the middle of the afternoon."

His grin widens. "You never heard of afternoon delight?"

Oh. He's teasing me. Still, there's a part of me that's afraid he'll change his mind, even if it was his suggestion.

I harness that bold side of me I've channeled the past two nights and shift on the couch so I'm straddling him. His eyes widen in surprise, and when I almost lose my nerve, his hands find my thighs, tugging me further onto his lap.

"You keep surprising me," he murmurs, one hand resting on my lower back to support me, the other rising to tuck a lock of loosened hair behind my ear. "I wish I'd seen this side of you before."

This side didn't exist before. Not until I'd already had an in with him as his fake date. Not until I worked up the courage.

And look how far I've come. I'm on the lap of this incredibly sexy guy, the one I've been crushing on forever, his blue eyes bright with desire as he gazes back at me. His dark hair sweeps off his face, stubble coming in on his strong jaw after not shaving for a couple of days.

I brush my thumb over the rasp on his jaw, loving that I have the freedom to touch him like this.

At least, I think I do.

"Is this okay? To touch you?"

He nods. "I want you to touch me." There's a gravel in his voice I haven't heard before, sending a shiver of lust over me.

My thumb drifts down from his jaw to his neck, over his pulse point, and his hand flexes on my lower back. My lips follow the same trail, unable to help myself, and he arches his neck to give me better access, his hands moving further down on my ass now.

"Mmm," I moan, the sound escaping me, and I grip his shoulders, loving the feel of his hard muscles under the soft fabric of his shirt.

He moves his head, capturing my lips, and I gladly settle into the rhythm he sets, his lips firm as they move over mine with skill.

I'm kissing Grayson. Making out with him, even. "I can't believe we're doing this," I murmur, unsure for a moment whether I actually said it out loud until he responds.

"I know. But I don't want to stop."

A thrill runs through me. "Me, either."

"Can I touch you?"

I can't get over the desire in his voice. This whole thing is a dream. "Yes, please."

His hands move up, snaking around to my stomach, then my breasts, squeezing lightly. Another moan escapes me, and I'd feel more self-conscious if it didn't feel so damn good, a pleasant ache forming, wanting more.

"You were so fucking sexy in your bra the last two nights," he says, molding his palms over me. "Such a tease."

"Do you like being teased?" I roll my hips against him, half-surprised at myself.

He groans, pulling me even closer on top of him. "Under the right circumstances."

I let go of his shoulders to unbutton the first two buttons of my shirt, revealing the edge of my bra.

His stare is glued to where I toy with the next button, slowly undoing it.

"Am I going to get the full show today?" he asks thickly.

I can't believe he's so into this. "If you want it."

As the third button pops free, he undoes the last of the buttons by himself and pushes my shirt off, as if he can't wait any longer. His hands grip my waist, bringing me in closer until his lips press into the center of my cleavage.

My breath stutters as his mouth moves over the swell of my breast to the edge of the cup. He takes his time, teasing me now, and I clutch his shoulders again, digging my nails in, the anticipation killing me.

He hesitates at the edge. This is a precipice we can't come back from. But I want it so bad.

And then thankfully, blessedly, he peels down the cup of my bra, exposing me. His gaze is hungry before he slowly sweeps the flat of his tongue over my nipple.

My lower belly goes liquid. "Oh my God, that's good."

He continues, the desire within me rising higher and higher, and as he pulls down the other bra cup and switches sides, I shift on top of him, needing relief from the growing pressure.

His erection is stiff underneath me, and I rub myself against his length, loving the low groan he gives in response. One of his hands settles on my ass again, establishing the rhythm, as his other hand squeezes the breast he's not sucking, rolling the hard bud of my nipple between his fingers.

This is... incredible. I've never experienced this level of craving. I spread my knees wider, settling further on him, riding him now.

He leans away from me briefly to ask, "Do you have a condom?"

His question breaks the spell I'm under, reality crashing over me. I'm half-naked in my living room on a Wednesday afternoon humping Grayson on the couch

"No," I answer, unable to believe we've gotten to this point. We kissed for the first time *today*, and we're already going to sleep together? "To be honest, I think I need a little time to wrap my head around, um, condoms."

He looks up at me, expression dazed, lips swollen. Oh my God, he's sexy. "You on the pill?"

"No, I mean… sex."

His face finally clears. "Yeah, of course. There's no pressure."

I nod, awkwardness settling in now that the rising tension has deflated. "I'm sorry."

"No, there's nothing to be sorry for. I'm sorry I assumed—"

"Don't be."

He shifts in place, his erection nudging me right where it feels amazing.

"Have you ever hooked up with someone before? Like a one-time thing?" he asks.

I shake my head, an uncomfortable sensation of inexperience and naivety rising within me. Grayson has clearly hooked up with a lot of women. He seems so comfortable doing this, like he knows exactly what to do.

His hands skim down my thighs, then to my ass and back again, almost as if it's an unconscious thing. "We can take things slower. I love sucking your tits."

It takes everything in me for my jaw not to drop at the offhand way he says it. And the way it makes my stomach dip in delight.

"I really like it, too," I admit.

What I'm not admitting is it's the first time a guy's done that. The first time a guy has done… anything. Would Grayson be weirded out knowing I not only haven't had casual sex, but any?

"What do you want to do?" he asks. "Keep doing what we've been doing?"

As good as that sounds, and as momentous as sex seems, I do want more. "Can I take your shirt off?"

He nods and lifts the hem for me, revealing a sliver of toned abs. He clearly works out, his skin warm and smooth as I pull the fabric up and off him. I skim my hands over the light dusting of hair on his chest and over his hard pecs, exploring him.

He watches me solemnly as I make my way over the tanned expanse, tracing each ridge of his abs, up his obliques to the heavy breadth of his shoulders. The muscles of his back are firm, and as I shift forward to reach them, he slips his hands around to unhook my bra, leaving me fully topless on his lap.

Pressing soft kisses to my breasts, he nuzzles me, shaping me with his big palms, and I melt into him, falling under his spell once more. When his tongue circles my nipple, I groan loudly, getting back to that state where I don't care what I sound like, wanting more of what only he can give me.

"You like that?" he asks, giving me a strong suck.

"Uh huh." I'm practically offering myself to him.

One of his hands trails over my stomach and down further. "What about this?"

His thumb presses firmly against the seam of my jeans, right over my cleft, and I buck against him as he continues rubbing the sensitive area.

"Yes," I moan, my touch on him growing bolder, restlessness building within me.

"I like it when you get like this."

I glance down at him, at the way he's looking back at me with lust and appreciation.

"It's fucking hot."

I swallow hard as a fresh wave of longing washes over me. "I'm so turned on," I admit.

"Yeah?" My admission seems to excite him. "Want me to touch you more?"

I nod, not even sure what he means, and when he unbuttons and unzips my jeans, I can't do anything but help him take them off, leaving me in just my underwear.

He rubs me over the thin fabric, heat pooling, and when he pulls my panties down and enters me with two fingers, I groan in a mixture of relief and eagerness.

I ride his fingers, already so wet. I'm so far out of my range of experience, it's laughable, but I wouldn't trade it for anything. Not as this delicious tension rises higher and higher.

He returns his mouth to my breast, sucking in time to the tempo of his fingers, and I dig my nails into his shoulders as my orgasm unexpectedly moves to the forefront, coming over me in a great rush.

"Grayson, oh my God." I shudder, still spasming when the doorbell rings.

We both freeze, his fingers still inside me, working me through it.

"Who is it?" he asks, as if I can see around the corner and down the short hallway through the door.

My thoughts are too scrambled to make sense of anything at the moment as I come down from my high.

There's a knock and then a faint, "Abby!"

The bubble we've been in bursts. "It's Harper and Owen." I look for my clothes, but can't find anything. "They're dropping off the last of the wedding favors for me to wrap." Seriously, just a bra would be helpful at this point. Harper's not going away until I answer the door. "I can't…" I push back the overwhelm that threatens. "Where's my bra?"

Grayson snaps into action, gently helping me off of him, then handing me my bra. I have no idea where he grabbed it from, but I'm thankful for him as I wrestle it on, then hang onto him for balance as he holds my jeans out for me to step into.

I call out, "Be right there," hoping it buys me another minute.

I get my shirt on and Grayson grabs his, then says, "I'll be in the bathroom."

We both look down at the impressive erection tenting the front of his pants.

"Good call." I glance around, wanting a mirror, but I don't keep one in the living room. "How do I look?"

Despite the urgency of the situation, his gaze rakes me up and down, his grin slow and sensual. "Fuckable."

There's a tug in my lower belly as desire trickles through me again, but he only kisses me quickly before escaping down the hallway to the guest bathroom.

I take a moment to center myself, smoothing my palms down my shirt. Grayson just fingered me to orgasm on my couch in the middle of the afternoon. And he's currently hiding out in my bathroom with a massive hard-on while his brother and sister-in-law are at the door.

Just another Wednesday.

CHAPTER SIXTEEN

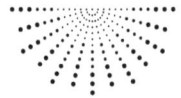

GRAYSON

*F*ucking Christ.

Adrenaline is coursing through me, still worked up. Damn, she gets me going. Something about that combination of innocence and seduction turns me on so fucking bad.

I glance down at my dick, debating what to do. This erection isn't disappearing any time soon on its own, not with the way she got my blood pumping.

There's the far off whisper of voices somewhere else in the house, but they're not anywhere near here. I could just...

I unzip my pants and reach into my boxer briefs, silently groaning at the relief that floods me. Not that Abby riding my fingers wasn't amazing, but I need a goddamned release.

Shutting my eyes, I brace myself against the bathroom counter, calling to mind Abby topless on me, begging me to keep sucking her with the sexy moans she was making. How is it that the girl blushes at the least provocation under normal circumstances, yet can do all this without a trace of self-consciousness?

I stroke myself, imagining it as her hand instead, the way she'd look up at me with that trusting gaze, maybe even dropping to her knees to suck me in her warm, wet—

The knock on the bathroom door has me jumping.

"Grayson?"

Thank God, it's Abby. I don't know what I'd do if my brother caught me in here masturbating.

"Yeah?" I choke out, still gripping my cock.

"They're gone."

"Okay, good." One less thing to worry about.

"Can I come in?"

My dick twitches, desperately wanting to invite her in and have her take me in hand.

"I'm indecent," I warn.

"Are you... taking care of yourself?"

I bite my lip, holding back a half-groan, half-laugh. "Yeah."

There's a long pause. "Can I help?"

Oh, fuck. She wants to do that? "Absolutely."

I open the door for her and she slips inside, closing it behind her with a quiet click. Her gaze is transfixed on my dick, her eyes widening.

She looks up at my bare chest and steps closer, pressing a hand to my abdomen. I hold my breath as her hand drifts down, brushing over my arm, my wrist, my hand, until one finger trails over the length of me.

I suppress a groan, wanting more of her touch.

"Tell me what you want me to do," she whispers, finally meeting my gaze.

There's excitement in her honey-brown eyes, but beyond that also a nervousness she can't fully hide. I won't fault her, though. Like we said, this is a first for both of us. Kristen's friends were always off-limits, but that was a decade ago, when we were teens.

Things are different now.

I take her fingers and wrap them around my cock, guiding her up and down my shaft. Her hold on me is soft, movements unsure.

"Rougher," I tell her, leaning down to capture her lips with mine. "Faster."

She picks up the pace, grip tighter.

"Yeah, like that." Fuck, that feels good.

She's unskilled but enthusiastic, kissing me back with passion, and I lose myself in her. My hips pump into her hand without conscious thought, and I cup her jaw with both my hands, tilting her head back. The intensity of our kiss deepens, and I let my tongue slip in, enjoying her soft sounds of delight.

Warmth rushes through me as she presses in closer, like she's getting turned on again. There's something about turning her on that fills me with a deep sense of satisfaction.

My hands travel down to her chest, squeezing a handful of her, and her rhythm falters for a moment before she continues. She's so responsive when I touch her.

"Wait a second," I tell her, releasing her grip from me so I can pick her up and place her on the bathroom counter. I take her top off then set her hand back on me, picking up the pace again.

Her chest is nearer to eye-level now, and I slowly slide her bra straps down, loving how her breath hitches, how she seems to unconsciously stick her chest out further.

My lips move to the shell of her ear, teasing her. "Tell me how bad you want my tongue here." I dip a thumb into one bra cup, rubbing her softly.

She makes a small sound of contentment, close to a moan.

"Come on, talk a little dirty to me." I know she's capable of it. "Anything you want, you only have to ask."

She hesitates, then whispers, "Touch me."

"Where?"

She brings her free hand up to cup her breast. "Here."

I brush a finger lightly over the area, and from the way she strains toward me, it's not giving her much relief.

"Is that all?" I ask, knowing full well it's not.

"Grayson."

I nearly chuckle at the exasperation in her voice. "What else do you want?"

"Your tongue. Like you said." She reaches back and undoes the hook on her bra, tossing it on the floor. God, I love when she loses her inhibitions.

Reaching out, I lightly pinch her nipple, rolling it between my fingers. "Here?"

She nods enthusiastically. "I want you to suck my nipples."

A tingle chases down my spine. That's my girl.

I waver a moment at the endearment that pops into my head, then brush it aside. It's only a heat of the moment kind of thing.

Bracing a hand behind her for support as I lean her back, I give her what she wants, using my tongue until her chest rises and falls in quick, uneven breaths. I lap at her, her nipples so fucking soft, then suck her into my mouth, adding little nips that have her hand speeding up on me.

The friction of her grip on my dick feels so goddamned good, but I want to see if I can make her come a second time.

And like she can read my thoughts, she slips down from the counter and unbuttons and unzips her jeans, sliding everything off until she's fully nude in front of me. "Get me off again?" she half-asks, half-demands. Her voice is hopeful, but expression set like she's going to come one way or another, even if she has to do it herself.

She doesn't have to worry about that.

She takes me in hand once more, setting the rhythm, and I drag my palm down her belly until it reaches the small tuft of curls at the juncture of her thighs.

"Anything you want," I whisper into her ear, pressing soft kisses against the length of her neck as I guide her legs apart and sink two fingers into her heat. "You're so wet for me," I murmur.

She nods, lost for words as her hips arch into my touch, seeking more. That's it. I want her desperate for me, the way I find I'm becoming for her, lust coursing through me.

I lean back, taking in her mussed hair and flushed cheeks. Like I told her earlier, she looks utterly fuckable.

She makes eye contact with me and smiles, leaning in to kiss me on the lips.

And that's apparently all I needed to send me over the edge, still worked up from before. My hips buck, a groan escaping me as I come on her hand and belly.

She bites her lip as she watches me, excitement on her face.

My chest is heaving by the time I'm finished, realizing my fingers have completely lost the rhythm inside her, and as I catch my breath, I redouble my efforts until her hips are rocking wildly into my hand again.

"You gonna come for me?" I ask her, and she helplessly nods in response.

Less than a minute later, her inner muscles convulse, her harsh, panting breaths like music to my ears as she drenches my fingers with her arousal.

She moans my name, and the urge to do some kind of caveman chest pounding strikes me. I've never felt possessive about a woman, but my name on her lips while she's in the throes of passion has an effect on me I wasn't expecting.

Especially since it's her. Shy Abby, of all people. Pride suffuses me that I could bring her to this state.

When she's finished, I gradually withdraw from her, glancing around the bathroom. I grab a washcloth from the neatly folded stack on the shelving unit in here, then clean us both up.

She quietly watches me as I wipe her stomach, and a part of me wants to ask her what she's thinking.

I've never asked a woman what she's thinking after sex.

Not that this was sex. It was, what? Third base?

But I've also never done anything like this with someone like Abby. If I date a girl and things don't work out, that's the end. I never have to think about her again. But Abby's connected to me in all kinds of complicated ways. Even if I don't live in Crescent Pass, she'll still be a part of my life.

Now where was that warning when I was suggesting to her we explore this attraction for the rest of the week?

She agreed that everything would be normal between us in the future, but that was before I knew the softness of her skin, the grip of her hand on my dick, the sound of her moaning my name as she comes. How can things ever go back to how they were?

And, more importantly, do I want them to?

Because at the moment, all I can think about is how much I want to do that again.

She moves to get dressed and I startle, wondering how long I was standing there motionless, caught up in my thoughts. Grabbing my shirt, I step out of the bathroom, giving her privacy, and finish getting dressed myself as I walk out to the living room.

On the coffee table is a small box of wooden coasters, engraved with Owen and Harper's names, along with Saturday's date. I pick one up, marveling at how it looks like a mini tree slice with unique grain patterns on each one. Did Owen make these himself? Goddamn, what can't the man do with a tree and a saw?

Leo jumps on the table next to the box and gazes up at me expectantly, but I can't tell if he wants me to pet him or is hoping for treats. I reach out and scritch the top of his head, liking how he sticks his face up into my palm for maximum pets.

"You two friends now?" Abby asks, joining us in the living room. Her hair is down around her shoulders and tousled, a glow about her. All I can think is that I put that glow there.

"Uh, yeah," I finally reply as Leo nudges my palm for more pets. I motion to the coasters with my hand that's not petting the cat. "Why did they bring these again?"

"Oh, I'm wrapping all the wedding favors for them. They'll end up looking like this."

She motions for me to follow her, and when I do, Leo jumps down from the table and walks with us to a closed room I haven't been in before.

Abby flicks on the light and picks up a wrapped box off the desk along one wall. She hands it to me, but all I can do is stare at the intricate folds in the paper that form the shape of a tree.

"Where'd you get this?" I ask, turning over the box in my hand. It's wrapped with quality paper, something you'd buy at a stationery store, but I still can't get over the detail and all the little tucks and pleats used to create the final effect.

"I made it," she says simply.

My brow furrows, thinking she's joking before I remember her saying she made that book display at the library with all the origami flowers. "That's… wow. Impressive is an understatement."

She huffs a breath of laughter. "It's folding paper."

"Seriously, you're an artist."

Her cheeks pinken the slightest bit, and I love that she can blush over a simple compliment when not ten minutes ago she was asking me to get her off without a hint of embarrassment.

"Everyone has different talents," she says. "If you're a financial analyst, I'm sure you can do some kind of Excel wizardry I couldn't dream of."

I laugh aloud at that. "Do spreadsheets turn you on?" I waggle my eyebrows for comedic effect. "I can create a pivot table that'll really make you blush."

A grin spreads across her face and she nudges at my shoulder playfully. "You know what I mean."

I capture her hand and bring her close. "I like seeing you blush."

She bites at her bottom lip, gaze downcast before she looks up at me with an impish tilt to her lips. "I like when you make me blush."

It's the most natural thing in the world for me to lean down and kiss her softly, her lips parting under mine. I had the passing thought earlier that it might be different between us after leaving that bathroom and entering this new, unexplored territory. But it's still good. Still exciting.

"Can I come over tomorrow night? After whatever's happening on the itinerary?"

She nods, her smile wide, like she's radiating happiness. "I'd like that."

Her smile brings a pleasant warmth to my chest, one I'm becoming more familiar with this week. No one's ever had an effect on me like this.

And I want more.

CHAPTER SEVENTEEN

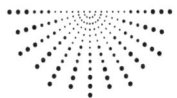

ABBY

"Oh, that tickles."

The woman using a pumice stone on Kristen's feet stops what she's doing and gives her a deadpan look. "Do you want me to stop?"

"Um, no. Sorry," Kristen mumbles, a sheepish expression on her face.

I stifle a chuckle, making sure I don't upset the nail technician working on my own feet.

Across the nail salon, Harper, Elena, and Kelly laugh about something as they get their manicures done, while Kristen and I are over here getting pedicures. They didn't have enough stations for all five of us to get the same thing done at the same time.

"Is Jamie feeling better?" I ask her, trying to keep my foot as still as I can while the technician trims my toenails.

"Yeah, he had a low-grade fever the other night, but he was fine the next morning and wanted to go to school. If it was Jenny, she would have milked that for days."

I smile. "Jamie's pretty responsible. He reminds me a lot of Owen."

"He is like him, isn't he?" She thinks about it for a moment. "If I had to compare Jenny to someone, I guess she'd be like Grayson. Class clown, center of attention type."

I consider it. "Hmm, maybe when he was younger. But he's not like that anymore."

She gives me a side-eye. "What, you're an expert on my brother after fake dating him for a week?"

I rein in my blush as best as I can. "If anything, I'd say Jenny's more like your mom."

She gasps. "You take that back." She's grinning, so I know she isn't serious.

"Think about it. She's pushy, won't take no for an answer…"

She groans. "You're right. I've created a monster."

Laughing, I tell her, "She's seven. There's still time for her to change."

She crosses her fingers. "Let's hope."

My technician finishes cutting and filing my nails, and squeezes a palmful of exfoliating scrub into her hand before massaging it on my feet. Ooh, that feels good.

"So my mom hasn't found out about you and Grayson yet?"

I go still, my heart suddenly racing. Does Kristen know what Grayson and I did yesterday? How could she? I can't imagine he would have told her.

"W-what do you mean?" I stutter.

"That you two are faking this wedding date thing," she says, like it's obvious.

Relief floods me. Duh, the original arrangement. Not this new one we have going on where we give each other orgasms at my house. "No, it's all good."

She harrumphs, settling back in her seat as her technician begins exfoliating her feet, too. "I still don't get why you're helping him," she grumbles. "It's not like you two are even friends."

How many times is she going to bring this up? Is it actually bothering her? "Are you mad?" I ask carefully.

She gives me a swift look then reaches over and taps me on the arm. "Of course not. But, to be honest, I've kind of been waiting for this to blow up in his face. I hate that you're caught in the middle, but he's always tried to cut corners. He deserves some comeuppance."

I relax again. "So you just want to say *I told you so*."

Grinning, she admits, "I do. You don't have siblings, so you don't know how it is, but saying *I told you so* to your brother is one of the most satisfying things on the planet."

"Sorry I missed out on that experience, then."

"So how did it go at Harry's? Was it boring?"

I had complained to her about the bar portion of the itinerary last week when Harper sent it to us, knowing I wouldn't be drinking.

"Actually, I got drunk."

She turns to me so fast, she visibly startles her technician.

"What?" she demands, laughing. "Tell me everything."

I explain how I got friendly with Elena, leaving out the part about how I admitted I like Grayson, and ended up taking shots. She laughs when I tell her I switched clothes with Kelly, again omitting because I thought Grayson might notice me more in a short dress, and then doubles over when I reveal how I accidentally flashed everyone when I spun around in the dress.

Her technician is not impressed with her client's behavior, but Kristen's delight in my utter mortification even makes me chuckle. If you don't laugh, you'll cry, right?

"Please tell me someone got that on video," Kristen says, wiping at her eyes.

"Absolutely not." I motion to the rest of our party getting their manicures. "They drank even more than me, so they weren't in any state to film things. I think Owen even took Harper's phone from her at one point so she couldn't do anything she would regret."

Kristen shakes her head. "I'm surprised Grayson didn't record the night, then. Seems like the type of thing he'd love. Or was he sloshed, too?"

"No, he didn't drink at all. He was pretty protective."

She gives me a quizzical look. "Really?"

"Yeah." I think back to that night, and now that I'm seeing it through Grayson's perspective, I'm glad he didn't take me up on my offer when I was drunk. That he waited to make sure I was in a clear state of mind before making a move. "He was very gentlemanly."

"Huh. Didn't know he had it in him."

I hesitate, unsure if I should say anything. "Maybe you don't know him as well as you think you do."

Her brow furrows. "I don't know my brother?"

"As an adult, I mean. People change as they get older. He's not the same carefree teen he was when he left Crescent Pass. I think it's easy to revert to the dynamic you had a decade ago when you lived together, but you're not the same person you were then, either."

Kristen's quiet as she listens to me. "Did he say something about us not knowing him now?"

"No," I assure her, not wanting her to think Grayson is mad at his family or anything. "He just seems a little... lonely."

He'd stayed for a while at my house after our *tryst*, keeping me company while I finished packaging all the wedding favor boxes. He'd offered to help, but it was abundantly clear after about five minutes that he's no good at wrapping.

I'd told him about funny things that happened at the library and caught him up on stories of his niece and nephew. He'd seemed wistful, commenting more than once that he wished he could have been there. And when he'd told me about his life in Seattle, it was mostly about his job in one of those tall glass buildings downtown and going to sports bars with his coworkers after ten-hour workdays. Or how he used to hang out with his friend Charlie a lot more before he got a girlfriend, and now he feels like a third wheel when he's with them. When he mentioned his condo is only a half-mile walk from the Space Needle, I expressed interest in seeing it and he had immediately said his place is always open to me. He'd remarked no one ever visits him in this heartbreakingly offhand way that I hadn't wanted to call attention to.

"He didn't outright say it," I continue, "but he seems to miss you all more than he'd admit. And sometimes feels excluded when he comes home, like he's out of the loop."

Kristen shifts uncomfortably. "Well, he moved away. What did he expect?"

I nod. "But the burden's always on him to stay close. He's the one who makes several trips a year here to visit, but no one ever goes to see him. And again, I'm only inferring. He didn't complain about any of this."

She runs her hand through her hair, considering my words. "Oh my God, I'm a shitty sister. All I've done is bust his balls his whole time here."

"No," I interject, but she cuts me off.

"I'll do better. And I'm taking the twins to go see him in Seattle this summer."

I hide my smile. "I bet he'd like that."

I settle back in my chair as my nail technician finishes the base coat and fans my toes to speed up the drying process.

"So you really are an expert on Grayson now, huh?" she teases.

God, I wish. Maybe then I'd know how he feels about me. If what we did yesterday was only a fun afternoon or meant something more. Meant everything to him, the way it did to me.

I know it didn't, though. Not with how casually he suggested hooking up in the first place.

But he did ask to come over again tonight. That's something.

"Hardly," I tell Kristen, knowing she's waiting for an answer. "But we've been spending a lot of time together this week. I guess it's only natural we'd find things out about each other."

Like how big his dick is, the feel of him incredible. Or how sexy he is when he comes, his hips jerking as he loses control. Or how he seems to already have mastery over my body, everything he did ramping up my pleasure to previously unknown heights.

Not that I would *ever* say any of that to Kristen.

"So what has he found out about you then?"

I swallow, thinking of something safe to tell her. Not the strip poker game or the drunken pass at him or their mom catching us kissing. "He had to help me with my dad the other night."

The admission comes out unbidden.

"Oh, Abby." She lays a comforting hand on my arm, knowing it's a sore subject for me. That I hate this awful thing happening to him, to the point that I rarely talk about it with others.

"It was embarrassing," I whisper. "Dad fell and Mom couldn't get him up."

She sighs in commiseration. "I'm so sorry. But I bet Grayson was glad he could help you. I give him a lot of crap, but when push comes to shove, he's always there to help if we need him."

I nod, not saying anything.

"Is your dad doing okay?" she asks hesitantly.

"Oh, yeah. No lasting harm."

Just the increased worry always going on in the back of my head about what's going to happen next to him. And at what point Mom won't be able to care for him anymore.

"Do you want to talk about it?"

Yes. No. "Maybe another time."

She nods in agreement. One of the things I love about Kristen is she never pushes if I ask her not to.

Unlike Harper, I've come to find. I eye her across the salon. What would she say if I told her what Grayson and I have been up to? It's a good thing she's been so preoccupied with her friends visiting and planning for the wedding or she definitely would have noticed something by now. She hadn't even commented on Grayson's car parked in my driveway yesterday when she dropped off the last of the wedding favors.

And then there's Kristen. She's always been clueless about my true feelings for her brother, and it's no different now. Guilt builds in my chest, knowing I'm essentially sneaking behind her back. Not that she's the boss of Grayson, but I'm fairly sure she wouldn't be happy about this. She'd say he's *cutting corners*. Hooking up with me without the commitment of a relationship.

But I'm okay with that. Right? That's what I told myself yesterday. And I don't regret what we did for a single second. But that uneasiness flashes for a moment again, thinking about what it'll be like when he heads back to Seattle. A fling that could never be.

What else can I do, though?

CHAPTER EIGHTEEN

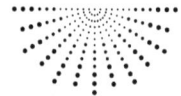

GRAYSON

Though it's quiet, subtle sounds still fill the near-silence. The faint, far-off whistle of a thrush. The muffled splash as an osprey dives into the lake to catch their prey. The occasional croak of a frog from the reeds, their call echoing across the mirrored reflection of the water.

Puffy clouds drift by, the smell of evergreens thick in the air—cedar, pine, and a faint earthy aroma of damp soil and fallen leaves. I inhale deeply, a wave of nostalgia hitting me. Not that I've been to this particular lake—of course Owen found us the most remote spot possible—but the last time we went fishing, Dad was here, too.

I glance over at Owen, his pole gripped loosely in his hand, his stare fixed out on the gently rippling water. He'd said as we drove out here this morning that he specifically asked Harper to fit this fishing trip into the schedule for me and him. That he knew this week would be crazy with everyone together and wanted to make sure we had some time for just the two of us.

And yet, in true Owen fashion, we've mostly sat in comfortable silence out in his canoe, releasing anything we catch back into the lake.

"You ever take Harper out here?" I ask, breaking the silence.

He half-grunts, half-sighs. "The last time I took her out on the water, she tipped the canoe trying to get away from a spider."

I hold back my laugh. "To be fair, you and I almost did that one time."

"When the fish got loose?"

It had been comical how it kept slipping through our fingers as it flopped all over the boat.

"Thought Dad might tip the boat, too, with the way he was laughing at us."

Owen grins, then sobers. "Wish he could be here."

"Me, too."

With Owen, there's no need to overexplain things. He knows I miss Dad as much as he does.

There's another beat of silence. "Eli told me he's planning to ask Kristen to marry him at Christmas."

Now that's a piece of gossip I didn't expect to hear from Owen, of all people. "Why Christmas?" That's eight months away.

"Kristen said she wanted to date for a year before getting engaged."

So he's taking it nearly right to the date. "He's that sure? They've only been dating for four months."

Owen shrugs. "When you find the woman you want to spend the rest of your life with..."

He trails off, but he doesn't need to elaborate further. He's the wrong person to be asking, marrying a woman he met only hours before in Vegas.

And now having an official ceremony over five years later.

"Did you know you wanted to marry Harper right away?"

"Yes," he says without hesitation. He's not one to waver from a course of action, though.

"And you think Kristen will say yes to Eli?"

He nods. "They're a good match. He's pretty devoted to her. And the kids."

"He seems like a decent guy." I'd thought that about him when I met him last Christmas. "Why'd he tell you he's going to propose?"

"I think he was sort of asking for my blessing. The way you would to a girl's father. That's what made me think of it when you mentioned Dad."

He should have asked me, is my first thought. I'm her older brother. Owen's the younger one. But I wasn't here to ask. He'd only met me one time, and briefly at that. Of course he'd talk to Owen instead.

"Funny that you're the last of us to get married when you're the oldest," Owen comments in an offhand way.

"I'm not getting married," I say, and it comes out flatter than I expected. Almost like I'm... disappointed.

I'm not, though. Like I told Abby, I'm not worrying about anything like marriage or kids until the right woman comes along.

An image pops into my head of pulling up into Abby's driveway after a long day at work, her waiting in the doorway with a little towheaded girl in her arms, both of them happy to see me.

Whoa... What the fuck?

"Yeah, I know," Owen says, oblivious to my concerning vision. "The last to be single, I meant. Just weird since you're the one who dates and Kristen and I don't."

"Kristen was married before," I say petulantly, not sure why I'm arguing.

He makes a noise of derision. "It was pretty obvious they were only together because of the twins."

Was it? I thought she'd loved James. But, yet again, I was barely around to know the difference. "I didn't know that."

"James wasn't good for her. Not the way Eli is."

Of course observant Owen would pick up on that. He's always the quietest one in the room, but ever watchful, noticing things others aren't even aware they're revealing.

Has he noticed what's happened between me and Abby?

"I guess I haven't been as lucky as the two of you," I reply, shying away from that thought.

"I assumed it was out of spite because of Mom."

A chuckle escapes me. "That, too."

The comfortable silence returns and after another hour with no bites, we call it quits for the day. After loading up the canoe on Owen's truck, we head back to town, the windows down, breeze blowing through our hair.

I look out at the trees on the edge of the highway, the low, mossy ground cover clinging to the forest floor, the soft green tones contrasting with patches of ferns unfurling their fronds. Wildflowers bloom in between the greenery, splashes of whites and purples against the darker trees. It's spring in Oregon, an annual rebirth of the forest. A new beginning.

This trip almost feels like a new beginning for me, too. Or maybe a turning point. Unexpected, but in a good way.

"Do you ever think about moving back here?"

I turn to Owen, his question seeming out of the blue. "What?"

"You've seemed different this week. Like you're finally enjoying yourself here."

Observant Owen strikes again.

"Just because I'm having a good time doesn't mean…" I swallow hard, the words stuck for some reason. "That I'd move back here."

"I know," he says easily. "I only wondered if you ever thought about it."

Before this week, no. And now… No, of course not. That's crazy to even think about.

"No," I tell him. "I haven't."

"What about Abby?"

I go still. "What about her?"

He takes his eyes off the road for a moment to look over at me, giving me an unimpressed eye roll. "Come off it. I've seen how you've been looking at her the past couple of days. When you think no one's watching."

My hands clench. How have I been looking at her? "We're putting on an act for Mom."

He makes a quiet scoff of disbelief. "Okay."

He seems content to leave it at that, but I'm not. "You don't think I'm that good of an actor?"

"No."

I should take offense to that, but I don't. Not when he's right. "What makes you so sure?"

He mulls my question for a moment, then says, "Your car was at Abby's yesterday when Harper and I dropped off the favors. And when she answered the door, she was all disheveled, her shirt buttons done up wrong. Then said she was busy and couldn't talk. Meanwhile, you were nowhere to be found."

Shit. He pieced that all together? "You're a regular Nancy Drew," I mutter.

He grins. "I prefer Hardy Boys."

I lean my elbow against the open window, chewing on my thumb. Why is he even noticing Abby so much when he's marrying her friend?

"This thing with Abby doesn't change anything," I say. "It's casual. And it only started yesterday."

"Okay."

There's silence for the next few minutes, but it's not comfortable anymore. Not for me. I'm stewing, obsessing over his not-quite accusation.

"Do you think it was wrong of me to start something up with her?" I finally ask, looking out the window. I don't want to see his judgment.

"No." His response is quick, and the uneasiness building in my stomach dissipates at once. I didn't realize Owen's approval meant that much to me. "But I'd be careful it means the same to her as it does to you."

"It does." She'd assured me yesterday she was fine with this arrangement. That she didn't expect anything after Sunday. "Does Harper know? Or Kristen?" That'd be the last thing I need.

"Not that I know of."

"Are you and Harper one of those couples that shares everything?"

His lips twist wryly. "I'll keep your secret."

"Bros before—"

"Don't finish that," he warns.

I grin, settling back into my seat for the rest of the ride.

CHAPTER NINETEEN

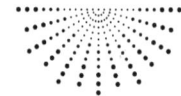

ABBY

For about the thousandth time today, my nails catch me off guard, the burgundy color stark against my pale skin. I never bother with nail polish, but Harper wanted us all to get manicures that match our bridesmaid dresses.

I smooth my hands over the soft cotton of my shirt as I pace the length of my living room and pull my gaze away from my nails toward the clock by the TV. Grayson said he'd be over after having dinner with his family. It's seven-forty now, but I force myself not to pick up my phone and clarify what specific time he'll be here. I don't want to come across as clingy or overeager.

This is a hook-up. Nothing more, I remind myself. A continuation of what we started yesterday. Something worldly adults do, rather than small-town girls who've only had one boyfriend.

And no sexual partners.

Actually, strike that. I've had one now. Grayson.

I bite my lip as the remembered sensation of his fingertips trailing over my skin spreads over me, raising pleasurable goosebumps. What will he do tonight? Better yet, what will *I* do? How far am I willing to go?

The doorbell rings, leaving me momentarily scrambling. I'm the same as I was Saturday, a nervous wreck at the thought of him coming over. Except, so much has changed since then.

He's gorgeous in his normal attire of faded tee and jeans, and my mind goes blank as I realize I don't know how to greet him. A wave like I would normally do? No, that's too casual. A kiss? Would that be too much? It's not like we're dating. Maybe a hug, in the middle of the two extremes.

Grayson solves my dilemma, though, by stepping in and giving me a toe-curling kiss. All the anxiety drifts away, no room left in my head for anything but the way his warm mouth feels on mine, the way my stomach pleasantly dips as he gathers me close to him.

When he breaks away, he shuts the door behind him. Did my neighbors get a free show?

"I missed you today," he says, kissing me again, slow and relaxed. Like we have all the time in the world.

"I missed you, too," I whisper against his lips, curling my body into his. "I... I kept thinking about the stuff we did yesterday," I admit. "How much I liked it."

His gaze alights with interest. "Yeah?"

I nod. I guess there was no need to get nervous about how tonight would go. I should have known Grayson would make things easy. It feels so right being with him.

"You want to go to your bedroom?" he asks, those slow kisses making their way down my neck now. A tingle races down my spine in response. Are we really doing this so soon?

I find his hand and lead him down the hallway to where I'd drunkenly stripped for him the other night. This time is a different story, though. This time I won't make an idiot of myself.

Hopefully.

I close the door behind us, the soft glow of my bedside lamp illuminating the desire already on his face as he threads a hand through my hair and brings my lips to his. His kisses are languid and drugging, my body relaxing as he coaxes me back under his spell.

"What are you willing to do tonight?" he asks.

His question implies there's no limit for him, but then again, I was the one who set restrictions when I said I wasn't ready yet to have sex.

Am I tonight?

I don't want to put pressure on myself, but this is a limited-time opportunity. If not tonight, then when?

"Ah, shit," he says. "I didn't get condoms."

A trickle of relief runs through me at the imposed limitations. "That's okay," I murmur. "I'm sure we can find other things to do."

I have no idea where I'm pulling this alluring voice from, but he seems to like it.

He nods, kissing me again, and backs me into the edge of the bed. "What are you comfortable with? Fingers again? Oral?"

I suppress the squeak that wants to escape my throat. "You—you want to go down on me?"

Why am I questioning this? I should be screaming *yes, please* as I rip my panties off.

He gives me a sly smile. "Give me some credit. I make sure a girl has a good time, too."

"That's good to know," I manage, arching my neck as he presses long, sensual kisses there. God, that feels amazing.

"So can I show you a good time?"

I swallow hard. "Yes." I want that more than anything.

His hands run down my back, grabbing the hem of my shirt, and I lift my arms to help him guide it over my head. He unclasps my bra next, his palms covering my breasts.

"Have I mentioned how much I like these?" he murmurs, bending his head to trail kisses over my upper chest.

I let out a sigh as he teases my nipple. "You said you like sucking on them."

His tongue circles me, then gently laps. "That's right, I did." He takes the hard bud of my nipple into his mouth and sucks, and I grip his shoulders for balance as my knees weaken.

It's just as good as yesterday. Maybe even better knowing what lies beyond the horizon, how incredible he can make me feel.

His hands continue southward, unbuttoning and unzipping me, then he unexpectedly picks me up and tosses me on the bed, a delightful frisson of lust spearing through me at the way he looks at me, like he wants to eat me up, the front of his jeans noticeably bulging.

I did that. I put that bulge there. And not even by touching him, just him getting turned on by my body.

He strips my jeans off, my panties next until I'm fully nude. I resist the urge to cover myself as his hands slide up my thighs, parting them.

"Ah, fuck, baby."

Warmth curls in my chest at the reverence in his voice as he stares at me, as if I'm something to be admired.

He drops to his knees, his mouth following the same path his hands took up my thighs, that warmth inside me burning hotter the closer he gets to my core. His thumb swipes through my folds and I shudder at the brief contact.

"Already wet for me," he murmurs.

I nod shakily, unsure what to say, what to do, on edge anticipating what he'll do next.

His hands wrap around my legs, pulling me closer to the edge of the bed, where he waits for me. Bending his head, he licks me along my seam, and I gasp in response, a flood of endorphins rushing through me.

Holy shit. I lean up on my elbows, watching his dark head at my pussy, licking me again, deeper this time. It's the hottest thing I've ever seen, ever experienced, and it's Grayson doing it. *Grayson.*

His gaze flicks up to meet mine. "You like watching."

Crap. Busted. But it's not like I can pretend I don't. He didn't even phrase it as a question.

"Yes," I admit in a low voice. "You're really sexy doing that."

He makes this *mmm* sound that has me quivering, especially as his big palms come up to hold my legs open wider.

He builds me up over long minutes until I'm a trembling mess, my fingers clutching at the duvet, my thighs shaking. The man knows how to use his tongue, licking and sucking at me in a perfect tempo that—

He backs away abruptly, pressing kisses to my lower belly.

"What are you doing?" I ask, unable to keep the demand out of my voice. I was so freaking close.

"You were about to come," he says, as if that's a complete explanation.

Um, yeah. Isn't that the point? "And?"

He nips at the juncture between my hip and thigh. "I'm not ready to be done."

"What?"

"I want to take my time with you." A fleeting kiss to my pussy has me arching toward him. "We have all night."

All night? He wants to prolong this that long? I'm so ramped up, I need release now. "How about you make me come now and then spend the rest of the night doing it a second time?"

I feel his smile more than see it. "I didn't know you were so bossy."

I'm not. Not at all. But something about being with him like this over the past few days has made me lose all my normal inhibitions. When he gets me past a certain point, I can't seem to control my mouth anymore and every little thing slips out.

I lean forward and slide a hand through the thick, silky strands on his head, guiding him down. "Make me come, Grayson. Please. We have all night. Just give me this first one."

There's so much longing on his face, it nearly breaks me.

He nods, licking me with a renewed fervor, and the desire within me quickly rises again, reaching critical mass. As his tongue flicks rapidly over my clit, it sends me over the edge, my fingers gripping his hair, keeping him with me.

I moan, letting the waves wash over me, delighting in my triumph as I go boneless against the bedspread. Aftershocks twitch through me as he kisses his way up my torso, pausing for a minute at my chest until another thread of desire weaves its way over me.

When he finally reaches my mouth, I return his kiss with enthusiasm.

"You taste like me," I murmur against his lips.

He pulls back. "Oh, sorry. I—"

"No, I like it." I bring him back down to me and wrap a leg around his hip to keep him close. "It's hot."

His hips push into mine, his hardness reminding me he's turned on, too. That I should do something about that. Giving him a handjob yesterday had been a first for me. A blowjob would also be a first, equal parts thrilling and terrifying. I can do this, though. I want to do this. I want everything with this man.

I snake a hand under his shirt, lightly scratching up his back, and he makes a sound of encouragement. He leans away so I can remove it, and I take my time roaming my hands over every inch of his muscled torso, the same as I did yesterday, committing it to memory.

"You're so sexy," I whisper, not even fully aware of what I'm saying until he responds.

"That's the second time you've said that tonight."

I glance up at the amusement on his face, and though I should be embarrassed at the admission, I'm not.

"You're the sexiest man I've ever met."

His amusement fades as he continues to look at me, until his seriousness matches my own.

"Abby…" His palm slides along my cheek until his fingers thread through my hair, cupping the back of my head. He kisses me like he's starving, like I'm the only thing that can slake his hunger.

I want to be that for him. I want to be the one who gives him everything he needs.

And that starts with tonight.

CHAPTER TWENTY

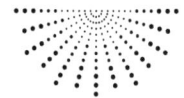

GRAYSON

This isn't fun and games anymore.

Not with how she's looking at me, her stare weighted with something heavy. Something I want to decipher but can't seem to.

Past hookups I've had have been light and breezy, both of us knowing we're here for a good time for the night. This is different. This is… deeper.

The idea should scare me. Should make me reiterate that we're just exploring this attraction. That it'll be over on Sunday.

Instead, I keep kissing her. I can't get enough of her lips. How soft they are. How they kiss me back with such enthusiasm, like she puts her whole body into it, her whole soul.

My hand drifts down her naked form, reveling in her smooth skin, mapping the hills and valleys. The urge strikes me to memorize each peak, each hollow, until there's no part of her left untouched.

"I want to make you feel good, too," she says, her hands still wandering over my chest, thumbs teasing my nipples. Fuck, I didn't think I'd like that so much.

"What'd you have in mind?" Please let her say—

"The same as you did for me."

A curl of anticipation twines through me. Her hand moves south, the need in me growing tighter as she heads exactly where I want her, over my jeans, shaping the outline of my dick through the fabric.

I inhale roughly. "Yeah," I tell her. "I want you to."

I help her remove my jeans and boxer briefs, realizing I haven't been fully naked around her yet. She looks her fill, her gaze filled with appreciation.

"Sexy?" I ask, trying to inject some levity into this, but she doesn't smile, only nods distractedly as she continues staring at my dick like it's the eighth wonder of the world.

She scoots down the bed and delicately wraps her hand around me, stroking it with light, barely there movements that have me wanting to strain toward her for more. When she increases the pressure I finally relax, then let out a groan as she guides my cock into her mouth, enveloping me in warm, wet heat.

"Fuck, that's good." I grip the duvet, needing to hold on to something, anything as she torturously teases me with light licks to the head and soft kisses down my length. And when she swallows me in further, I resist the urge to jerk my hips forward as her tongue makes this slow, circular motion that has me wanting to beg for more.

Maybe I'm just worked up from going down on her. Yeah, that's all this is. It's not that she's exceptionally good. It's not that this is better than anything in memory. It's only that I desperately need release.

Her head bobs up and down, and I sweep her hair back behind her ear, adjusting her so I can see my length disappear down that pretty mouth of hers. Damn, that's hot.

She releases me briefly. "You like to watch, too?"

My voice is hoarse as I tell her, "Yes."

"Will you tell me what you like? Exactly what you want me to do?"

All the moisture recedes from my mouth as I nod in agreement. Yes, I fucking want that.

She looks excited at the prospect.

I guide her hand to the base of me. "Make your fingers a tight ring here and pump." She does as I say. "Now do what you were doing before and suck me harder."

The suction of her mouth is incredible, taking me deeper and deeper until she can't take me anymore.

"Yes, like that. Just like that."

Fucking Christ. I squeeze my eyes shut, afraid to look at her. If I do, I'll come right now, my hips already bucking.

"Are you turned on again?" I ask, hoping to God she is. That I'm not the only one experiencing this kind of intensity.

She hums an agreement, never straying from her task.

"Put your other hand between your legs and touch yourself."

A moment later, she makes another happy hum, and I give up the fight and look down, doing my damndest to direct my gaze past her bobbing up and down on my cock to where her fingers play with her pussy.

An electric thrill runs down my spine. "You like getting off while you suck my cock?"

She nods, moaning around my dick, and I can't hold it at bay anymore, giving myself over to the pleasure.

"I'm so close," I tell her, sliding a hand in her hair to grip the back of her head gently. "I'm going to come in your mouth, okay?"

There's a third hum of approval and it's what breaks me, warmth rushing from me as the orgasm overtakes me. She swallows down everything I give her, my hips pumping, unable to stop, but she seems to like it, making excited noises that keep spurring me on.

When I'm finished, she releases me with a pop, and even in my stupor, I still have the presence of mind to guide her up my body.

"Straddle my face and grip the headboard," I tell her, waiting until she obeys before I lick her pussy again, loving how her thighs bracket my ears, how her moans gradually increase in volume.

I eat her out as she tells me how much she likes that, as she rides my face, all restraint gone. Her pussy lips are swollen, arousal coating my tongue as I instruct her to bear down harder on me and bring my thumb up to flick over her clit. Her body goes still, then collapses on top of me as she comes, jerking and twitching as she whimpers.

I softly suck on her clit, enjoying the way it prolongs her pleasure, the way she vibrates with satisfaction. When she goes boneless, I reposition her so she's snuggled into my side, her arm lazily draped across my chest.

"That was unreal," she mumbles. "So good."

It was good. Incredibly good. Unbelievably good. If I'm being honest with myself, it might have been the best sex I've ever had.

And we hadn't even technically had sex.

I close my eyes, head reeling with the realization. No, no. That can't be true. I've got an overflow of dopamine swimming through my veins right now. I can't trust anything I'm thinking at this moment. If I did, I'd be curling further into her side, whispering that I can't get enough of her. That I want to do that again as soon as possible. That I can't believe we haven't been doing that all these years.

That's not what this is, though. We aren't dating. We aren't making up for lost time. We're fooling around for a few days before I go back home. That's it.

The thing is… I have a bad feeling I'm the one about to get fooled.

CHAPTER TWENTY-ONE

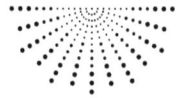

ABBY

"So I want the silk wrapped around the chair, then tied in a bow in the back." Harper looks between me and Kristen, miming making a bow with her hands. "But like a pretty bow, not a regular bow. Something you'd see in a wedding magazine."

Kristen gives Harper a skeptical look. "How about I help Eli with the aisle runner?"

Kristen escapes before Harper can give her an answer. Guess she didn't want to be responsible for ugly bows.

Harper turns to me with an increasing air of desperation. "Do you get my vision? Do you know what I mean? I need tomorrow to go perfectly."

I squeeze her shoulders. "I got this. Don't worry. Go help Elena and Kelly with the reception tables."

Across the yard, the two women are struggling with overlarge tables.

"Yes, good idea. Let me check in with Owen first."

A few feet away, Owen and Grayson are setting up the wedding bower, where Harper and Owen will stand during the ceremony tomorrow. Owen carved the whole thing himself, and it's presumably heavy from the way their muscles are straining. Grayson's sleeves are pushed up to show off his flexing biceps, and I bite my lip, remembering how he'd been naked in my bed last night. How he'd made me come twice with his tongue. That's four orgasms in two days. Some kind of record, for sure.

I blink, realizing I'm gawking at him. It's one thing to do it in private, but another to do it here in front of his family. Oh God, in front of his *mom*.

Glancing around, I don't notice Cheryl right away, until I look behind me and spot her setting up the directional signs. Okay, crisis averted.

I get to work fulfilling Harper's vision, carefully sliding the sashes of silk around the chairs and tying each in a perfect bow. No shoddy work here. After tying, I tuck tiny sprigs of evergreen into them, making sure each one is perfectly symmetrical.

"Need an assistant?"

I glance up at Grayson, my gaze tracing his crooked grin, longing filling my chest.

He kneels so he's eye-level with me where I'm hunched on the ground around the back of this chair. "Wish I could kiss you good morning," he says in a voice quiet enough for only me to hear.

A smile breaks free over my lips. "That'd probably cause some kind of controversy."

"Probably," he agrees, still grinning. "What's the taskmaster having you do?"

"I have the very important job of tying chair bows."

"Ah." He nods, as if duly impressed. "Wouldn't be a wedding without chair bows."

"It really wouldn't."

He picks up one of the evergreen sprigs and tucks it behind my ear. "You sleep okay?"

He'd gone home late, the two of us staying in bed for hours, talking until our voices were hoarse. Touching each other, turning each other on again, learning the other's likes. And for me, *discovering* my likes. Apparently, my inner thighs are a serious erogenous zone. The only reason he didn't stay all night was he didn't want Cheryl to wonder where he was.

I can't stop smiling, loving his attention. "Yeah. For some reason, I was exhausted."

His gaze dances with playful interest. "Hmm. Any clue why?"

"Well, there was this guy…"

"A guy, you say?"

I nod. "And he really knew what he was doing. Completely wore me out in the best kind of way."

The light in his eyes sharpens, turning darker. "You liked it?"

"It was the most amazing night of my life," I tell him honestly, the truth slipping closer to the surface. How much longer until I reveal everything? That this was never an act for me. That I wanted him since the beginning.

"What'd you like the most?"

"Your tongue," I answer without thinking. "And the way you told me what to do."

He exhales slowly, the look in his eyes now devilish. "Are you trying to turn me on in front of my family?"

I place a hand on my chest. "Me? I would never."

He chuckles, but it comes out choppy. Like maybe I'm actually having an effect on him.

There are sudden footsteps and then Kristen is there, crouching next to us. "You two need to tone it down."

Grayson and I both go still, exchanging a worried glance before looking at her.

Did she overhear us? I thought we were keeping our voices low enough. Oh my God, I'm going to die if she did.

"What's got your panties in a twist?" Grayson asks.

Kristen waves a hand to encompass the two of us. "The fake flirting. You don't have to sell it so hard in front of Mom. She's about to shit a brick, she's so happy."

I relax. Well, if she thinks the flirting was fake, she likely didn't hear what we were actually saying.

"It's nauseating," she continues, plucking the evergreen sprig out of my hair. Hey, I liked that. "She's going to start planning your wedding next."

Grayson purses his lips. "Shouldn't you be happy she's not planning *your* wedding?"

"I would be, except Abby's my best friend. I don't like her being caught up in your scheme. And I don't want Mom asking her if she likes cream or white better for the table settings of this imaginary future she's planning for you two."

As much as I appreciate her protectiveness, I don't need it right now. She's going to ruin everything.

Grayson takes back the sprig of evergreen and carefully places it in my hair, right where it was before. I swear his fingers linger on me, and there's no mistaking his gaze does. A rush of warmth fills me.

"We've got it under control," he tells her. "And cream is obviously the superior choice."

Kristen rolls her eyes as I stifle a smile.

"I love you, but seriously. Don't leave Abby to clean up your mess."

She stands and walks away, returning to help Eli roll out and secure the aisle runner.

Grayson sobers, and I hold out a hand to stop whatever he's about to say. I don't want doubt or regret to be a part of this. Only happiness. Excitement. Anticipation for what's still to come.

"There's nothing to worry about," I tell him. "Nothing I can't handle. This doesn't have to change anything."

He eyes me for a moment. "Are you sure?"

"Yes, absolutely."

I must say it with enough conviction because he nods and after a minute returns to his former mood.

"So, tell me more about this guy..."

"I appreciate you letting me sleep over," Harper says, spreading some kind of face cream over her cheeks. "Owen and I wanted to be traditional about at least one thing."

I fluff up a spare pillow for her, placing it on the left side of the bed. "You really think you're going to avoid seeing him before the wedding? Don't we still have last-minute things to set up in the morning?"

She shrugs. "That's the plan. If it doesn't work out, it's not the end of the world, but it's supposed to be bad luck for the groom to see the bride beforehand."

"Yeah, but that originated when arranged marriages were common and the bride's family didn't want the groom to back out of the deal in case he thought the bride was ugly. Same reason why brides wear veils until the *I do*'s are said. The guy doesn't see her face until after he's committed."

She blinks at me. "Sometimes I forget you're a librarian and know way too many random things."

I'm not sure if I should take offense to that, so I consider it a compliment instead. "At least we don't have to worry about Owen backing out. He's already got you locked down."

She smiles. "That he does. And I've always wanted to walk down an aisle in a fancy dress, so I'm glad he's indulging me."

My house has been designated *Operation Bridal Team* for tomorrow morning. All the girls will get ready here so we can spread out and make a mess without having to worry about cleaning up before driving to the ceremony in Harper and Owen's backyard. Their house has already been deep cleaned within an inch of its life since people will need to go inside to use the restroom. Harper's anticipating busybodies like Ruth to poke around, so she didn't want the added stress of cleaning up again when time will be at a premium.

Harper puts the jar of face cream back in her bag of cosmetics, then takes out some kind of tool that she rolls around on her face. I'm not sure what it's supposed to accomplish, but she seems well-versed in using it.

"God, I can't wait for it to be tomorrow already. I don't know how I'm going to sleep tonight."

I'll definitely sleep well. Today was exhausting setting up all that stuff. But I know she's excited. "It's like the night before the first day of school."

Harper gives me a pitying look. "Oh, honey. No. Most kids dreaded that, not looked forward to it."

Well, to each their own. "Sleepovers weren't a thing the night before school, at least."

"No, they weren't. And I feel like I've barely talked to you this week, so I'm glad I get to spend tonight with you. I've been so caught up with wedding stuff and Kelly and Elena visiting."

I wave off her concern. "No, it's fine. All of this is once-in-a-lifetime stuff, but I'll be here when it's over."

Available, as always. Nothing going on. This magical week over.

"Have things been going okay with Grayson?"

I nod, not trusting myself to speak. If I do, I might blurt out the whole story. Not that I want to purposely keep her in the dark, but the more people that know, the better chance there is of it getting back to Kristen.

And I'm still not sure if I want Kristen to know. She's been so against me even helping Grayson this week. She might combust if she finds out what we've really been up to.

"You two looked super flirty setting up the chairs earlier. Too bad it's fake."

"Yeah, too bad," I murmur.

"Can you imagine if you actually fell in love this week? How romantic that'd be?"

I'm quiet. Is that what's happening? Do a few orgasms equal love?

I nearly laugh out loud at my delusion.

"Oh, shit. I'm sorry." Harper reaches out a hand to me. "That was crappy to say. My mouth didn't catch up with my brain."

"It's fine." I shrug. "It's the dream, right?"

"Right," she says hesitantly.

"How did you know Owen loved you?" I ask abruptly.

She appears startled for a moment at the change of subject. "He told me. Begged me not to go back to Chicago."

I nod. In that scenario, it'd be me begging Grayson. But he's given no indication he wants to stay. And why would he? Other than the sense I got that he's a bit lonely up in Seattle, he has a great job in a cool city. Crescent Pass doesn't have much to offer, other than his family being here.

And me. Would that ever be enough to sway him?

Squeezing my eyes shut, I dispel the thoughts as best I can. There's no use in worrying about things I can't change. I just have to enjoy it while I still have it.

I pick up my phone to charge it on my nightstand and see there's a text from Grayson.

Grayson: *Wish I could be there tonight. No fair that Harper gets to sleep with you before I do.*

I grin, my heartbeat picking up. My fingers fiddle over the screen before I go for it.

Me: *My bed's open tomorrow night.*

It's as direct of an invitation as I can make it, and my gaze zeroes in on the three little typing dots at the bottom of the text thread.

Grayson: *I'll bring the condoms.*

Heat washes over me, and I pray Harper is still focused on her nighttime skincare routine rather than the hot flash I'm experiencing. This week has been a learning curve in the best kind of way, and tomorrow I'll put everything I've learned to good use. It's my last chance to do anything with Grayson before he leaves, and dear God I'm going to take advantage of it.

Me: *Till tomorrow, then.*

I plug in my phone and turn it facedown so Harper can't accidentally see any more messages that may pop up.

"You ready to sleep?" I ask her, wanting it to be tomorrow already, too.

She nods and gets under the covers. "Tell me more about arranged marriage bridal customs. Maybe it'll bore me enough so I fall asleep."

"First of all, rude. Second of all, you came to the right place. Back in the day, marriages were strategic alliances between families, not based on love."

She yawns. "It's working already."

CHAPTER TWENTY-TWO

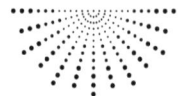

GRAYSON

Somehow, the guys got roped into doing all the last-minute wedding setup, but I honestly don't mind. Putting out place cards at table seats is distracting me from Abby's texts from last night, saying her bed will be open for me tonight. I swear she enjoys teasing me.

My phone buzzes in my pocket, and speak of the devil, it's Abby.

"Hey, gorgeous," I answer, only realizing afterward I might be on speakerphone if she's with all the other bridesmaids. Oh, wait, that still checks out if we're keeping up the act in front of Harper's friends. It seems so long ago that we were purely acting, when in reality, it's only been a few days.

"Hey," she says, a pleased note in her voice. "I need your help with something. Can Owen spare you?"

I glance over at Owen securing the fresh flowers he picked up from the florist onto the wedding arch. A few feet away, Eli is putting centerpieces on the tables. Yeah, I think they'll be fine without me. Nothing here is life or death.

"Yeah, what's up?"

"The bakery called Harper because their truck broke down, so they can't deliver the cake. She's kind of freaking out about it."

That seems like a simple enough fix. "You want me to drive to town and pick it up?"

"It's a bakery in Kirkwood, so it'll take a while to get. And Harper wants two people to go, one to drive and one to sit in the backseat to make sure nothing happens to it."

Geez, she's paranoid.

"I'm the only one completely ready," she continues, "so I offered to go with you. If you're not too busy setting up. Or still need to get ready yourself."

I check my watch. Two hours until the ceremony. It'll take at least half an hour to drive there, maybe five minutes to pick up the cake, then another half an hour back. Me, Owen, and Eli aren't dressed yet, either. We didn't want to set up in our suits. How long can it take to put on a suit, though?

"Yeah, I can make it. I'll swing by your place to pick you up."

"Okay, see you in a few."

I tell Owen the new plan and he shoos me toward my car, not wanting Harper to freak out about this any longer than necessary.

When I get to Abby's, I text her and wait in the driveway, only half paying attention before she walks out of her house in a slinky burgundy dress that has my head turning. Holy fuck, she looks hot.

I get out of the car and walk toward her, taking in the way the silky material clings to her, the peek of cleavage at the neckline, how she even seems to carry herself differently wearing it. Her blonde hair is styled in loose curls, makeup done more heavily than I've ever seen it. But that's not what draws me to her. It's something about *her*. Something irresistible. How did I never see it before?

"You look incredible," I tell her, loving the blush that creeps over her cheeks.

She stops in front of me but doesn't move any closer to kiss me in greeting.

"Worried Kristen's spying on us?" I ask, nodding toward the front window.

She smiles. "More that I'll mess up my lipstick. I'm not used to wearing it."

"I would *love* to mess it up."

She playfully nudges my arm. "Come on. We can do that after we get the cake."

Good thing she's being responsible, because all I can think about as we leave Crescent Pass and get on the highway is getting her out of that dress tonight. Hell, maybe even at the wedding. Would anyone notice if we snuck away? Owen's house will be open. I doubt he'd care if we use his room to blow off some steam.

Sliding the silky fabric up her legs, bending her over the side of the bed. Finding her wet for me, wanting me to take her. Or maybe her kneeling in front of me, smearing that lipstick all over my cock.

Fuck, I cannot be getting turned on right now. I'm driving. And Abby would be mortified at the depraved things I'm thinking of.

Then again, she's been a lot wilder than I expected. And she'd certainly sucked me off enthusiastically the other night.

No, what am I thinking? This is Owen's wedding day. As his best man, I should focus on that. And then tonight, when it's over, I can have Abby. A perfect end to a perfect week.

My gut twists at the thought of driving back home tomorrow, but I push it aside.

"You have any kind of bridesmaid speech planned for the reception?" I ask her, trying to think of a safe topic.

She gives a quiet scoff. "No, me and public speaking don't mix."

"But you're a librarian. Don't you do storytimes for kids or something?"

"That's different. Children aren't there to judge you."

"None of the adults would either." There's nothing about her that's unlikable.

She smooths her hands over the silk fabric of her dress. "I know. I guess I'm just used to... being in the background."

"Not in that dress."

I take my eyes off the road for a moment to find her smiling at me. "You know what I mean."

"Do you want to be in the background?" I can't relate, but Owen's always been that way.

"Yes… and no. But mostly yes. I don't know, it's complicated."

I suppress a grin. "Why?"

She's quiet for a minute, seeming to collect her thoughts. "Do you remember years back these memes that talked about the mortifying ordeal of being known?"

"Um, vaguely?"

"It's from a larger quote from a *New York Times* piece. It talks about how if you want to reap the benefits of being loved by someone, you also have to submit to them knowing everything about you. The good and the bad."

My interest sharpens. "Do you think there's something bad about you?" What could be bad about Abby?

She shakes her head. "No, that's not what I'm trying to say. More that the article always stuck with me, because I identified with it so much. I never put myself out there because I don't want people to judge me. Or maybe don't want to find out how little they think of me." She glances at me quickly, then away.

I frown. "Why would they think that?"

She throws her hands up. "I didn't say it was logical. Don't you have anxiety?"

"No."

She stares at me. "Seriously?"

I shrug, scratching at my jaw. "Maybe when it comes to my mom."

"I'd probably have a nervous breakdown if Cheryl was my mom."

"It's a wonder Kristen and Owen aren't in an asylum already. They have to deal with her way more than I do. You're lucky your parents are chill."

A sigh escapes her. "Well, they come with their own set of challenges."

Oh, shit. I forgot. "I'm sor—"

"No, don't be."

There's a beat of silence. "How's your dad doing?" I ask, remembering how tired she'd seemed on the ride home from her parents' house.

She shrugs. "As good as he can be."

"And your mom?"

"Same."

It's funny, as quiet as she used to be, this week she hasn't stopped talking to me. Except for this. "The other night, you said we'd talk about this another time."

She makes a *hmm* sound. "I did say that, didn't I?"

And yet, she still doesn't speak. Okay, message received. "You don't have to—"

She reaches over and places her hand on my leg. "No, I want to. I just don't know what to say. My dad's not himself anymore. And it only keeps getting worse."

My heart twists for her. "How long has this been going on?"

"It started about six years ago."

Wow, that long? I wonder why Kristen never mentioned anything. Then again, why would she? It's not like I've ever asked about Abby.

"Do you talk to Kristen about it?"

"Not really. She has her hands full with Jenny and Jamie. I have... nothing."

There's something painful about the way she says it, loneliness seeping through her words.

"That's not true." If Abby thinks she has nothing... What do I have?

She chuckles, but there's an edge of bitterness in it. "That sounded dramatic, didn't it? I only mean I don't have the same kind of responsibilities as she does. With kids and a significant other and everything."

"That doesn't mean you're not allowed to talk about it."

"I know, but what is there to say? I help out every week but there's nothing I can do to help *him*. I have to watch as he slowly becomes this other person, and all the while I'm waiting for the other shoe to drop, for something really bad to happen. Like the fall."

There's that twist in my chest again, stronger this time. I wish I could take this burden from her.

She wipes her eyes, and I'm suddenly aware this is the wrong time to discuss a sensitive subject. She just had her makeup done for the wedding. "Hey, let's talk about this later. When we're not rushed for time." Kirkwood's exit isn't that far away.

"When? You're leaving tomorrow."

And there's another stab in the chest. I'm going to need some antacids at this point.

As much as I hate to admit it… we're running out of time.

CHAPTER TWENTY-THREE

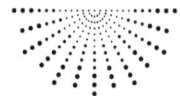

ABBY

"Abby, Abby!"

I glance around, the urgent voice startling me. Jenny rushes across the lawn in a heap of pale pink tulle and presents her back to me.

"Can you tie the ribbons? Mom said you're an expert at it."

My heart settles. Okay, it's not actually an emergency.

"Yeah, of course." I pick up the sash ties and put the bow back to rights. Who knows how it even got untied to begin with?

"Did you see me throwing the petals earlier? It was good, right?"

Jenny had taken her flower girl duties seriously, going so far as to practice for the last few months. The only thing is, they didn't have an endless supply of petals at home, so Jenny used Legos instead. She was driving Kristen up the wall.

"You were the best flower girl I've ever seen."

"Really?" She spins around and jumps up and down, clapping her hands. "Jamie will be so jealous."

Oh, God. I don't want to get in the middle of whatever sibling rivalry she has going on. "Well, he was the best ring bearer I've seen, too."

Her excitement dims. "I guess. We were both pretty good."

"You were a great team."

"But which one of us was better?"

I sigh. "Jenny, I'm not answering that."

I don't know how she manages it, but she somehow gives me a sly grin even as she pouts.

"Okay, but I can tell you're secretly thinking me."

My lips compress, not wanting her to see me smile.

She scampers off toward where her brother is, and my gaze follows her, snagging on Grayson over by the bar set up near the house. He's catching up with friends from high school, and though he invited me to talk with them, I begged off, wanting to sit down for a bit.

The ceremony went beautifully earlier, everything going according to plan. Afterward, we ate, then danced on the makeshift dance floor they've set up until my feet hurt in these heels I'm not used to wearing. Tonight has been perfect, but I can't help the growing discontent in me.

I should be enjoying this night, soaking up the once-in-a-lifetime experience. But no matter how much I try to stay in the present moment, my mind keeps fast-forwarding to tomorrow, when all of this goes away. Like Cinderella after the ball—back to rags and a big-ass pumpkin after midnight.

What I should be focusing on is what happens tonight directly after the wedding. I invited Grayson to my bed, and with the way he's been whispering in my ear all night, he's more than ready.

A wave of shivers washes over me, equal parts anticipation and trepidation. I have no idea what the hell I'm doing. I've somehow muddled through everything so far, but this is the big one. The one where I can't hide behind bravado anymore. He'll know, right?

Maybe... Maybe he won't care. Some guys like sleeping with virgins.

I cringe, my face heating. That was embarrassing to even think.

Over by the bar, one of the girls in the group, Lucy, touches Grayson's arm, smiling up at him. She had an obvious crush on him back in high school, though I don't remember them ever dating. She's married now, but still hanging on Grayson's every word.

He smoothly moves his arm so she's forced to drop her hand, and my heart warms. Not that I have any claim on him, but she better not try to mess with—

"Hi, honey. How are you doing?"

I glance over at Cheryl, who takes a seat next to me at one of the tables. Does she suspect I was thinking about her son?

"I'm good. Just resting my feet."

"Oh, I saw you two cutting it up on the dance floor earlier."

I smile, but don't respond. It's still too weird that she caught me and Grayson kissing at the winery.

"You were beautiful up there next to Kristen and the other girls."

"Oh, thank you. Your reading during the ceremony was lovely, too."

She waves off my praise but looks pleased. "So, where's my son? Please don't tell me he's abandoned you already."

"Oh, no." I motion toward the bar. "He's talking to some old friends."

"And things are going good with you two?"

I nod, not sure how else to respond. It doesn't seem as important to lay it on thick in front of her now that the situation between me and Grayson has changed.

"And after he leaves?"

"I don't know."

The words sound stupid, but what else is there to say? I knew what I was getting into.

She makes a *hmm* sound. "You leave that to me."

"Oh, no—"

She cuts me off. "Don't you worry about anything. I've always known you two were meant for each other."

She absolutely did not always know that, because she's never once hinted at anything between us. And Cheryl isn't known for keeping her thoughts to herself. Besides, her support might actually be a point against me in Grayson's book. He's always stubbornly gone against whatever she says.

She saunters away before I can argue against whatever idea she has, then I roll my eyes, accepting my fate. We're done after tomorrow, anyway.

With that nihilistic attitude, I join Grayson at the bar, slipping my hand through the crook of his arm. I swear Lucy gives me a dirty look, but I serenely smile as if I don't notice.

Grayson asks if I want to dance again as the DJ announces it's the last song, and leads me out to the center of the dance floor as something slow and melodic comes over the sound system.

"Looks like Operation Fake Wedding Date was a success," he says as he wraps an arm around my back, his other hand holding mine.

"Maybe a little too successful."

He gives me a questioning look.

"I think your mom is going to launch an offensive in my favor."

"Ah." He nods in understanding. "What'd she say?"

"That she's always known we were meant for each other."

I intended for the words to come out lighthearted, as if we're both in on the joke, but they don't. There's something weighty in them, as if there might be a glimmer of truth in the notion.

Grayson is silent, no sign that he finds humor in it, either. "I'll take care of her," he finally says.

We're quiet for the rest of the song, swaying back and forth to the melody. A few feet away, Harper and Owen are dancing, too, smiling at each other in a lovesick way that has my chest aching. I want that so badly. Want someone to look at me the way Owen is looking at his wife. With caring and devotion and a love that goes beyond anything I've ever experienced.

No. What I want is for Grayson to look at me like that.

A tear slips down my cheek, and I hastily wipe it away before he notices. No sad thoughts tonight. Not while I still have the chance to be with him.

"You ready to get out of here?" he asks when the song ends.

"Yeah."

My stomach fills with butterflies as we make our goodbyes and head over to his car on the far side of the lawn. He opens the passenger door, his hand on the small of my back. It burns hot through the silk of my dress, and as I turn to slide into the seat, I catch the look in his eyes. It's not the same look Owen gave Harper. There's desire, yes, but not the same kind of soul-deep love.

"I can't wait to peel this dress off of you." His thumb travels over my waist, down to rub my hip bone.

His words send a rush of arousal through me, even as the hollowness in my chest expands. Harper and Kristen are going home tonight to be with men who love them. Who'd do anything for them. Who'd die for them.

I'm going to have sex with a man who's leaving tomorrow.

I lean forward and kiss him, wanting a connection. Wishing this was the man I'm starting the rest of my life with.

He seems surprised but kisses me back before gently breaking away. "I thought you wouldn't want anyone to know about this."

There are still plenty of others milling about, getting in cars, taking in the last of the wedding festivities. "I don't care if anyone knows." And in this moment, it's true. Sure, it could cause problems later. Questions from people I'd rather not answer. But I want Grayson, more than anything. More than he's willing to give, if I'm being honest with myself.

"Okay." He backs me up against the car and kisses me again, bringing me flush against him, his hand cupping the nape of my neck. He doesn't hold back, probably giving everyone around us a show, but I don't care about that. This is what I wanted. A public acknowledgment of what's been developing between us. For it to be real. The kind of thing that could grow. That could be lasting.

"I've wanted to smear that lipstick all day," he whispers against my lips, his hips rocking against mine. There's a growing bulge there and a responding throb in my core.

"My place?" I ask, my voice breathless.

He nods in response and gets me situated in the passenger seat before rounding the car to drive us home. He holds my hand on the short drive back, playing with my fingers, my belly making pleasant swoops imagining what'll happen in a few minutes. Him taking my dress off like he said he wanted to, covering me with that big body, entering me...

My palms turn sweaty. It'll be fine, I tell myself. Out of everyone in the world, Grayson would be my first choice for this. I shouldn't be nervous.

My hands shake slightly as I use my keys to open the door to my house, but once we're inside, he's kissing me again, sliding the straps of my dress down.

"Have I mentioned how phenomenal you look in this?" he asks, finding the zipper in the back.

I nod, my tongue thick in my throat.

His lips press against my neck as the zipper slides down in one fell swoop and the dress falls to the floor.

"Fuck," he drawls, looking at me with appreciation. He must like the lingerie I picked out.

The next thing I know, I'm in his arms, being carried to my bedroom. He flicks on the dim light and sets me flat on the bed, his hands already roving my body, his lips following soon after. My bra disappears and his mouth replaces the fabric, giving gentle sucks that have me straining toward him.

His fingers are in the straps of my panties next, pulling them down, pausing by my feet to take off my shoes, too. He stands back, taking in the sight of me as he loosens his tie and takes off his jacket.

"Goddamn you're sexy," he murmurs, unbuttoning his shirt. "You wet for me?"

I nod, watching him disrobe. I'd like to take his clothes off myself, but if I move, I might completely lose my nerve. I want him to take control this first time. To have him show me what to do.

His pants are off now, leaving him in his boxer briefs, and as his thumbs hook in the sides, a thrill runs through me. This is it. Showtime.

His cock bobs in front of him as he stands nude before me, but I don't get a chance to look my fill before he's bending down, fishing around in his pants pocket for something. He pulls out three condoms, connected at the edges like they're arcade tickets, and I blink rapidly. *Three?*

"What is it?" he asks, and I realize I'm gawking at him.

"Are we using all of those tonight?" I mumble. Once is crazy enough, but he wants to have sex three times?

He chuckles. "They don't sell singles at the store. Haven't you bought condoms before?"

I shake my head, feeling dumb.

He rips open the foil on one and puts it on, his actions easy and skilled. How many times has he put a condom on before? How many women has he had sex with? And how on earth has he not realized I'm not at his level? Is it misleading to not tell him I'm a virgin?

He climbs back on the bed, hovering over me, and kisses me again. His lips are so sure, so right, and I try my damndest to lose myself in him, the way I have before, but the rising anxiety won't let me.

"You okay?" He leans back. "You're shaking."

I nod, too rapidly to be believable. "Just a little nervous."

"We don't have to—"

"No, I want to. I want this."

He studies me. No, no. Don't look closer. "What's going on?" he asks.

Shit. He's not going to accept a throwaway answer. "I just…" My fingers twist in the sheets underneath me. "I haven't done this before."

My heart is jammed up in my throat, but he doesn't react.

"Yeah, you said you hadn't hooked up with anyone, only had relationships."

I swallow hard. I never said that second part. He must have filled in the blanks in a way he found reasonable. "No, I mean I've never had sex."

He stares at me, silence filling the air between us. There's a squeezing sensation in my ribs, compressing tighter and tighter until I'm sure everything inside is going to spill out as my hope that this wouldn't be a big deal vanishes.

His face is carefully neutral, other than the tips of his ears turning red. What is he thinking?

"Please say something," I whisper. Dear God, anything.

"We shouldn't do this."

Okay, anything but that.

CHAPTER TWENTY-FOUR

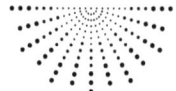

GRAYSON

She's a virgin? *A virgin?* Who the hell is a virgin in this day and age at twenty-eight years old? She's not religious, is she? No, she wouldn't have done all that other stuff with me if she was, right?

I glance down at my dick, still eager and ready for Abby. It didn't get the memo that there's no way I can do this. I cannot be her first. Not the guy who's leaving tomorrow. How much of a shithead would I be if I took her virginity and left town the next day?

She sits up, pulling the sheet over her, and leans against the headboard. "I'm sorry I didn't tell you before."

I shake my head, not sure what I even mean by the action. My thoughts are swimming too fast inside my brain.

"It doesn't have to be a big deal," she continues, almost as if she's trying to convince herself. "It's an old-fashioned concept, anyway."

She's not wrong, but I still can't help but feel like she should wait for someone else. Someone important. Someone who will stick around and be here for her. Someone here in Crescent Pass.

Even as I think it, everything in me rejects it. No guy here would be good enough for her.

"I..." I drag my hand through my hair, hating this. "I can't take your virginity."

Her cheeks flush, lips flattening. "Why?"

My fingers grip the back of my neck, nails digging in, forcing myself not to reach for her. How the fuck can I make this better? "Abby..."

And just like that, she's on edge. Her nostrils flare, and the change that comes over her would be magnificent to watch if I wasn't caught in the crosshairs. "Seriously, why? Am I going to be spoiled goods for the next guy or something?"

I recoil. "No, I didn't mean it like that."

"Then how did you mean it?"

There's a tightness in her expression I hate. "It should be with someone important."

"You are important."

There's a hitch in my chest, but I push it aside. "I'm leaving tomorrow," I force myself to say.

"I know." She chuckles, an edge of bitterness to it. "Trust me, I know."

"Then what if you meet someone and you regret—"

"Meet someone? Who am I going to meet? All the droves of guys waiting to get with me?"

"You know what I mean."

"No, I don't."

"This was supposed to be casual," I tell her. "A fun hook-up. Taking your virginity is a hell of a lot more serious than that."

Her face reddens further. "Fine. I'll go get it out of the way."

She removes the sheet and scoots off the bed, grabbing her bra.

I watch her wrestle it on, then slide her panties up her legs. "What are you doing?"

"I'm going to get laid so you don't have to worry about being the first."

My muscles tense. "That's not funny." I can't help the growly way it comes out, but she doesn't seem to take notice.

"I'm not laughing," she replies coolly, picking her dress up off the floor.

I force my jaw to unclench. She wouldn't actually... No, of course she wouldn't.

She taps her pointer to her chin. "Hmm, who do you think would help me out on such short notice?"

"Okay, I get it," I grit out, but she ignores me.

She snaps her fingers. "Oh, I know. How about Greg? He's always looking for some action."

Greg? Fucking *Greg*? The guy who hits on every girl with a pulse?

I take the dress from her and throw it behind me. "You're not doing that."

She meets my eye, all challenge. "Why?"

"Because you're mine."

Silence hangs heavy in the air as she stares at me, her breaths picking up in speed. Shit. I shouldn't have said that. It was just... instinctual.

I turn, scrubbing my palm over my jaw, and sigh deeply. "I'm sorry. I know you're not mine."

"No, I liked it." She steps closer, her fingertips trailing up my arm, leaving pleasurable shivers in their wake. "I want to be yours."

I squeeze my eyes shut. She cannot say stuff like that to me. The caveman part of my brain lights up, telling me to make her mine for real, to fuck her until she never wants another man but me. That strange possessive urge I've felt around her the past few days pulses faster and faster.

This wasn't supposed to turn out like this. This was meant to be an easygoing fling. Not have my heart pounding out of my chest as her touch moves up to my shoulder, her body close enough I can feel her heat.

"Make me yours," she murmurs. "I want it to be you."

I can't focus on anything but the way her breath whispers across my skin, the soft press of her lips to my jaw, up and over to my mouth.

The gentle tease of her lips on mine, gradually growing more urgent. It's over when she groans sweetly, my resistance crumbling. I can't deny her anything.

I want to be yours.

I want it to be you.

The words play over in my mind as I take control of the kiss. In the depths of my soul, I want it to be me, too. Even if I'm a bastard for doing it.

She kisses me back hungrily, sweeping her fingers through my hair, her eagerness revving me up.

"Abby…" I try to grab onto my reasoning from before, but it's just out of reach. I'm already being pulled under by her, an innocent siren who doesn't know the power she's gained over me.

"Please, Grayson." Her hands wrap around my shoulders, drawing me into her.

Then again, maybe she knows exactly what she's doing.

"Are you sure you want this?" My voice is shakier than I intended, something about this feeling so momentous.

"Yes."

Her complete conviction is what breaks the last of my resistance. I unhook her bra and strip her panties off, then lay her on the bed. I take my time at her chest, sucking on her nipples until she's curling herself around me in response, one leg hitching over my hip. My dick rubs against her core, reminding me why we're here.

I bring a hand between us and softly circle her pussy, entering her with two fingers and working her up until her hips are rocking, wanting more. "You ready?"

She nods, some of her bravado receding, but there's still so much trust in her gaze, I can barely stand it. What have I done to earn that kind of trust?

And will she ever look at me that way again after I leave?

I rub my dick along her seam, once, twice, holding myself back. I need to be careful, to not rush this. I want this to be amazing for her.

Slowly, I feed myself into her, going so slow it's a special torture. She's so tight, the pressure incredible, but I don't want to hurt her.

"You okay?" I ask, pausing to let her get accustomed to my size.

She nods, her neck arching off the pillow as my hips jerk of their own accord, wanting so badly to thrust already. "I'm good. Everything's good."

I bend down, kissing along the shell of her ear. "I think we can do better than good."

Her chuckle turns into a moan as I push in until I'm seated to the hilt, then draw nearly all the way out.

As I slowly fill her again, I ask, "That okay?"

"Yes. Good. Great. Amazing. Keep doing that."

She shifts under me, her hips tilting into mine, and I let her find the angle she wants, starting up a steady pace. I rock into her, over and over, the pleasure increasing, and as I look down at where we're joined, I'm transfixed. There's something incredibly sexy about watching her pussy take my cock, especially knowing I'm the only one to do this with her. It probably makes me a sick bastard, but I don't care at the moment. She's mine. She said she wanted to be mine.

I glance up, meeting her eyes, and as our gazes connect, I swear something passes between us. A connection I didn't know was possible. I've never felt this with another woman.

I shut my eyes, an icy river of fear washing over me for a split second. That's not what this is supposed to be. This connection… nothing good can come of it. Not when I'm leaving tomorrow.

"You like it when I fuck you?" I ask, being purposely crass. This is just sex. Nothing more.

She moans an assent, and when I open my eyes again, I concentrate on the way her breasts bounce gently to the rhythm I've set, the way her pussy clenches my cock, the scent of sex in the air. I focus on my own breaths, harsh in the quiet of the room, the soft slap of our skin meeting, how incredibly smooth her waist is where I grip it.

I don't look in her eyes again. I'm afraid to, if I'm being honest with myself. I don't know what will be reflected there. What I want to be there. And what might not be there at all. Maybe I imagined the whole thing. Or maybe it was one-sided.

I lean forward, angling my face out of her line of sight, and pick up my pace, enjoying the gasps she makes, the way she clutches at me. Putting my weight on one arm, I reach a hand between us and rub her clit, concentrating on making her come. After a few minutes of effort, her rhythm goes erratic, her hips out of sync as she orgasms in a long groan, her arousal coating me. I follow soon after, letting myself go, gripping her tightly to me so she takes all I give her. All I *can* give her. This is it.

Pulling out, I roll onto my back, staring up at the ceiling. What was that? That moment of connection? I imagined it, right? That kind of thing doesn't actually happen.

Abby shifts to her side, facing me, and spreads her hand over my chest. "You okay?"

Shit. I should be the one asking her that. "Yeah, of course. You good?"

She leans in to kiss me. "More than good."

"You're not sore?"

She shakes her head. "I'm fine."

She snuggles into my side and I instinctively wrap an arm around her, listening to her breathing even out until I'm pretty sure she's asleep. I carefully disengage and head into the bathroom to clean up, then brace my hands against the counter, staring at myself in the mirror.

I liked sleeping with Abby. Really fucking liked it. More than liked it. And even with forcing myself to focus on what we were doing and not the emotion behind it...

I shy away from that thought. I don't want to think about that right now. Don't want to think about leaving tomorrow. Don't want to think about how I slept with an amazing woman knowing I can't give her what she deserves.

I grip the counter harder. We both knew what we were getting into when we agreed to do this. This shouldn't come as a surprise now.

So why do I feel like the worst piece of shit?

CHAPTER TWENTY-FIVE

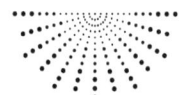

ABBY

A muffled banging noise wakes me, and it takes me a moment to make sense of what I'm seeing, my vision blurry. Grayson's holding his foot, leaning against the dresser, his face twisted in pain. Only his lower half is dressed, his shirt clutched in his hand.

"You okay?" I ask, sitting up. I slouch back down when I remember I'm naked, covering myself with the sheet. That's right. We slept together last night.

Warmth spreads through my chest remembering how good it was, how he handled my body with ease, knowing exactly what to do to make me come. Then feeling him pulse inside of me as he came, too, and the way he'd clutched me tight to him, keeping us connected. Falling asleep in his arms, exhausted from the hustle and bustle of the wedding.

The warmth fades. None of that will happen again.

He nods. "I stubbed my toe. Sorry if I woke you."

"No, it's fine." I glance at my bedside clock. Wow, it's almost nine. We slept in late. "Are you, um… What are you doing?"

He lets go of his foot, straightening himself up. "I have to get going. I promised my mom I'd help her out with some stuff around the house before I drive back."

A bowling ball settles in the pit of my stomach. He's leaving already? I thought we'd have more time. I thought… Well, more like I wished.

I knew this was coming. Knew it'd be on us in the blink of an eye. I can do this. I can be strong.

I nod, pasting on a smile. "Yeah, of course." I grip the sheet tighter to me, feeling exposed. Can he see right through my fake smile?

He slips on his shirt and crosses the room to sit next to me on the bed. Without hesitation, he kisses me, his warm palm cupping my jaw, and the tension in my belly loosens.

"I've had an amazing week with you," he murmurs.

"Me, too."

He takes my free hand, brushing his thumb over my knuckles. "I'm not good with emotional goodbye kind of things," he says with a self-deprecating laugh.

My stomach sinks even further. "I wish you didn't have to go," I whisper. It's all I can seem to get out through my suddenly parched lips. All I'm willing to admit out loud. I knew what I was getting into when I agreed to this. How hard it would be afterward.

And I still did it anyway.

He nods. "I know. But it's not like I'll never be back."

Neither of us say what our next meeting might be like. If we'll pick up where we've left off. Or if everything's over once he returns to Seattle.

I'm fairly sure it's the latter. I can't remember if he outright said that when we first made this agreement, but I'm not going to ask for clarification either. If he wanted to stay, he would. I won't beg him.

How pathetic would that be?

There's a burning pressure behind my eyes, but I refuse to let any hint of moisture break through. There'll be time enough for that later.

"I'll see you next time, then." I force my lips to tip up at the corners, to put on a brave face for him.

"Yeah, next time." He's still playing with my fingers, looking down at them instead of me. He suddenly squeezes my hand, then sets it down. "Fuck, Abby, I…"

Nothing follows that statement, and my heart pounds in my chest as he leans forward and kisses me again, hoping he's changed—

He stands and crosses the room, pausing at the door. "I'll let myself out."

I nod, not that he sees, and then he's gone, my front door opening and closing a moment later.

The tears leak out then, an unrelenting river that won't stop. My ribs grow tight, my hands fluttering up to my face helplessly, my breath hitching into sobs I can't control. I've held this at bay all week, and the reality of it comes crashing down on me now. Grayson's gone. He really left.

I lay there for I don't know how long, crying in a way I don't remember ever doing, until Leo's fluffy face nudges my arm.

"Hey, bud," I mumble, thankful for him as he curls up in my lap. I focus on petting him instead of the crushing weight of Grayson's leaving, and his purrs eventually calm me enough to where I can get dressed and ready for the day.

I wander through my house, but all I see is Grayson. Sleeping together in my bedroom, making out on the couch in the living room, playing strip poker in my kitchen, getting each other off in the guest bathroom. Even my craft room is affected, where he sat and kept me company while I finished packing up wedding favors, talking and laughing with me.

I hope there will come a day in the not-so-distant future when I can be in my house without remembering him, but today's not that day. I need to get out of here.

Grabbing my phone from my nightstand, I open a text from Kristen I must not have heard during my crying jag.

Kristen: *Breakfast at Cascade?*

She sent it half an hour ago, and I quickly text her back, hoping she didn't already eat. This is exactly what I need. Something to take my mind off of Grayson.

Me: *Meet there in fifteen?*

She responds with a thumbs-up emoji, and I finish getting ready and get out the door, driving to Cascade Cafe, our only restaurant in town.

Now that she's dating Eli, Kristen has actually had more free time than usual, since the kids love hanging out with him. She's already sitting in one of the back booths, her dark head bent over a laminated menu.

"Hey," I say, sliding into the opposite side of the booth.

She looks up and smiles, but there's something troubled in her eyes.

"What is it?" I ask without preamble. Now that I think about it, it's kind of weird she asked me to breakfast when I've seen her nearly every day this week.

"What do you mean?"

I give her a look and she sighs. "How do you always know?"

"You have an expressive face. And we've been best friends for over twenty years."

She lays her menu on the table. "What is it exactly you're doing with my brother?"

I stare at her, momentarily dumbstruck. What does she know?

Lucy, the cafe owner, chooses then to come over and take our orders.

"Did y'all have a good time at the wedding?" she asks, clueless to the tension.

I nod mutely as Kristen makes some kind of small talk with her.

"I saw Grayson last night," Lucy is saying. "Been forever since I've seen him in town."

That's right, she was there. I didn't realize Harper was close enough with Lucy to invite her. Then again, Harper must come to the cafe a lot since she hates cooking.

"Yeah, he's been here this week. Longest he's been back since Dad's funeral, I think," Kristen says.

I'm silent as they finish talking, only chiming in when Lucy asks if I want my usual order of the combo platter. When she leaves, I take a sip of my water, avoiding Kristen's eye.

"You're being weird."

I finally look at her. Did I actually believe I could hide this from her forever?

"I saw you two kissing last night," she says when I don't respond. "That seems pretty far to go to convince my mom you're wedding dates. Especially when the wedding was already over."

I nod. It's not like we were being circumspect at the end there. I stupidly even wanted people to see us. For there to be some kind of proof that this connection between me and Grayson really happened. "We, um..." How do I even begin to explain this? It was one thing for her to tell me about stuff with Eli. It's another for me to tell her the same about her brother.

"Did you get drunk again?" she asks, searching for an explanation.

"No, nothing like that." God, I don't want her to think Grayson took advantage of me. "We sort of started something up the past few days. The way you and Eli did when you first got together."

Her eyes widen. Crap. I shouldn't have said that last part, even if it's the truth.

"It's over now, though," I continue hastily. "Just a fling, I guess."

I trace my finger through the condensation on my water glass, willing my mouth to keep shut. I don't need to start blabbing about how amazing it's been with him or how I've kept my crush on him a secret from Kristen all these years.

Pressure builds behind my eyes, coming easily since I already spent God knows how long earlier crying. I look down at the table, praying she doesn't see what I fear is all over my face.

"Do I need to go beat up my brother?"

I startle, nearly spilling my drink.

"Because I will for you."

"W-what?" I ask, confused.

"He broke your heart, didn't he?"

My eyes are hot, moisture pooling at the edges. "No... well, maybe a little." I press the heels of my palms to my eyes, trying my best not to let anything break through. "It's not his fault, though. It's my own."

My voice cracks on the last word and my shoulders shudder with the weight of keeping everything inside. We're in a public place. I cannot cry in front of everyone.

I blindly fumble out of the booth and head to the single restroom in the back, but I'm barely in before it opens behind me and Kristen's there, pulling me into a hug. Latching onto her, I let my head sink onto her shoulder, tears leaking onto the soft cotton of her shirt.

"It's okay," she says soothingly, her tight embrace calming me.

I didn't realize how much I needed this. It's only a hug, but right now it feels like a lifeline. Especially since I feared she'd have a different kind of reaction to the news about me and her brother.

A minute later, I'm better. I rub my fingers over my eyes, clearing away the wetness. "How'd you know I was upset about it?"

She gives me a small smile. "Like you said, we've been best friends for over twenty years."

I nod. "I'm such an idiot," I mumble. "I knew he was leaving."

She makes a *hmm* sound, neither a confirmation nor denial. Then again, she obviously doesn't see what I see in him.

"I guess I hoped something would magically change before he left. The way Eli stayed for you."

I haven't said that out loud before. Have barely let myself think it. I was trying so hard to prepare myself for the reality of him leaving, I stuffed down any secret wish that he would stay. It's the truth, though. Of course I wish he would've stayed.

Even if I knew it was impossible.

"Abby..."

There's so much pity in her voice, another wave of sadness nearly washes over me, but I hold it at bay. "I thought you'd be mad at me."

Her brows furrow. "About what?"

My hands twist together, a bad habit I've picked up from Kristen that she does when she's nervous. "Me and Grayson. You didn't like that I was even helping him."

She waves me off. "I was being stupid. But to be fair, I did say he'd leave a mess behind. I just thought it'd be with Mom, not you."

A weak chuckle escapes me. "He has some explaining to do with her, too. She made it sound like she has some kind of master plan last night."

"Of course she does," Kristen mutters. She looks at me and rubs her thumbs under my eyes. I probably look a wreck. "You good now? Can we leave this gross bathroom and go talk about this?"

I nod and follow her back to our booth, where we get an odd stare from Lucy. I can't tell if she's concerned that we both emerged from a single stall or maybe my face looks like a puffy, red mess, but I don't care. Knowing I have Kristen's support has done more than I realized to ease some of the tension in me.

Kristen asks me how this all started and I do my best to explain without fully admitting to the years-long crush I've had on her older brother. I also gloss over the… intimate parts, fairly sure she doesn't want to hear about that, either.

She spears a forkful of pancake when we get our meals and quietly listens, and when I'm finally all talked out, she shakes her head.

"I can't believe you slept with Grayson. Then again, I can't believe Harper does the same with Owen."

"That's what we're focusing on?"

"Right, right. Sorry. So…" She picks at the food on her plate for a second before setting her fork down. "You have feelings for him? Like, serious ones?"

I nod, unable to deny it.

"And you don't think he does?"

One of my shoulders lifts in a half-shrug. "He left. That says everything, doesn't it?"

Her lips twist. "Harper left. But she came back."

"Please don't."

She blinks at me, and I realize it came out harsher than I intended.

"Don't get my hopes up," I say in a softer tone. I can't deal with hope right now. "He made it clear from the beginning he was going to leave today."

She frowns but doesn't argue. "Did you know then you'd be this unhappy?"

A sigh escapes me. "Yeah. But I still thought it'd be worth it." The last few days have meant everything to me. "You did the same with Eli, right? Before he said he'd stay."

Her mouth flattens, like she doesn't want to agree with me, but she nods.

I pick up a piece of bacon and take a half-hearted bite, the usual rich flavor bland and dry.

"I can talk to him—" Kristen says, and I cut her off.

"No. Don't tell him I said any of this. I don't want him to know I'm upset. It's pathetic enough, as is."

It's one thing to secretly pine after a guy. It's another for everyone to let him know, too.

She hesitates for a moment, then nods. "If that's what you want."

Breakfast continues in a somber fashion until I get a text from Mom asking if I'll be over today like I usually do to help out with Dad. I like giving Mom a break from being a full-time caretaker for him.

And though I'm happy to help my parents, it's another reminder that it's back to the real world starting today. Back to work tomorrow, back to my normal life. This past week has been play-acting, pretending I'm with Grayson. Knowing it was a dream as it was happening. Now it's time to face reality.

There is no me and Grayson. And there never will be.

CHAPTER TWENTY-SIX

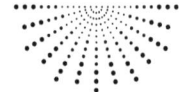

GRAYSON

I put the ladder back in the garage and double check Mom's list again, making sure I did everything she asked. Cleaning out the gutters was the most time consuming, but I didn't want to make Owen have to do it when he does a ton of other stuff for her throughout the year.

"All done," I call out as I head inside. "I'm going to shower real quick." I'm not driving home for four hours smelling like this.

Mom's disembodied voice echoes from the kitchen. "Okay, I'll have lunch ready when you're finished."

I join her ten minutes later to find sub sandwiches and thick slices of leftover wedding cake on the kitchen table.

"We're having cake for lunch?" I ask, pulling out a chair.

"Someone has to eat it."

"Jenny and Jamie didn't offer?"

Mom smirks. "Kristen didn't give them the chance for some reason."

I swipe my finger through a glob of buttercream frosting, relishing the sweetness. That bakery in Kirkwood knows what they're doing.

There's a pang in my chest as I remember driving there with Abby yesterday morning. How beautiful she'd looked in her bridesmaid dress. How easy it was to talk with her, the two of us picking up conversation like we've been doing it forever. How close we've become this week.

I swallow hard, the frosting turning sickly sweet in my mouth, nearly overbearing.

"Did you have fun at the wedding?" Mom asks as I grab a sandwich and put it on my plate.

"Yep." I brace myself for her next question, knowing it's coming.

"So what's going on with you and Abby?"

And there it is. God, where do I even start?

Then again, nothing's going on anymore. We said our goodbyes.

"We were just wedding dates," I mumble, taking a big bite of sandwich to avoid responding any more.

She gives me an unimpressed look. "Is that so?"

I nod, chewing slowly, but she simply stares at me, waiting for more. Shit.

"It was never supposed to be anything more," I add, needing to justify myself. "It was only for this week."

That's what I keep repeating in my head, over and over. At some point I might actually believe it, too.

"Hmm." There's a wealth of meaning in the sound, but I don't want to decipher it. I shouldn't have bothered to shower and eat lunch here. I should have left as soon as I put that ladder away, avoiding interrogation.

If I'm lucky, she won't mention how she caught me kissing Abby at the winery, how I've been flirty with her since. And especially that I didn't sleep here last night. She had to have noticed.

"So you two aren't anything?"

My lips compress, the sandwich turning to sawdust as my throat goes dry. This thing with Abby… It can't be anything more. I don't live here.

I shake my head once, looking down at my plate.

"Well, good."

My head snaps up, nearly giving myself whiplash. "Good?"

She nods. "I haven't spent much time with Abby lately, but I forgot how delightful she is. There's a new P.E. teacher at the elementary school I think she'd hit it off with. I'll give him her number."

The food in my stomach turns over, sending a wave of nausea through me. "What?" I manage to get out through dry lips. She's going to set Abby up with someone?

She calmly takes a bite of cake and chews before answering. "Brandon. He replaced Coach Jensen at the beginning of the semester. Lovely boy. Has the thickest eyelashes I've ever seen on a man, but he somehow pulls it off."

My head is spinning. Who the fuck is this Brandon guy?

"He obviously likes children if he works with them," Mom continues obliviously. "And I'm sure Abby will want to start a family sometime soon. I mean, a teacher and a librarian? What could be more perfect?"

I let go of my sandwich when I realize I'm crushing the bread. "I don't think Abby's interested in dating," I say, needing to come up with some kind of reason for her not to give this guy Abby's number. How could my own mother do this to me?

"Why not? She went to the wedding as your date. So she must be open to dating."

"That was..." I clear my throat. "As a family friend."

She gives me a bemused look. "She kisses her friends like that?" Shit. I knew she'd bring that up at some point. "No, she's clearly interested in dating. And she deserves some happiness. Especially if there's nothing going on between you two."

I go still. Oh. So that's what this is about. She's calling my bluff. I either tell her I like Abby or she'll set her up with someone else.

I *am* interested in Abby, but how is it fair to lead her on? She lives here and I live in Seattle. Even if we were both open to long distance, isn't the end goal always to eventually be in the same place?

Would Abby move to Seattle?

No, how could she? Her family is here and they need her help.

Then that leaves me. And though I've known Abby nearly all my life, we only started hooking up four days ago. *Four days.* How could I upend my whole world based on four days?

Besides, this is all assuming Abby even wants anything else with me. There's a good chance she's perfectly fine with how we ended things.

My chair skids across the floor in a loud screech as I stand. "I have to get going," I mutter as I abandon my lunch.

Mom's unconcerned expression turns flustered. "So soon?"

Oh, so she doesn't like her bluff called either? Well, too bad. Neither of us is getting what we want.

A fresh stab of guilt and hurt lances through me as I grab my suitcase from the guest room, what used to be me and Owen's room growing up. Mom converted Kristen's room to a playroom for Jenny and Jamie years ago.

"I'm having a Mother's Day lunch here in two weeks," Mom says, bustling behind me as I stalk down the hallway toward the front door. I usually like looking at our school pictures lining the walls, but I'm too worked up to pay attention this time.

"Owen and Kristen will be here," she continues, ignoring my non-response. "I'd love it if you could make it down."

Which implies *you better be here, or else.* "Yeah, I'll come."

I open the front door and pause. That means I'll be in town again. I could see Abby.

There's a jittery sensation in my stomach, anticipation racing through me. Is this what a junkie feels like when they're about to get their next fix?

No, maybe what I need is a clean break. If I keep seeing her, keep thinking about her, won't it only prolong this hurt?

"Are you okay, honey?" Mom asks hesitantly from behind me.

I pinch the bridge of my nose. "Yeah, I'm fine. See you in two weeks."

I give her a quick hug and get in my car. My stomach is twisted up in knots but I ignore it, speeding out of town towards home. If I get back into my normal routine, the otherness of this week will disappear. Crescent Pass will disappear.

Abby will disappear.

~

"Charles, can you get those pro forma statements to me by end of day tomorrow?"

My boss, Robert, is all business as usual at the head of the conference table, but everyone else on the team is lounging in their chairs, relaxed during our informal daily check-in.

"No prob, Bob," Charlie says, giving him a salute. He's playing with fire since Robert hates nicknames. He won't even call his employees by anything less than their full name.

Robert gives him a sideways glance. "You sound like Grayson."

I'd take offense to that... if he wasn't right. It does sound like something I might normally say. Not today, though.

"Well, Grayson's had a stick up his ass the last two weeks," Charlie says casually, "so I have to fill in for him."

There are a couple of good-natured *ooohs* from around the table, but I ignore them. Charlie's also right about that. Unfortunately.

Robert turns to me. "Why do you have a stick up your ass?"

"No reason," I mutter, avoiding his eye.

"If you ask me, it's because he had to spend a week in Podunk City," Charlie chimes in. "And then has to go back again this weekend."

I'm silent, grinding my molars. I usually enjoy riffing with Charlie, ragging on each other until one of us busts out laughing.

But there's no laughter today.

"You have to return?" Robert asks. "Do you need more time off?"

"No, everything's fine."

That's blatantly untrue based on the way my jaw clenches and my shoulders bunch around my ears, but I don't think anyone will call me on it.

I give Charlie a death glare when Robert turns away, and for the first time in the last two weeks of busting my balls for my shitty mood, he looks like he realized he went too far.

The atmosphere is tense for the rest of the meeting, and I fully own up to making it that way, but I can't seem to bring myself to make my usual jokes and quips to lighten the mood. My body's on edge, my skin prickly. I can't shake this feeling that I've made a huge mistake. I just don't know what about.

My eyes squeeze shut. That's not true. I know exactly what about. But what can I do?

I'm the first one out of the conference room door when the meeting is over, pounding down the hallway. If I walk fast enough, maybe I can escape my own thoughts.

But as I return to my office, I find I'm not alone. Charlie trailed me, and as he shuts the door behind him, he says, "All right, I was going to save this for when you're being nicer, but maybe this will get you out of your funk. Bianca is willing to set you up with one of her model friends. We can go on a double date after you get back from Podunk City."

"Will you stop fucking calling it that?" I explode, slamming the folder of papers in my hand onto my desk. They fly loose, spreading out every which way over the desk and floor.

Charlie blinks at the mess, shocked. "What's wrong with you?"

"Nothing," I grit out, unwilling to put this growing restlessness into words.

"Bullshit. I'm dropping a prime opportunity in your lap, and all you can focus on is what I call your hometown? Which you call, too, by the way?"

Yeah, but not since this last trip. Not since everything changed.

"And don't tell Bianca, but these girls are smokeshows. Even hotter than her. You'd be lucky if any of them gave you a chance."

My nostrils flare. "I'm not interested in dating your girlfriend's model friends. And you shouldn't be talking about other women being hotter than her. She should be the hottest thing you've ever seen. You wouldn't even think about other girls if you loved her."

It's silent in the small space after my outburst, other than my harsh breaths. I'm all worked up, completely unnecessarily. I barely know what I said, and as I replay it in my mind, my mouth dries. I shouldn't be taking what I feel about Abby out on him.

Not... not that I love her. I don't. How could I? I left her.

And even then, it hasn't been enough time. Like I told myself the day I left, it was four days. Four amazing, intense days that seemed to go beyond the laws of physics, of time itself. A lifetime of being with her was packed into those four days I learned her body, learned what makes her gasp and groan. Learned how uninhibited she can get, how her skin flushes with pleasure when I turn her on, how she can make me rock hard with only a sultry look.

And before then, there were the days of getting to really know each other, beyond the superficial things. Then the years of shared history, of her always being a part of my life, a fixture in Crescent Pass I'd taken for granted. Never realizing what was under my nose the entire time.

"Do you have a thing for Bianca?"

Charlie's question startles me out of my reverie. What? That's what he got from that? "No. Christ." My gaze flicks up toward the ceiling, a headache brewing behind my eyes. "I met someone in Crescent Pass. I..." I swallow hard. "I miss her."

That's the understatement of the century, but I don't want to get into it. Charlie and I aren't the *let's dissect a relationship* type of friends, anyway.

"Oh, so that's why you're crabby. You want to get laid. Well, go do that this weekend and come back in a better mood."

I stare at him, speechless. We've been friends for years and that's his advice? Has he always been this insensitive?

"Right. I'll go do that," I tell him, wanting to drop the subject. "I need to get started on these forecasts for Robert."

"Yeah, okay." He lingers for a moment, looking uneasy. He's not used to me brushing him off, but I don't have the bandwidth right now to smooth things over. Especially if he's going to be so callous. I tell him I met someone and his only response is I must be hard up?

I mean, I am hard up, but that's not the point.

After he leaves, I slump down in my desk chair, scrubbing my hand over my face. I can't keep going on like this. Powering through every day at full force, not letting myself stop for fear I'll think about—

I pick up my phone, a reflex I can't seem to break. I set it back down like I have a hundred other times over the past two weeks. I want to text Abby. To hear if she's thinking about me, the same way I can't stop thinking about her, despite my best efforts.

I want to hear her soft voice, for nothing else than to tell me about her day. What happened at the library, what she had for lunch, if she has plans with her friends after work. I want everything from her, while giving nothing of myself in return. I want her to tell me she misses me, without admitting I think of her every night lying in bed. How I can't sleep because I swear I can smell her on my pillow, even though that's impossible. She's not part of my Seattle life. My real life.

She's part of a fantasy life I left behind. One that was never real.

What good would it even do to reach out to her? To ask to see her again when it'll lead nowhere?

My head drops into my hands. I need to talk to someone about this. Bottling up my feelings obviously isn't working out well if it's affecting not only my personal life but my work now, too. But who?

I mentally flip through a list, dismissing each one. They're all surface-level friendships, where we bitch about work or the latest hockey game, not about being afraid that you're falling in lo—

No. That's not what's happening.

My palms go itchy, something loose jumping around in my stomach. I'm... I'm misremembering things. It wasn't really that good with Abby. It was only new and exciting. If I went back again, it wouldn't be half as great as I think I remember.

Maybe... Maybe I need to put it to a test. To be with her one more time to prove to myself that it's not good as—

I nearly laugh out loud at my delusional self, grasping at straws like this. Honestly, though, I don't care at this point. Just the thought of being with her again has a rush of warmth flooding my chest.

My decision rolls over me, my timeline for heading to Crescent

Pass this weekend drastically moving up. Even if there's a chance Abby won't be interested. Even if I gave her a shitty goodbye and left her. Even if she hasn't reached out to me, either.

    I can't keep going on like this. I need to figure things out.

    One way or another.

CHAPTER TWENTY-SEVEN

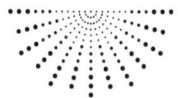

ABBY

Harper slides the pile of poker chips in the center of the table toward her, the winner again in our weekly poker night she insists on doing. Big surprise that she's the best at the game when it's always her idea to play. At least it's at her house this week, so I don't have to worry about cleaning up.

Kristen and I let her have her fun, though. Neither of us cares about losing at poker. For Kristen, it's one night a week she gets to herself, away from the twins. And for me, it's one night a week I'm guaranteed to hang out with friends, rather than lounging on the couch with a book and Leo curled up on my lap. Not that that's a bad alternative, but variety is the spice of life.

I have to admit, the past two weeks have been more difficult than usual, though. I've had to employ all my best distraction techniques to avoid thinking about—

Nope, not thinking about him.

Damn it, I just did.

I've started five new books recently, abandoning four of them when they didn't absorb me enough. There was also the kitchen cabinet reorganization, the paper crafting project for the library's summer reading display, the binge rewatch of The Office…

The list goes on but there's only so much I can do to keep my mind off Grayson. Memories of him surface in every part of my house, every corner of my brain. And though I've never considered myself a prideful person, I don't seem to have it within me to be the first one to reach out to him. He made it clear in the beginning that what we were doing was only while he was in town. And his radio silence since then is confirmation he meant what he said.

Trying to keep this going when he clearly doesn't want to will only make me more miserable.

"Do you have any plans this weekend?" I ask Kristen and Harper, again attempting to distract myself from my thoughts.

The two exchange a look and Harper says, "Just a lunch at Cheryl's on Sunday for Mother's Day." Her voice is overbright, like she's trying to sell me something.

Kristen picks at her nails, avoiding my eye.

Wow, could they be any more obvious?

"It's okay if Grayson is coming," I say. "You don't have to hide it from me."

I filled Harper in on what happened between me and him, along with a few of the more salacious details I didn't share with Kristen.

"We weren't sure if it would upset you," Kristen admits, looking guilty.

"It's your brother," I tell her matter-of-factly. "And I know he'll be back in town occasionally. It's not a big deal."

Did I expect him to return so soon when sometimes he goes a year between visits? No, I didn't. Did I expect him to call me to say he'll be here on Sunday? Again, no.

Even so, there's a tightness in my chest that wasn't there before. I knew this would happen. I was prepared for it.

And I still wouldn't change anything we did. I'm glad I got the chance to be with him, even if it was short-lived.

Despite the Grayson-shaped hole in my heart that isn't going away any time soon.

"I hope you have fun at the lunch. I'm visiting my mom that day, too."

Harper smiles, glancing between us. "See, we're all adults about this."

Kristen purses her lips. "I still think I'm going to kick his ass."

A laugh escapes me, mostly at the thought of her doing anything to Grayson, who's half a foot taller and has at least forty pounds of muscle on her.

"Anyone want a drink?" Harper asks, standing. "Shots for you, right, Abby?"

I grimace. "Count me out."

They both grin and Kristen follows Harper into the kitchen to see what she has when my phone rings. I pull it out of my purse, expecting it to be my mom, but it's not.

It's Grayson.

My hand is shaking as I accept the call. Why is he calling me? Did he somehow know we were talking about him? "Hello?"

"Hey," he says, his voice warm and soothing and everything I've been striving to put behind me since he left. "Are you busy?"

In the kitchen, Kristen says something and Harper laughs, over-loud in the otherwise quiet space.

My thoughts are scrambling, still trying to figure out why he's calling, when he adds, "Are you out of the house?"

I pause, thrown off by the sharp change in his voice. "Yeah."

He starts to say something then stops, clearing his throat. "Are you out with Brandon?"

Brandon? Who's Brandon? Oh, wait. "The P.E. teacher?"

"Yeah."

How does Grayson know him? I've only met the guy once, and only because the library did a partnership program with the elementary school a couple of months ago. "Why would I be out with him?"

If Grayson calling me after two weeks of no contact wasn't confusing enough, now he's adding this?

"So you're not out with him?" he asks, instead of answering my question.

"No, I'm at Harper's."

"Oh." The relief in his voice is palpable. "Mom said she might set you up with him, but I assumed she was bluffing."

It's only then that the dots connect. That sharpness in his tone was… jealousy. He's jealous? At the thought of me going out with someone?

"And if I did go out with him?" I find myself asking, standing and moving to the front door. I slip outside before anyone notices.

I'm playing with fire, putting this question to him when I should immediately deny it. But if I'm being honest, I want him to be a little worried about me. I want to know I still mean something to him.

There's a long pause. "You're free to do whatever you want."

Disbelief and hurt and resignation all jumble up in his voice, and a pinch of guilt winds through me.

"But…?" I ask, wanting him to admit to something. He had to have called for a reason.

The pause this time is even longer. "But I'd hate it," he finally says, tone low and growly in a way that instantly lights me up.

I brace myself against the porch railing, looking out at the shadowy lawn, the moon overhead casting everything in grays and silvers. My ego is sufficiently stroked knowing he feels some kind of way about me, but we're still at an impasse.

"Why did you call?"

He lets out a soft sigh. "Can I come over tonight?"

I frown, holding my phone away from my ear to look at the time. It's nine o'clock. "When?"

"I'm half an hour from Crescent Pass."

My brows pop up. What? I thought Harper and Kristen said he'd be here Sunday.

"What do you want to come over for?"

I'm frozen in place, intensely listening for his answer.

There's rustling over the line, then he says, "I can't stop thinking about you."

My breath catches in my throat. There it is. What I wanted to hear. What I've wanted to hear for years. But now that I have his notice… Do I want to put myself through the last two weeks again? Trying to forget about him once he leaves?

"Have you thought about me at all?" he asks, and my eyes squeeze shut at the desperation that leaks into his voice. My heart twists knowing he must have been in pain, too, but that doesn't stop the relief that splashes hot in the pit of my stomach. I wasn't the only one feeling this way. He feels it, too.

"Of course I have." My fingers are trembling, gripping the phone tighter to my ear. And even knowing what's in store for me afterward, I can't help giving in. It's all I've ever wanted. "Please come over."

He makes a small sound of satisfaction, almost as if it's involuntary. "Thank you." He says it like it's a benediction.

The gratitude ties my tongue for a moment. This means something to him. "I'll see you soon," I say, unsure what else to say. How much to prod. To ask him how much it means to him. *Why* it means so much. If I do, I might have to admit how much it means to me, too.

But he said he can't stop thinking about me. Could this be the start of something… more?

I slip back inside but say nothing to Harper or Kristen about my plans. There's still a hesitancy in me, like I don't believe Grayson's really going to show up. That maybe I imagined that whole conversation.

I make my excuses ten minutes later when things are winding down anyway and race home. I'm in a whirlwind of activity as I change into sexier lingerie and frantically shave my legs while I brush my teeth. I replace the sheets on my bed and light a candle, then blow it out. It's too obvious.

Then again, that's what he's coming over for, right? For sex? We didn't say that outright, but it was implied.

Is it a good idea to fall into this addiction again? I can't answer that right now, my body swimming with anticipation. And the only relief is Grayson.

The knock at the front door is a live wire through me, and when I let him in, the door's barely closed behind him before he's kissing me hungrily, like I'm the air he breathes, his fingers entwined in my hair, palms cradling the sides of my face. It's all-consuming, drugging, but I can't get enough of it, the kiss going on and on.

We've picked up right where we left off, no hesitancy, no awkwardness. Only need. The hurt of the last two weeks fades away, until it's so small it's silly to think it ever happened. That there was anything in my life but this man kissing me, my heart full to bursting with having him here.

"I want you," he murmurs against my lips, his big body backing me up against the front door. "All I've thought about is you the last two weeks." His lower half makes contact with mine, a groan releasing from him. "Tell me I'm not crazy. That you feel it, too."

"I feel it." This pull between us. It's only gotten stronger.

His hands travel south until they rest on my ass, squeezing. He lifts me then, encouraging me to wrap my legs around his waist as he carries me into my bedroom.

My breasts press against the hard muscles of his chest, and I'm suddenly overheated, wanting these clothes off. Wanting there to be nothing between us. To return to that state we were in two weeks ago, connected in a way I'd only dreamed about.

When he sets me on the bed, I drag him down with me, until that hard body is covering me, a delicious weight I can't get enough of. He angles his hips, rubbing himself against me, and I sigh happily, the warmth spreading through me like a balm to my soul. The contact is electric, even through our clothes, and pretty soon we're making out like a couple of sex-starved teenagers. That's what it feels like, though. As if I've been starving all this time and didn't realize it. Not until he showed me what it could be like. How good it could be between us.

I dip my hands under the hem of his t-shirt, up over the ridges of his abs, drawing it up and over his head. My gaze touches every inch of his uncovered torso, the heavy cuts and vast expanses of muscle I want to spend days exploring. I'll make do with tonight, though, my fingers trailing up his obliques, his skin warm, his hips still rocking against mine, desire building.

When I bring my hands between us and undo the button to his jeans, he draws back.

"Wait."

CHAPTER TWENTY-EIGHT

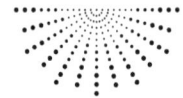

ABBY

*W*ait? What does he mean, wait?

"Ladies first," he murmurs, his hands slipping under my shirt to pull it off.

My sudden panic eases. Oh, that's all he meant. Well, I'll never say no to that.

His fingers skate over my ribs on his way back down, and he makes quick work of my pants, leaving me in my lingerie.

He sits back, his hands on his thighs, gaze roaming all over me, like it's a physical touch. Goosebumps break out over my skin, anticipating what's coming.

He continues to stare, his thumb rubbing over his mouth. "I thought I might've misremembered how beautiful you are." He reaches out to wrap his fingers around my ankle. "But you are so fucking sexy."

Pleasure suffuses me, from the top of my head down to the ankle in his grasp. He bends and presses a gentle kiss right above his fingers, then makes his way upward at a snail's pace. My calf, my knee, my thigh, openmouthed, sensual kisses that have me shaking with the promise of what's to come. But just when he's at the top of my inner thigh, so close to where I want him, he leans back and starts over on my other leg.

A frustrated groan escapes me, and I can feel his smile curl into my shin as he takes his time, occasionally nibbling the tender skin, pausing when he finds a particularly sensitive spot. He's acting like we have all the time in the world, and while technically we're not in any rush, he has me so turned on, I'm throbbing for him.

When he stops halfway up my thigh to lave kisses there, I take matters into my own hands, snaking a hand down to rub myself over my panties.

"Abby," he warns, in a low, possessive voice that sends a thrill through me.

I act oblivious. "Hmm?"

His hand comes up to gently flick my fingers away. "That's mine."

Another thrill, my heartbeat picking up in speed. "Well, you didn't seem that interested."

"I'm *very* interested. Let me savor this."

He moves marginally faster up my inner thigh, until he's poised over me. He nuzzles me over my underwear, the silk wet with my arousal. I'm past the point of caring how desperate I appear, ready to beg him to lick me already when his big palms spread my thighs wider, opening me up to him.

I whimper as his mouth covers me, sucking me through the thin fabric. Any contact is better than none, but as his finger gently pulls the silk aside to expose me, I give a pleading moan when he only blows cool air over me, wanting his tongue so badly.

"You want me to lick that pretty pussy?" he asks, his eyes mischievous as he looks up at me. Underneath the playfulness is red, hot desire, though. He can't pretend he doesn't want it as much as I do.

"Yes." I squirm, trying to get closer, but it's useless. His grip on my thighs is like iron. "Should I beg?"

He makes a soft sound of satisfaction. "No begging necessary. Hold your panties to the side."

I do as he says, and I'm rewarded with a slow, gentle lick. He continues at that pace, torturing me the same way he did kissing up my leg.

"Are you savoring this, too?" I angle my hips further toward him, but his hands quickly bring me back down, keeping me on the edge, wanting more.

"You have no idea," he murmurs, his steady rhythm driving me insane.

When we last did this, my pleading had him speeding up, giving me what I wanted, but he's not as easily swayed now. He takes his time, building me up slowly over long minutes until my thighs are shaking, lust pent up and coursing through me, seeking release.

"You're close," he says, more like it's a statement than a question.

I nod, gripping the tangled bedsheets underneath me with my free hand.

"You've been so good, letting me do what I want. You ready to come?"

"Please," I croak out, filled with a pressure that's near to bursting.

One of his hands lets go of my thighs, two fingers entering me smoothly with how wet I am, and curl forward as his tongue focuses on my clit, at a pace that has me moaning.

"Oh my God, yes. Like that. Just like that."

I brace my free thigh against his cheek, practically humping his face with the way my hips are rocking, the pressure spiraling out of control.

My hands find his head, gripping his hair to make sure he doesn't stop, and he hums in delight.

It's the final thing that breaks me, and I cry out as I ride my high, my body jerking against his mouth as he continues to lick me exactly where I need him, prolonging the pleasure.

When I finally pull him away, his gaze is hungry as he removes his clothes, watching me. There's little finesse to it, taking everything off as quickly as he can.

"You still have those condoms?" he asks, opening my bedside

drawer. His cock bobs in front of him, and I have to force myself to drag my gaze away to process the question.

"I moved them under the bathroom sink." I didn't want to be constantly reminded of them when I clearly wouldn't be putting them to use.

He nods and is off the bed in one fluid motion, retreating to the en suite bathroom.

I take stock of my body for a moment. The easy warmth running through my veins. My still pounding heart. The wetness between my thighs.

Peeling off my panties, I fling them onto the floor as Grayson returns, rolling a condom on.

"Do you need a minute? Or can you take me?"

"I can take you."

He sits against the headboard, guiding me to straddle his lap, and positions himself at my entrance.

"I am so fucking hard for you," he whispers, his hands on my waist, bringing me down on his length inch by inch.

I wasn't on top last time, and the position feels wholly new, the way he's filling me up a completely different experience. There's a beautiful kind of tension, especially as he lifts me nearly off and back down, until my ass meets his thighs. The friction is exquisite as he sets a pace for us, but even better than that is watching his expression change, the emotions that play out, from anticipation to relief to need again.

"God, I've missed you," he murmurs, kissing me deeply.

My heart fills with a yearning so intense, I nearly stutter with it. "I missed you, too." I settle into the rhythm, up and down on his dick, my hands on his shoulders for balance, relishing the wide expanse of warm, tanned skin. "More than I thought possible," I admit, letting some of that longing out.

"Yeah?" He leans back, studying me. "I was afraid I was the only one."

"No, you weren't."

I'm not sure what he sees on my face, how much I'm revealing, but he seems to like it by the way he urges me closer, his kiss fervent, his tongue winding with mine.

His hands come up to undo the hook on the back of my bra, and he removes it, replacing the cups with his big palms, gently squeezing me.

It really feels like we're making love, the way we're connected like this, even if we haven't said anything about that. My heart feels it, though, undeniably. This time with him has sharpened all my feelings, the highs greater than they've ever been, and the lows just as intense. We're past the lows now, though. He came back to me.

My hand moves to rest over his heart, the fast thump under my fingertips proving he's with me, that he feels this, too. That this is the start of something more. He wouldn't have come back, otherwise. Wouldn't have admitted how much he missed me, how he couldn't stop thinking about me.

Sweat blooms over me, considering saying those three little words. They're sitting right there on my tongue, waiting to escape. Would they bring us closer, connecting us forever? Or scare him off, all of this too much, too fast?

My lips tremble, wanting this off my chest, but before I can say anything, he groans and maneuvers us so my back is on the mattress, his weight anchoring me as he thrusts with faster strokes, need curling in my lower belly.

It distracts me enough that the words dissolve, waiting for another time. Maybe when he makes me come again, the stars just within reach. Or after we're finished, lying lazily in his arms, our heartbeats in sync. I have forever to tell him. This isn't the end.

The passion rises as he continues to pump into me, filling not only my body but my soul. And when he picks up the pace, my back arching off the bed with how incredible it is, I give myself over to him completely.

"That's it, baby," he murmurs, pressing into me, over and over. "You're so good at taking my cock, aren't you?"

I nod, wetness escaping out of the corner of my eye. I'm too far gone for words.

His teeth graze the tender skin of my neck, then he soothes it with kisses. He praises me, telling me I only have a little more to take and then I'll come again. That he'll be right there with me.

A helpless sound escapes me, wanting that so badly, for him to be with me in any way I can get.

"Please," I beg, not sure what I'm even begging for. I know I just told myself this isn't the end, but the truth is, it could be. When he leaves again, it might be forever. I can't do it again. "Please," I repeat. "Stay with me."

He burrows his face into the curve of my neck. "I'm with you. I'm here."

No, that's not what I mean. Not only for now. For always.

"Fuck, Abby." His hand moves down to grip my hip, securing me to him. "I'm about to come."

I exhale, clenching him tightly, absorbing the harsh grunts he makes into my skin, relishing the way his hips jerk against mine. His orgasm washes over me, kicking off a release within me, too, and I sink into the mattress, letting the waves sweep me under.

I'm boneless, drifting, trying my damndest not to let the worry ruin this. Trying to stay in the present moment.

But the tears leak out anyway.

I turn my face into the pillow, unwilling for him to see me like this. Desperate and pathetic. Wanting him more than he wants me. I know he wants me physically. That he missed me. But that doesn't equate to anything lasting.

He thankfully heads into the bathroom to clean up, not noticing my internal crisis, and when the door shuts, I pull my hair, silently screaming at myself. Why can't I be satisfied with what I have? I have a hot guy in my bed giving me multiple orgasms and it's still not enough? I got another night with Grayson. Can't I be happy with that?

I get up and head to my dresser, pulling on a fresh pair of panties and an oversized shirt as I wipe away all traces of tears.

The bathroom door opens, and he pauses in the doorway. "Clothes on already?" He grabs his boxer briefs off the floor and slides them on, but doesn't add anything else to his ensemble as he crosses the room and slips his arms around me from behind.

My eyes squeeze shut, basking in the simple pleasure of being in his embrace, his heat surrounding me. And even though every part of me screams not to ruin this moment, I still ask, "When are you leaving?"

His grip tightens briefly before relaxing again. "Sunday. We could spend all day together tomorrow. If you don't have plans."

I turn in his arms, hugging him. "I'd love that." My hands smooth down his bare back, stopping at the waistband of his boxer briefs. "I, um…" I take a deep breath, just going for it. "I have a three-day weekend in a couple of weeks. For Memorial Day. Maybe I could come up and visit you in Seattle?"

I say it as nonchalantly as I can, as if it's a passing thought. As if it doesn't mean what it could—the start of something more.

He leans back, surprise on his face. He cups my cheeks and smiles. "Yeah, of course. No one ever visits me."

"I'd like to."

His smile gently drops into something more serious, his gaze searching mine. "That would mean a lot to me." He kisses me, that connection alive and kicking, and I melt into him with relief.

I need to play the long game here. Maybe I can have everything I ever wanted if I'm patient enough. If I give it time to grow. I've waited years for Grayson. I can wait a little longer.

Even if I want it all now.

CHAPTER TWENTY-NINE

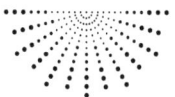

GRAYSON

"Do you know where we're going?"

Towering Douglas firs and hemlocks dominate the space above us, their deep green needles creating a dense canopy overhead. Every so often, the forest opens up to offer a glimpse of the river winding below, a soothing murmur that guides us toward our destination.

"Of course I do," I answer. At least, I'm pretty sure. Owen's directions had seemed straightforward enough, but he's the mountain man, not me. I gave that up years ago.

"You said yourself I used to live in these woods," I add. That was a decade ago, but still.

"Okay, I trust you." There's amusement in her tone, but I appreciate her faith in me all the same.

Shouldering my backpack higher, I intertwine our fingers together, encouraged when she squeezes my hand in return. I bring her hand up to mine, pressing a kiss to the inside of her wrist.

I haven't been able to stop touching her today. Holding her waist as I lift her over a moss-covered log in the path. Curling my hand around her hip when she wanders a little too close to me. And that's in addition to how I woke her this morning, my head between her legs, her moans of satisfaction music to my ears. She'd returned the favor, and I swear it was even better than last time.

It's a far cry from the last morning after I spent the night. But today isn't a goodbye. Not if she wants to come see me in Seattle. She has no idea how much her offer calmed that part of me that's been restless the past couple of weeks, missing her. And though I still don't know what the hell I'm doing when it comes to Abby, I'm thankful for it all the same. All I know is… I don't want this to be over yet.

"Oh, look at that."

Abby's pointing to a great blue heron at the edge of the river, still as a statue waiting to catch a fish. Its beady eyes focus on the water in front of it, and just when I'm about to look away, it dives forward, spearing a fish in its long beak.

"Did you see that?" Abby exclaims.

"Pretty cool."

The path leads down closer to the river, the water reflecting the green of the surrounding trees.

"How long is this river?" Abby asks, reaching out to nearly touch a dragonfly buzzing by.

"I'm not sure. I know it splits from a bigger one further north."

"Maybe it runs all the way up to Seattle."

I chuckle. "That's a pretty far distance. I think the river there starts up near Mount Rainier. It doesn't cross over into Oregon."

"Hmm." She stares out at the water, ducks gliding along the current up ahead. "Well, I still like to think there's something that connects us between where I am and you are. Maybe the river breaks off into little streams and lakes that eventually meet up."

I'm fairly sure that's not how it works, but I pull her closer and say, "I think you're right." The idea is hopeful. Maybe we aren't as far apart as it seems at first glance.

The turnoff to the clearing is right where Owen said it'd be, past a pair of fallen logs that form an X-shape. Abby uses my hand for leverage up the steep incline, then pauses.

"Oh my God," she mumbles, breaking away from me, her fingers trailing over wildflowers. "It's like the meadow scene."

I glance around, with no idea what she's talking about. "What?" I pick a spot in the center and set my backpack down, then pull out a blanket and spread it on the grass.

"From *Twilight*."

"Uh, never saw it."

She looks at me over her shoulder. "I'm guessing you didn't read the book, either?"

She's kidding, right? "You did?"

She snorts, as if my question is ridiculous. "Of course."

I'm not sure whether to frown or laugh. "But you're a librarian. I thought you were only allowed to read serious literature." I pull out the picnic lunch I packed us, setting it on the blanket.

She gives me a pitying smile. "At the end of the day, I want to turn my brain off, not try and figure out symbolism and stuff." She settles next to me and picks up a strawberry from the container of fruit.

"So what do you read?" I ask.

"Oh, a bit of everything. Sci-fi, thrillers, fantasy, chick lit, mystery. But mostly romances."

Really? "The smutty kind?"

She blushes, avoiding my eye. "Maybe."

Well, damn. No wonder she's amazing in bed. "Any scenes you'd like to act out?"

She laughs, delighted, and my heart pounds watching her. I can't remember having this good of a time since... the last time I was here in Crescent Pass with her.

We gorge ourselves on the picnic lunch, talking about everything and nothing in a way that makes the mundane seem like a once-in-a-lifetime treat. The conversation ranges from the innocuous like recent weird dreams we've had, and Abby teasing me when a bug lands on my face and I freak the fuck out, to the more serious, resuming our discussion from the other week about the struggles she faces with her parents aging and her father's condition. And though she apologizes for feeling like she's unloading on me or complaining, I stop her.

"Abby, you can always talk to me. About anything." I like that she's comfortable enough with me to share this kind of stuff. When I think about it, I have very few relationships like that in my life. And now that I have it with her... I don't want to give it up.

She looks at me, solemn and serious in that way I always found her before this week. Before I got to know the real her. She plucks a blade of grass, folding it with her deft fingers the way she works her origami projects.

The moment passes and I'm left with a disquieted feeling. Almost as if I... failed at something. As if she doesn't believe my offer. "I mean it," I add, as if that lends me any credibility.

"I know," she whispers. When she looks back at me, I swear there's both sadness and acceptance in her gaze, but it's gone before I can make sure it was there. "Here, lay with me."

She positions me at an awkward angle so my torso is fully flat on the ground but my neck is cranked all the way to the side to look at her.

She mimics my pose and murmurs, "And so the lion fell in love with the lamb."

"What?" What is she talking about?

She gives me a small, secretive smile. "It's nothing. Let's just enjoy the rest of the day."

And we do, something about being back here melting my tension away. I've missed the simple things. Spotting wildlife. Scenic views. Finding wonder in the surrounding beauty.

I study Abby as she looks up at the sky. The soft curve of her lashes. The gentle slope of her nose. The lushness of her lips, the bottom one ever so fuller than the top.

Both Abby and Crescent Pass have brought the wonder back into my life. And when I leave again...

No. Not ruining today with that. Not when I have the first measure of peace I've had in weeks.

Thanks to her.

"Hi, honey." Mom enfolds me in a hug, somewhat surprising me considering how we left things the last time I saw her, calling bluffs without acknowledging it aloud. "How was the drive?"

"Fine." I didn't tell her I arrived Friday night and spent the last day and a half with Abby. I don't want her getting involved and messing with my head. Things are jumbled enough as it is. "Happy Mother's Day."

I hand her the bouquet I picked up from the florist in town, and she makes a big production of finding a vase to put it in.

"Show off," Kristen mutters, coming down the hallway to greet me. She's smiling, so I know she's not serious, but as she hugs me, there's a sharp pinch to the back of my upper arm.

I jerk away, rubbing at the spot. "What the hell?"

"That's for messing around with Abby behind my back."

The blood drains from my face. "She told you about it?" I thought only Owen knew about me and Abby. Then again, the two of them are best friends. Of course she'd tell her.

"Only after I asked her why you were making out after the wedding over by your car."

I rub the back of my neck, glancing away. Oh, yeah. That. "I, um… I had a feeling you'd react badly."

She crosses her arms, glaring at me. "You've put me in an awkward position. Am I supposed to choose between the two of you now?"

"What? No. I—"

"Because she was super torn up about you leaving. She was crying in the middle of the cafe the morning you left, for God's sake."

My stomach drops. "She what?"

Kristen blinks, face going blank. "Shit. You didn't hear that."

"I most definitely did. What do you mean, she was crying?"

Her hands wring together, a nervous habit she's had for as long as I can remember. "I wasn't supposed to tell you that. She didn't want you to feel bad."

Which makes the bowling ball in my stomach sink even lower. I never wanted to cause her pain.

"I was thinking of her every day I was gone," I confess, a gravity in my voice I wasn't expecting.

My sister stares at me, her head tipping to the side the slightest bit, as if I'm some alien creature. To be fair, we don't share these kinds of things with each other.

"I spent this weekend with her," I add, unable to help myself. "I couldn't stay away."

She huffs out a surprised breath, touching her fingers to her mouth. "You have feelings for her? Like, serious ones?"

I swallow roughly, my throat suddenly tight, and nod. It's the truth. I can't deny it to myself anymore.

Her face clears and she reaches forward to hug me. "Holy crap, Grayson."

My knees sway for a moment, surprised at the sudden lightness that fills me at Kristen's acceptance.

"I know things are complicated," she says, her arms still around me. "But I hope you two can work something out. I want you both to be happy."

"All right, too mushy. You crossed the line."

She laughs and leans away. "Fair enough. So, spoiler alert, I told the twins we're coming up to visit you in the summer and it's all they're focused on now."

I sling an arm over her shoulder as we head down the hallway. "Wait, seriously? You all are going to come up to Seattle?"

"Yeah." She pokes me in the ribs. "Your girlfriend convinced me."

I pull up short at the entrance to the kitchen as Kristen continues on, crossing the room to join Eli, Owen, and Harper at the table. *My girlfriend?* Abby's not my girlfriend. Actually, I don't know what she is.

But I really like the sound of it.

CHAPTER THIRTY

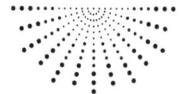

ABBY

"This is so sweet, thank you." Mom enfolds me in a hug, and as the scent of her perfume teases my nose, nostalgia overtakes me. "I can't wait to look through this."

"What's that you got, Brenda?" Dad asks, tearing his gaze away from the TV.

"It's a photo book," Mom says, standing and showing him the book I made for her, filled with childhood pictures of us. "Wasn't that nice of Abby?"

Dad looks at me next, a pleasant, generic smile on his face. I can't tell if he recognizes who I am. The days he does are getting farther and fewer between. "Very nice."

His attention returns to the television, his only source of entertainment these days. He can't focus enough to read books anymore.

"Never mind him." Mom bats a hand in his direction, then wavers in place, holding her hands out to steady herself.

"You okay?" I ask, almost out of my seat to help her.

She regains her balance and sits next to me again. "I'm fine. Just light-headed for a moment. I haven't slept well the past few nights."

"I can come over later and stay up with Dad if you want to head to bed early."

"No, no." She pats my knee. "I'll be fine. Only a little tired is all."

"Okay." I relax back into the couch cushions.

"Oh, while I have you, what's your work schedule like the weekend of the twenty-seventh? I was hoping to book a hairdresser's appointment but wanted to make sure you could stay with your father."

I hate that she's chained to the house so often. It's too much trouble for her trying to take Dad out anywhere, other than necessary doctor's appointments.

"Actually, I have plans that weekend."

She idly flips through the photo book, pausing at a picture of the three of us at a zoo. I look to be about seven or eight years old. "Which day? Tanya's available both days, so I can go on the one you're free."

Admittedly, it's highly out of the ordinary for me to be busy an entire weekend, so I'm not surprised when she widens her eyes as I tell her, "I'll be out of town."

"Where are you going?"

I look down at my lap, my heart pounding out of nowhere. "Seattle. I'm visiting Grayson."

She snaps the book shut and turns to me excitedly. Dad coughs and resettles in his recliner, but otherwise isn't paying attention to us.

"Grayson, hmm?"

I can't help the smile that creeps over my face. "Yeah."

"As a friend? Or something more?"

"Something more. I don't know what exactly," I add when she opens her mouth to prod. "But more than friends."

She reaches over and squeezes my hand. "Well, that's exciting. I hope you have a fun time."

Oh, I think we'll definitely have *fun*. But I'm not going to talk to my mom about that.

We chat some more and when it's quarter to four, I tell her I need to leave. Grayson said he'd stop by my house again after lunch at his mom's to say goodbye. A proper one this time.

Grayson is already in the driveway when I get there, leaning against the hood of his car.

"I thought you said four," I say as I get out.

He offers me an easy smile as he approaches. "Just wanted to see you sooner."

The near-constant butterflies in my stomach this weekend escape their cage to beat their wings madly. I love the romantic things he's been saying.

"Did you want to come in?"

The look he gives me is pure devilry. "If I do, I might never leave."

I smile, but inwardly think that wouldn't be a bad thing.

He kisses me with a familiarity that has my toes curling, until I hear a sharp, "Abby Walsh!" that has me startling away.

Ruth Cooper is across the street in a lime green tracksuit that has my eyes watering, her hands on her hips in outrage.

Crap. I forgot she's started walking the neighborhood this time of day.

"And—Grayson Taylor, is that you?"

He doesn't seem nearly as flustered as I am. "Yes, ma'am."

"What are you doing sucking face with my librarian? Haven't you already made your annual visit?"

Sucking face? It was a simple kiss.

"It was great to see you, too, Ruth," he calls out, waving a hand. He presses his free hand into the small of my back and guides me up the walkway toward my door. "On second thought," he mutters, "let's go inside."

I bite my lip to hide my smile as I unlock the front door, especially when Ruth shouts, "Don't think I'm going to keep this from your mother. I have her number."

"I'm sure you do." This is said as he closes the door behind us. Though I know I'll hear about it the next time Ruth is at the library, I can't help but revel in her shocked expression as he shuts her out.

I set my keys and purse on the front entryway table. "Looks like the ruse is still going for your mom."

"It's not a ruse," he murmurs, pulling me in close to him. "It's the real deal. At least, for me."

My heartbeat picks up. "For me, too." I wanted to bring something like this up, but I wasn't sure how. "After you leave here today…"

"Mm-hmm?" His lips whisper over my neck, leaving goosebumps in their wake.

"And I come visit you in a couple of weeks…"

"Can't wait for that."

"What…" I'm distracted for a moment by his palms sliding over my backside. "What happens afterward?"

His touch doesn't falter a bit. "I want to keep seeing you."

Relief fills me. "I want that, too."

"How do you feel about long distance?"

"If it's with you, I'm willing to do anything," I tell him honestly. "I want to be with you."

His hand comes up to cup my cheek, his thumb brushing over my cheekbone. "I'm sorry I had my head up my ass last time I was here. I was so focused on leaving and I didn't know how you felt—"

I lay my fingers against his lips. "We're together now. Let's go from there." I'm tired of rehashing the past. I want to focus on the future.

He gives me a lopsided grin. "So we're together."

I nod, biting my lip to keep my own goofy smile at bay.

"When I was talking to Kristen earlier, she called you my girlfriend and I…" He rubs at the back of his neck, uncharacteristically shy. "I liked the sound of it."

"I like it, too." I kiss him, reveling in the sweetness. "I want to be yours."

He groans and returns my kiss, wrapping himself around me. "You can't say stuff like that right before I'm supposed to leave."

And without even needing to defend myself, he picks me up and carries me to the bedroom, where he stays much longer than he intended before finally returning to Seattle.

A RIVER CONNECTS US

∼

Grayson's fingers intertwine with mine, his arm a deliciously heavy weight over my side. "I'm so glad you're here."

His voice is a deep rumble in my ear, and I sink further into him, my back to his front, one of his thighs wedged between my own. I don't think I've ever been this comfortable. Then again, I'm still getting used to the post-coital stupor he puts me in.

"Me, too," I say, snuggling deeper under the covers. "Though I've only seen one room so far."

I feel the curve of his smile against my neck. "Well, it's a very important room."

Upon arrival at his condo tonight, I was immediately given a thorough introduction to his bed. There will be time for exploring his place later, though. We have the next three days to be together.

The last two weeks have been among the happiest and most miserable of my life. Grayson and I have been in constant contact, texting throughout the day and on video calls with each other at night, but even being practically glued to the hip with him virtually, it hasn't replaced the visceral ache in my chest when I go to bed alone.

Tonight I can finally breathe easy. I'm here with Grayson. My *boyfriend*. I still can't get over that. If I could tell teenage Abby where I am right now, she might pass out from sheer elation.

"How was the drive up?" he asks, rubbing his thumb over my knuckles.

"Um…" To be honest, it sucked. I've never driven that far of a distance before and only plying myself with candy and a new audiobook made the trip somewhat bearable.

"Say no more," he says before I can come up with a palatable answer. "I'll make the drive to Crescent Pass from now on."

"No, that's not fair to you. We should do it equally."

"Abby." He squeezes my hand. "I don't think you realize how much I've missed you. I'll gladly do it if it means I get to see you."

My heart dissolves into a puddle in my chest. I turn in his arms until I'm facing him, taking in his familiar features, the warmth of his gaze. "That's sweet of you."

He shakes his head, grinning. "It's selfish. I'm a crabby bastard when I don't get my Abby fix. Just ask Charlie."

I match his grin. "Will I meet him this trip?"

Grayson said he's been on the outs with him the last couple of weeks after some kind of blow up, but Charlie's been trying to get back in his good graces.

"Yeah, we're going to dinner with him and his girlfriend tomorrow night."

"After the Space Needle?"

He nods. It was the one thing I asked to do this weekend, not knowing much else about the city.

"So what you're saying is you made an itinerary?"

He groans. "Damn itineraries. I'll never escape them, will I?"

"Hey, don't completely write them off. Harper's wedding week itinerary brought us together in a way."

He considers my words. "You're right. Itineraries are my new best friend. I'm making one every day."

I grin, leaning in to kiss him, but I'm interrupted by my phone ringing.

"It's nobody," Grayson says, kissing my neck. "A telemarketer."

"At nearly midnight?" I reach over to the bedside table where I put my phone earlier. I always answer it, half-worried it's going to be something about my dad. "It's a Kirkwood area code."

"See? Not even local."

I roll my eyes and answer. "Hello?"

"Hi, this is Dr. Chen from St. Mary's. Is this Abby Walsh?"

"Yes," I manage to say, my brain taking a moment to catch up. St. Mary's is the closest hospital to Crescent Pass.

"Your mother Brenda is here. You're listed as her emergency contact."

There's a sudden ringing in my ears. "Okay," I say dumbly. What's going on?

"She had a heart attack."

I don't hear anything else after that as the ringing intensifies. The next thing I know, my phone is on the bed, slipped from my grasp. I stare at it, my brain telling my hand to pick it up, to listen to what the doctor is saying, but I can't. It's like I'm paralyzed.

There's something else in addition to that awful high-pitched ringing, but I can't place it. Not until Grayson's in my face, capturing my attention. He's repeating my name, worry etched in his expression, but I'm unable to respond. Anything I try to say gets stuck in my throat.

He picks up the phone, his lips moving, but I can't tell what he's saying. There's only this terrible pressure in my chest, weighing heavier and heavier, until I'm sure it'll burst. I rub my hand over my heart, suddenly realizing my face is wet, that I'm crying. Am I having a heart attack, too? Is this what Mom felt like?

Oh my God, I didn't even ask if she's okay now, or if she… if she…

"Grayson," I call out, my mouth working again. I look around frantically but he's not in the bed anymore. Where did he go?

He pops his head out from the walk-in closet, pulling on a pair of jeans, the phone still pressed to his ear.

"Is Mom alive?"

He nods and I fall back against the pillows, unimaginable relief spreading through me. The ringing stops, my ears miraculously unblocked, and I focus on Grayson's conversation with the doctor, asking about treatment and recovery, visiting hours—all the things I should be doing. He got a notepad and pen from somewhere and is writing everything down, but all I can think is how lucky I am he was here with me when I got this call.

I wipe away my tears and get out of bed, finding my clothes thrown haphazardly on the floor from earlier when Grayson stripped them off me. I fumble to get my bra on, and then Grayson's there, helping me, my hands shaking too badly to do it myself.

"I should have been there," I say, not sure if I'm talking to him or myself. "I wasn't there for her, even though I always am. The one time I leave…"

"This isn't your fault," he murmurs, putting my shirt over my head. "We'll get there as soon as we can."

He pulls a duffel bag out from under the bed and brings it with him to the closet. I crane my neck to peek in, finding him packing his clothes into it. When he's finished, he grabs my still unopened suitcase in the corner and carries them both out of the room.

"What are you doing?" I ask when he returns, not processing everything that's happened in the last five minutes.

"I'm driving you back to Crescent Pass."

I blink rapidly. "You're coming with me?"

His brows furrow. "Of course I am." He says it like it's a given. Like it's non-negotiable. "I'll bring you to the hospital in the morning when visiting hours start, and I'll stay at the house with your dad since someone will need to be with him."

Tears leak out again, wetting my cheeks. He would do all that for me? Without me even having to ask?

I reach my arms out and he's there, allowing me to cling to him, crying into his shirt. "I love you," I sob, unable to keep it in any longer. Not when he's everything I've ever wanted. What did I do to deserve this man?

He soothes his hand down my back, murmuring something, but I can't hear it over my sobs. All I know is I'm never letting him go.

CHAPTER THIRTY-ONE

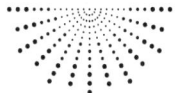

GRAYSON

"Hey, Robert. I need a favor."

My boss grumbles something, but asks what it is.

"I'd like to work remotely for a few days, if that's all right with you. My girlfriend's mom had a heart attack, so she's at the hospital with her, but someone needs to be at the house with her dad, who has dementia."

There's silence on his end for a few moments, until he says, "You have a girlfriend?"

That's what he got out of my request? "Yeah."

"Wasn't Charlie trying to set you up with someone?"

Robert needs to keep up. That was weeks ago. "He didn't know I'm seeing someone long-distance."

"Long-distance? Where are you?"

"In my hometown in Oregon."

"Oh. Where you were for the wedding?"

What's with all the questions? "Uh huh. So, remote working? Is that okay? If not, I'll need to take PTO."

"Yeah, sure. Not for more than a week, though. Otherwise, everyone on the team will want to work from home, too."

"Got it. Thanks, Robert. This helps a lot."

Abby's been going through so much the last few days, I want to take what I can off of her plate.

"No problem. And I'm sorry about your in-laws."

The word startles me for a moment, but for all intents and purposes, I guess that's what Brenda and Stephen are to me now, even if we're not legally bound. By being with Abby, they're a part of my life, too.

"Thank you."

I hang up and set up my work laptop on the small desk in Abby's childhood room. We've been staying in here since our arrival three days ago, and though the twin-sized bed and cramped space aren't ideal, I'll take it any day over being alone in my condo.

My family has stepped up big time in helping out, bringing us food, checking in on Leo at Abby's house, and Kristen and Harper have been spending time with Abby at the hospital. Brenda is supposed to be discharged later today, which to me seems way too soon, but Abby says the doctors are pleased with her mom's recovery.

And thankfully, hanging out with Abby's dad hasn't been too bad, either. He pretty much watches TV all day, and as long as I deliver him his meals in his recliner, he's fine for the most part, other than repeatedly asking where his wife is. The first day I gave a long-winded explanation, but after about the sixth time, I started telling him she'd be home soon, and he seemed content with that.

I keep the bedroom door open and check in on him throughout the day, glad when it's five-thirty and I can log off. I put a casserole in the oven that Mom gave us on Sunday to reheat, and about five minutes later, Abby shows up with her mom, leading her in slowly.

"I'm fine," Brenda is saying, waving off her daughter's help. "You don't have to be so anxious."

Abby's lips compress, but she doesn't say anything as she hovers over her mother.

"Brenda," Stephen says in delight, noticing her. It takes him a moment to get out of the recliner, but he manages it, shuffling across the floor to hug her.

As much as I'm sure their relationship has changed over the years, it's still nice to see the affection and love they have for each other.

Brenda hugs me next, thanking me profusely for taking care of everything here while she was gone. Like I would do anything else when Abby needed me, though?

"Dinner will be ready in fifteen," I tell them. "Is anyone hungry?"

"I could do with something that's not hospital food," Brenda says, heading toward the kitchen. "How about I set the table and you two relax before dinner?"

"Mom, I can—"

"Honey, I'm fine. The doctor said light household chores are okay if I feel up to it. And I do. I've been going crazy lying in that hospital bed for days. Now, shoo."

"She'll be the death of me," Abby mutters as she listens to her mother and heads toward her room.

I keep my smile to myself as I follow, glad I'm not the only one dealing with a bossy mom.

"She insists we can go back to my house tonight," she continues, closing the door behind her. "Her and Dad will be fine here overnight and then I can come over again in the morning."

"Are you okay with that?" I ask, thinking longingly of Abby's comfortable queen-sized bed.

She shrugs. "I guess. I don't want to stress her out more. I just want to help."

"I know." I wrap my arms around her and she notches herself into place against my chest. It's crazy how natural that feels already. "And she knows that, too. You're both trying to look out for each other."

She nods. "Thank you again for everything you've done. You've looked out for us, too."

"You don't have to thank me. You know I want to be here for you."

She sighs contentedly, but soon pulls away. "When do you need to leave?"

And there's the thing we haven't talked about yet. I told her I would definitely be here today, but would have to talk to my boss about the rest of the week.

"Robert gave me a week to work remotely."

"That's generous. I guess I'll need to drive you back since we took my car down here."

I shake my head. "I can have Owen drive me. You should be here for your mom."

She nods but doesn't say anything, looking at the ground.

"I'm not in any rush," I add. "I'd love to stay through the weekend, if that's okay with you."

She smiles, visibly relieved. I hate that she's worried about me going back, though. "Yes, absolutely." Her hands brush up my forearms. "I don't want you to leave."

"I don't either." The thought of returning home without her makes my stomach roll.

"Maybe you should stay forever, then." She says it in a joking way, but I can sense the seriousness behind it.

Logically, we haven't been together long. It's only been a little over a month since we first got together. But for how long I've known her and how I feel about her… I want to stay forever. With her.

And as much as I wanted to leave Crescent Pass as a teenager, there's something different about being here now. I can appreciate the slower pace of life, the connection to nature. My family is here, too, and I'm tired of being on the outside looking in with them. I want to be in on the inside jokes and fun stories. I want to be part of the memories.

It just took being with Abby to realize that.

"I…" I'm not sure how much to say, since this is only a vague plan. "I was looking at my company's vacancy report today. It's what they send out to current employees wanting to laterally transfer for reassignment before a position officially opens up for promotion."

"Yeah?" I don't miss the hopeful gleam in her eye, as if she already knows where I'm going with this.

"There's a remote position on another team. It's not quite a step down, but I'm pretty sure I can negotiate to keep my current salary."

She covers her mouth with her hand, though I'm not finished.

"Would you…" I'm suddenly sweating, even knowing Abby wants me here. "If I moved here—"

"Yes." She crashes into me, kissing me with abandon. "Yes, yes, yes."

The knot of unfounded worry in my belly dissolves. "It's not a done deal." I laugh as she continues to kiss me. "I haven't even put in the transfer request."

She loops her hands over my shoulders. "Just that you would want to move here means so much to me."

"Of course I do." I stroke a hand through her hair, remembering that awful night when the doctor had called. As I'd told her I was taking her back to Crescent Pass, she'd cried and said she loved me, but I still don't know if she actually meant it or it was simply something that came out in the heat of the moment. She hasn't brought it up since, and I've been afraid to ask, in case it was the latter.

But as she looks up at me, her expression satisfied and dreamy, it seems the most instinctive thing to tell her, "I love you."

The joy that radiates over her face is indescribable. Something I'll remember for the rest of my life.

"I love you, too," she responds, and everything clicks into place as my lips touch hers.

I'm mindful that we have to go out and eat a casserole with her family any minute now, not letting our kiss get too out of control.

"I wish we were alone," she says, breaking away before I get visibly turned on. I'm practically salivating at the sultry look she gives me.

"Tonight." It's not a question, but a promise.

She nods in agreement, reaching for my hand to squeeze it. "You make me happier than I've ever been. And as awful as the past few days have been with my mom, it would have been a million times worse without you here to support me through it."

"I'll always be here for you." Even if the transfer falls through, I'll figure out something else. Because now that everything I never knew I wanted is within reach, nothing's taking it from me.

EPILOGUE

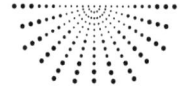

ABBY

3 MONTHS LATER

"Wait, wait." Grayson holds up a finger, looking between me and Harper with incredulous delight. "You had a crush on me in high school?"

I glare at Harper, who gives me a sheepish expression, before I meet Grayson's eyes. "Um, maybe we could talk about this later?"

Eli smirks as he takes a sip of his beer, but wisely stays silent.

"Did you know about this?" Grayson asks Owen.

Owen scoffs. "As if I paid attention to anyone's love life."

"Don't look at me." Kristen holds her hands up. "This is news to me, too."

My face is roasting, hot enough to cook an egg on. "Okay, triple-date-night-whatever-this-is is over." I get up from my seat, but the chorus of objections has me sitting back down.

Grayson leans into me. "We'll definitely talk about this later," he murmurs, low enough for only me to hear.

Okay, not helping my mega blush.

It's scary good how well Grayson has fit into my friend group here, but then again, half of them are his siblings, so it only makes sense. And not only that, but fitting into my life in general. Like he's always been a part of it.

Which he has, of course. But his transition from occasional cameo to main character has been pretty seamless. Once he switched teams at work and went fully remote, it wasn't long before he found a renter for his condo and made the move to Crescent Pass. He debated about finding a place of his own, but I convinced him to stay with me while he looked at his options. And once he was here, it felt so right that any talk of him leaving fell by the wayside.

I still pinch myself sometimes, praying that the past few months haven't all been a dream. A miraculous, wonderful fantasy where the guy of my dreams is in love with me, each day better than the last.

I'm content to sit back and watch Harper and Grayson dominate most of the conversation as the six of us sit outside Owen's cabin around the fire pit in the backyard, the summer air warm and pleasant.

As Grayson is telling a funny story about a hiking song he, Jenny, and Jamie made up on a recent hike he took them on, Kristen looks over at me and squeezes my hand. We don't need words for me to know what she's thinking, because I'm thinking the same thing. How nice it is for Grayson to be here now, spending quality time with his niece and nephew. As much as they used to idolize their Uncle Owen, Uncle Grayson has quickly risen in the ranks to be a contender for favorite uncle.

Weekends are spent with family, and he seems to be making up for lost time, creating new memories with the twins, reconnecting with his brother and sister and their significant others, and of course basking in the adoration of his mother now that he's returned home. And that's in addition to helping out with my parents, who thankfully need us a little less since Mom has recovered.

What I love most, though, is our time after work on the weekdays, just the two of us. My home is filled with laughter and happiness and so much love, my chest aches with it sometimes.

After a half hour, as the night is winding down, Grayson whispers to me, "You ready to get going?"

I nod, giving him a lazy smile.

"And you'll tell me about this crush, right?"

Oh God, I already forgot about that.

He brings my hand to his mouth to kiss my knuckles, grinning mercilessly.

We make our goodbyes a few minutes later and head around the house to where Grayson's parked by Owen's workshop. He opens the passenger door for me, his gaze twinkling with mischief.

"No teasing," I warn, settling into the seat.

He mimes zipping his lips before shutting the door, but that's only for show. He wouldn't be Grayson without a little teasing.

He at least waits until we're off Owen's property and on the main road before asking, "So on a scale of one to ten, how likely were you to tell me about this crush?"

"Hmm." I tap my lip, pretending to think. "Negative one, because I was taking it to my grave."

"Why? It's hot."

I chuckle, unable to help it. "No, it feeds your ego. Which is already in danger of exploding, it's so big."

He laughs, just like I wanted him to.

"Seriously," I say. "If you'd known back then, how would you have reacted?"

His lips twist. "You mean when I was desperate to put Crescent Pass behind me? Okay, fair point." He holds a finger up. "But you at least have to tell me why you had a crush on me."

I turn toward him, and though his focus is on the road, my gaze lingers over the upward tilt of his mouth, the crinkles next to his eyes, his happy and relaxed aura.

"Well, I thought you were incredibly handsome."

"Still am," he agrees with mock solemnity.

"Okay, ego."

He grins, biting his bottom lip.

"And I liked that you were smart and funny. How kind and thoughtful you were to others. That you always helped your family."

His smile gradually drops as I continue on, something both pleased and abashed in his expression. I love the rare times I'm able to discomfit him in a good way like this.

"You were fun to be around," I tell him. "You brought life and energy into a room when you entered. You still do that." I reach over and intertwine my fingers with his. "And I guess I wanted all of that energy and focus on... me."

He makes the turn onto our street, silent as he processes my words. It's not until we're parked in the driveway that he responds.

"If you had told me all that back then, I wouldn't have known what to do with it. Definitely would have fucked it all up somehow." He unbuckles and leans over the center console to kiss me, nice and slow. "I wouldn't have appreciated you the way you deserve," he whispers against my lips. "Wouldn't have fallen in love with you the way I have now."

He reaches over and unbuckles my seatbelt, too. "Wouldn't have known you're everything I've ever wanted."

Heat crawls over my cheeks, still stunned by the romantic things he says, even after months together.

He opens his door and quickly rounds the car, leading me out and up the driveway. When we're inside the house, he's kissing me, bracing me against the back of the front door.

"I know what to do with it now," he murmurs in my ear, sending a thrill down my spine. "You have all of my energy and focus. You have everything of me. I'm all yours."

His hands slide down my torso, his touch lighting me up, every time like the first. I'll never get tired of this.

"I love you," I tell him in between kisses.

"Love you more."

Impossible. But as he carries me back to our bedroom, I'm willing to agree to disagree. Though I've loved him longer, I don't doubt his love for a second. Not when he shows me every day.

Like he said, he's mine. Just like I'm his. And the best part is, it'll be that way for the rest of our lives.

ALSO BY ALLIE WINTERS

Want more Grayson and Abby? Get a free sweet and sexy bonus epilogue when you sign up for Allie's newsletter at alliewinters.com/extras.

All books by Allie Winters:

The Crescent Pass Series

Three spicy small-town romances set in the Pacific Northwest following the Taylor family siblings

A Forest Between Us (Crescent Pass #1)

A Mountain Divides Us (Crescent Pass #2)

A River Connects Us (Crescent Pass #3)

The Bishop Brothers Series

Follow three billionaire brothers as they find love in Manhattan

Resisting the Billionaire (Bishop Brothers #1)

Marrying the Billionaire (Bishop Brothers #2)

Seducing the Billionaire (Bishop Brothers #3)

Suncoast University Series

Four steamy new adult novels that will have you swooning

Let Go (Suncoast University #1)

Watch Me (Suncoast University #2)

No One Else (Suncoast University #3)

First and Only (Suncoast University #4)

Lessons Learned Series

Set in Penny Reid's Educated Romance World, these angsty new adult romances explore human development in the heart and mind

Under Pressure (Lessons Learned #1)

Not Fooling Anyone (Lessons Learned #2)

Can't Fight It (Lessons Learned #3)

Standalone

A fiery standalone entry in Penny Reid's Green Valley Heroes series, All Fired Up is an enemies-to-lovers romance that has sparks flying

All Fired Up

ACKNOWLEDGMENTS

Thank you to my husband for your endless support and encouragement of my writing. For all the late nights you've patiently listened to me blathering on about plot points and book covers and word count goals—I'm endlessly grateful.

Thank you to my beta readers and editor for your kind words and keen eyes. Already looking forward to sending you the next one.

Thank you to the bloggers, reviewers, bookstagrammers, and anyone spreading the word about this book. Your time and efforts are invaluable. If you enjoyed the book (or even if you didn't!) please consider writing a review. I love to hear your thoughts.

And the biggest thank you to my readers for waiting a while for Grayson and Abby's book. Before starting this one, I had almost quit writing altogether, but I hated the idea of leaving a series unfinished. A number of readers let me know they were anticipating this story, so I eventually got to work making it happen, and in the process had my usual moments of being 100% sure I would never figure out the whole book. But I also had my moments of the characters seeming so alive in my head and the scene flowing out onto the page seamlessly, my fingers unable to type as fast as the story was unfolding. It's moments like these that I live for when I'm writing and what I love to share with my readers. I hope you love Grayson and Abby's happily ever after as much as I do.

I'm excited to start a new series soon, moving over to the Three Sisters Bakery in the small town of Aurora, Pennsylvania, where we follow Rachel, Sydney, and Hailey, and the men who change their lives forever—coming your way in mid-2025.

ABOUT THE AUTHOR

Allie is also the author of the Lessons Learned series, the Bishop Brothers series, and the Suncoast University series. She lives in sunny Florida with her husband, daughter, and two cats. A librarian by day, she spends her nights writing happily ever afters. She enjoys reading, playing video games, and all things Disney.

Follow for all the latest book info and news:
    Website: alliewinters.com
    Newsletter and bonus epilogues: alliewinters.com/extras
    Instagram: instagram.com/alliewintersauthor
    Facebook: facebook.com/alliewintersauthor

Printed by Amazon Italia Logistica S.r.l.
Torrazza Piemonte (TO), Italy

69458756R00136